T0196001

Confessional
Matters

A Bertrand McAbee Mystery

Joseph A. McCaffrey

authorHOUSE®

AuthorHouse™
1663 Liberty Drive
Bloomington, IN 47403
www.authorhouse.com
Phone: 1 (800) 839-8640

Published by AuthorHouse   02/20/2020

ISBN: 978-1-7283-4174-3 (sc)
ISBN: 978-1-7283-4173-6 (e)

DEDICATION

To the memory of my brother - Bill

CHAPTER ONE

The Vatican, July 1996

Scarzi scrolled down the all-too-long list of sinning clerics, a list that was updated once a week by Dominican Sister Catherine Siena, the most exasperating, detail-oriented person he had ever encountered. He would joke with his intimates that once you found yourself on Sister Catherine's list, that removal of your name was beyond God's power. In fact, he claimed with his most innocent expression, he was quite sure that the fornicator St. Augustine, and, his alcoholic mother St. Monica, were in one of her files.

Even the settlement of a complaint, or complete exoneration, or death itself would only move you into a new, tightly crafted sub-category. Scarzi honestly knew of no way to get off the list once this Dominican nun put you there. And it wasn't a list on which any self-respecting Roman Catholic cleric would choose to be.

On an average, there were 15 new listees every week. Only when he opened each name file would Sister's asterisk be removed, probably her way of checking on his diligence. On this day there were 12 names which were transmitted from around the world by diocesan bishops. Scarzi figured that for every name that was sent, another was being quashed in some manner-even though the Pope had issued a stem and unequivocal command that he expected a full reportage to Scarzi's little known, but easily inferred, Vatican Office of Clerical Affairs (a title that Scarzi knew drew derision and scorn).

Bishop Guillermo Scarzi was born in Verona, Italy, in 1921, and except for an occasionally difficult month or two here and there, he had never doubted his lifelong devotion and vocation to the Church. Very bright, he progressed nicely through the seminary, and at the age of 25 was ordained a priest. From there he was sent to the Dominican University in Rome, called at that time the Instituto Internazionale 'Angelicum,' for a degree in Canon Law. He never went back to Verona as he was selected by German Cardinal Friedrich Von Horst to work in the Office of Doctrine at the Vatican where he became a lifelong bureaucrat. After John Paul II (the Polish Karol Josef Wojtyla) was elected, he was given his current post and shortly after, consecrated a Bishop in 1980. Both he and John Paul II were classmates at the 'Angelicum' from 1946-1948. They were very close friends, although he regretted that their relationship had suffered immensely since the Pope's elevation.

He forced himself to focus on the screen. The first case concerned a Belgian parish priest whose name was found on a mailing list of pedophiles. Scarzi would be kept informed.

The second case concerned a Tutsi priest in Rwanda who had been implicated by a United Nation's task force in a number of reprisal murders against the Hutus. Scarzi would be kept informed.

And so it went. Each time he would close the file, the asterisk would disappear as if to say the Holy Roman Catholic Church was now in control of the matter. The only thing that was being controlled was Scarzi's despair over the impossibly long, tangled, and ponderous list.

When he got to the eleventh name, it didn't register all at once-Taylor, William, Priest, Diocese of Davenport, Iowa, USA. He tiredly gazed at the name, vaguely aware that there was something about this one. "Caro mio!" He hit the file key and the contents came forth to the now fully alert Scarzi.

> Taylor, William (b. 1921 DeWitt, Iowa), ordained 1945, Davenport, Iowa. Education: B.A., St. Ambrose College, Davenport, Iowa, 1941; Major Seminary, St. Paul's, St. Paul, Minnesota; Ph.D., Theology, Angelicum, Rome, 1949.
> Instructor - Theology - St. Ambrose College, Davenport, IA - 1949-1952
> Assistant Professor- Theology- St. Ambrose College, IA- 1952-1956
> Associate Professor- Theology- St. Ambrose College, IA- 1956-1963
> Professor - Theology - St. Ambrose College, IA - 1964-1965
> Parish Priest- St. Anne's Church, Long Grove, lA- 1965-1975
> Parish Priest- St. Anthony Church, Davenport, IA- 1975-1985

> Parish Priest - Sacred Heart Cathedral, Davenport, IA - 1985-1993
> Parish Priest - St. Mary's Church, Clinton, IA - 1993-1996
> Suspended - Trappist Monastery - Dubuque, IA - Present

Scarzi stopped for a minute in reflective silence. Billy Taylor! Taylor was the closest man to sheer spirituality whom Scarzi had ever met. As students at the 'Angelicum,' both he and John Paul II had walked around Rome and sat and talked and laughed on many occasions with Billy, and when John Paul was in a reminiscing mood, Taylor would invariably find his way into their conversation, and the Pope's mood would visibly lighten up. Scarzi had last seen Taylor about five years ago when he was on a visit to a conference in Chicago. In fact, he had spent two days with Taylor in Davenport, Iowa. As he recalled, that stiff-necked Irish Bishop of the Davenport Diocese was put out by his staying with Taylor, instead of at the Bishop's residence.

And Taylor had not changed. He was still charming but fixed on spirituality. Scarzi remembered the constant interruptions of the telephone and the self-sacrificing generosity of Taylor, who was all things to all people. And always he remembered Taylor's belief that all things happen for a reason, and that faith is the acceptance of that truth. "We are on a pilgrimage through a wasteland. There is no other way to see life." Taylor, still brilliant, was like a man who spent his entire life removing the clutter of personhood-so as to find the one simple truth-the return to God.

He went back to the screen, nervously and hesitantly wondering what could have befallen this apparent saint.

The Situation

Father William Taylor and the Diocese of Davenport were served papers for a civil complaint by one John Antle, who claims to have been sexually molested by Taylor while Father Taylor was at St. Anne's Church in Long Grove, Iowa (1970, 1971).

The charge is based on repressed memories which had surfaced during therapy. Antle's case is being handled by Carl Youngquist of Minneapolis who has been identified as a longtime bigot, hostile to the Church.

The Diocese was approached for a settlement before the papers were served. Bishop O'Meara steadfastly refused.

When questioned by Bishop O'Meara, Father Taylor denied any wrong doing but has refused to fight the matter publicly.

The Current Status

The Diocese has retained the services of the Blaine law firm to defend both itself and Father Taylor. Because it is felt that Father Taylor's ministry is now hopelessly compromised, he has been removed from his parish duties and sent to the Trappist Monastery in Dubuque, Iowa, where he will stay until the matter is adjudicated. All this is done under the orders of Bishop Brendan O'Meara.

-Monsignor George Duncan, Chancellor,
Diocese of Davenport
-July 12, 1996
"May God's Will Prevail"

Scarzi shut off his computer and went to his lounger where he sat and leaned back. He removed his glasses and stared out the window, which, if he had stood, would have given him an extended view of St. Peter's Square, but which now gave him a view of the hazy blue Roman sky. He felt totally exhausted and shattered. Although he knew that in probably 50 percent of the cases that he found on his screen there was truth to the charges, in this instance, nothing could shake his belief in Taylor's innocence. And yet this holy man, Taylor, would now be subjected to a spectacle that probably the guilty didn't even deserve. He wiped his moist eyes with a handkerchief and fell into a slumber.

Iowa, July 1996

Brother Joseph Fahy was a veteran of the Korean War. He had experienced both the surges of MacArthur and the ugly reprisals that the Chinese Communists had inflicted. He was wounded twice before being sent home to his native Chicago, where he joined the Chicago Police Department in 1953 at the age of 22. In 1956 he entered the Trappist monastery just outside Dubuque, Iowa. Now, at the age of 67, he served as the Director of Guest Services, which included handling arrangements for the numerous men who would come to the 1,000-acre farm/complex for weekend retreats or extended stays, depending on their need.

Father Edward, the Abbott, told him that a special guest would arrive by the name of Father William Taylor, he was to put him in the cloistered section, ask for his car keys, and then remove the car and park it in the barn, about a half mile east of the monastery. "And Brother Joseph," Father Edward looked sternly over his reading glasses, "no fraternizing! He is never to leave the grounds, and keep an eye on him. I want daily reports. To everyone here he is a guest. Do not let it be known that this man is under a cloud. Understood?"

"Yes, Father Edward."

Every once in a while Brother Joseph regretted not pursuing the priesthood, because sometimes he'd like to tell one of these pushy priest bosses to go to hell with their attitudes of superiority. But he'd catch himself, knowing that he'd have to admit to this type of thought in the weekly chapter of faults where each monk would have to confess before his brothers to his communal errancies.

He was on the telephone when a black-suited, Roman collared man was suddenly before his desk. He had never heard him come through the doors, a first for the sharp-eared Brother Joseph. Completing his conversation, he looked up and asked: "Can I help you, Father?"

"Yes, Brother. My name is Father William Taylor. I believe you're expecting me for a prolonged visit."

"Ah! Yes, Father, welcome to our monastery. I'm Brother Joseph."

Father Taylor, rail thin, stood about 5 feet 9 inches,

his full head of hair was gray, he wore rimless glasses, and all of his features were pointed and contrasted boldly with each other; his sharp, well-defined jaw, his lips which were tight but had the hint of a smile, his small but well-defined nose, and then the eyes-almost completely black and fully piercing. Brother Joseph had to come back to Taylor's face four times and only with a highly conscious and disciplined intent could he hold the look of this man.

"Allow me to assist you, Father." They went out to the graveled parking lot and removed two bags from Taylor's late-eighties Buick Skylark.

Taylor turned to Brother Joseph and said with a soft smile, "I guess there's no good reason to lock this around here."

Brother Joseph smiled back as best he could and with a blush said, "Father, I have been instructed to ask for those keys from you and to park the car elsewhere on the property." For just a minute, he thought that Taylor's eyes went dead, but he recovered.

With a smile he patted Brother Joseph's arm and handed him the keys, "I understand, Brother."

Brother Joseph had seen his share of eccentrics and personalities over the years. Already he was struck by the quiet power of this man.

For almost two weeks, he observed Taylor, not so much for Father Edward but out of curiosity, since it seemed that Taylor was quickly out-trappisting the Trappists. It was the custom for Brother Joseph, after ringing a bell in the death-like silence of the monastic wing, to knock on each door of the cloistered section at 5:00a.m. to say, "Bless the Lord" and listen for the response "Thanks be to God." Of course, years ago it was done in Latin: "Benedicamus Domine" and responded to by "Deo Gratias." After two days of English, Brother Joseph, unconsciously, switched to the Latin and from Taylor was given the Latin response. From then on, Brother Joseph stuck to that routine, because, in the case of Taylor, it seemed right.

He watched Taylor from his chair stall as the monks went about their business of chanting the ritualistic services beginning with Matins at 5:30 a.m., moving to the mass, and finally the process of meditation. Taylor easily took to the rhythm of the place and in a short time was well beyond any period of adjustment. During meditation, Brother Joseph saw the intensity in Taylor's rigid body as he smiled with eyes closed and with a look of serenity that was as natural as a field of corn on a sun-filled, Iowa summer day.

When the monks went to breakfast at 7:30a.m., Taylor drank a small glass of orange juice, ate two pieces of toast, and drank a cup of black coffee. He'd leave then and go back to his cell, complete his work assignment, in Taylor's case cleaning the showers and toilets (at Father Edward's insistence), from 8:00a.m. to 10:00 a.m., and then engage in another prayer session until 10:30 a.m. and then he'd walk until 11:45 before prayers and lunch. He'd then walk for a good two hours, probably nap or read for a short while, prayers, dinner, another walk, and then reading and praying again and sleeping. There weren't many options in this controlled day, as he kept to himself and adapted to the nurtured silence of the place.

Brother Joseph could see that the other monks were noticing this quiet man and could tell that respect was manifest in their eyes. Brother Joseph concluded that Taylor took to the Trappist schedule because either it was not that far from the way he ordinarily acted or he welcomed the contrast to his most recent schedule.

Meanwhile, he was prodded on a daily basis by Father Edward, and he could tell that Father Edward was initially disappointed when Brother Joseph would report about Taylor's discipline and character.

In the second week of Taylor's stay, Brother Joseph did something that he had never done before. He took advantage of his situation with Father Edward who on this particular day was in Des Moines on some monastic business. Assigned to cover Father Edward's office, he removed the key to his filing cabinet, which Brother Joseph knew was concealed under the desk lamp, and he opened the file cabinet. He found Taylor's file in the second drawer of the neatly arranged cabinet.

It had three pieces of communication. The first was a letter to Father Edward from Bishop O'Meara of the Davenport Diocese. It read:

> Dear Father Edward:
>
> Pursuant to our conversation of yesterday a.m., let me thank you for your cooperation on this Taylor matter.
>
> As I mentioned, I can't presume to know whether or not the man is guilty of pedophilia those many years ago (c. 1970), but let it be known that usually where there is smoke, there is fire. Furthermore, in numerous court cases where dioceses have

shown hesitancy in responding proactively liability has been exacerbated.

I don't want him treated as a criminal, of course, but I also want him kept on your grounds until the matter can be adjudicated or some resolution comes about.

It is said by some, but I have my doubts, that he is quite holy and therefore will not flee your grounds. I don't know, but your vigilance about the matter will be appreciated. If, for some reason, he does leave, please advise immediately.

The charge of $30 a day is agreed to and is most generous of you. An occasional report would be appreciated.

Yours in Christ,
Bishop Brendan O'Meara

Brother Joseph shook his head back and forth and wondered about the truth of the charges. His general feeling on the matter, however, was one of disbelief. And Bishop O'Meara? With the likes of him in your corner, you didn't need enemies.

The next letter, a copy, was from Father Edward to Bishop O'Meara.

Dear Bishop O'Meara:

It has been ten days since the arrival of Father Taylor. He seems to have fit in well and goes about his business in a reserved and disciplined manner. Brother

Joseph, a pretty shrewd old monk with a police background, seems to admire him. I certainly see no signs, as of yet, of any problem with him. I will keep you advised.

In Christ,
Father Edward, Abbott

And then, finally, a letter that must have come within the last day or two based on its date.

Dear Father Edward:

Received your note. Thank you. Glad to hear that Father Taylor seems to be toeing the line. Perhaps it's his ability to appear to be holy and unthreatening that is the source of our current problem. Please continue to be vigilant. By the way, I can understand this Brother Joseph of yours saying that there's nothing to report, but if he has fallen to a state of admiration, perhaps you need a more balanced observer.

Yours in Christ,
Bishop Brendan O'Meara

Brother Joseph could feel himself getting hot before catching himself and chastising himself for opening files that were not his business. He wavered from hurling some curses at the Bishop before placing the files back in the cabinet. "Balanced observer, my ass, Bishop O'Meara," he muttered before ordering himself a self-imposed rosary in atonement for this most recent outburst.

As he walked through the cloister, he dwelled on the

pederasty charge. He had a feeling of disgust and anger about the crime, but he could not relate the activity to Father Taylor, and yet he didn't know Taylor some 25 years ago, and he didn't know how grace and atonement and God's love played into the life of Taylor if indeed he was guilty. And if he wasn't guilty, was this some purification process that God kept in store for this seemingly holy priest? And ultimately, who really knew who was holy? But this man-how interesting! His Bishop had already washed his hands of him, and God knows how many of his parishioners and fellow priests were jumping off the cliff in order to disassociate themselves from this quiet, inner-oriented man.

He shook his head, pursed his lips, and went into his office. There were never enough rooms to meet the massive demand for spiritual services of the monastery. Catholics, Protestants, Jews, you name it, only Father Billy Taylor was remanded *to* this holy place to which they all came willingly.

CHAPTER TWO

Iowa, July 1996

Chip Blaine was the founder and czar of his law firm that was begun back in 1980 after an ugly split from the Sain & Lake firm, which had more or less dominated the Quad Cities region for decades. They had preached to him that it was only fair and fitting that he receive 20 percent of what he had earned for the firm. After seven years of that nonsense, he left and took with him a cadre of attorneys in their early-to-late thirties. "Let the old bastards fend for themselves. I'm not in the business of supporting them." And while the Sain & Lake firm still had considerable clout, Blaine compared it to an old bull walrus who couldn't protect his brood. It was just a matter of time.

At the age of 51, Blaine was the king of the hill. For those who came up against him, it was a no-holds-barred battle. His firm, now with 27 attorneys, had finally passed the Sain & Lake group, and his personal standing in the community was immense with just about every charity, board, and local corporation wanting him as a director. In addition, he had now become an official of the American

Bar Association and was the past President of the State of Iowa Bar. He considered himself to be the heavy hitter between Chicago and Des Moines on the horizontal axis and Minneapolis and St. Louis on the vertical axis.

He liked the fact that he drove an F-150 Ford pickup that was eight years old and had 130,000 miles on it. He felt that it showed his disdain for custom. It was one of many of his cultural eccentricities. After all, what other successful attorney had the balls to drive this broken down piece of crap!

Seated next to him was a two-year associate in the firm and a recent graduate from the University of Iowa Law School, Kim Rice. She was third in her graduating class and a real babe. She gave him all the right signals-respect, awe, obeisance, and she blushed at some of his subtle overtures. She was beddable material and perhaps on some overnight, he'd move on her.

Blaine reflected on Bishop O'Meara, with whom he was about to meet. O'Meara was appointed Bishop of the Davenport Diocese eight years previous. Twenty years ago he had come to the Diocese of Peoria, Illinois, as a young priest from Ireland to help the Diocese offset its dwindling supply of priests. The Peoria Bishop had taken a liking to him and in five short years, he was appointed his Chancellor. When the Davenport position opened, the conservative O'Meara was appointed as a continuation of the effort by the Vatican to bring American Catholicism to heel by appointing conservative bishops. Particularly liberal dioceses like Davenport groaned under this shift.

The Diocese of Davenport took in a number of Iowa's counties along the eastern rim of the State, from Clinton to the north and Keokuk to the south on the Missouri border and then pretty much across Interstate 80, which cut through the middle of the State, to about 90 miles west where it adjoined the Des Moines Diocese. To the north of the Davenport Diocese was the Archdiocese of Dubuque, which in the organizational chart of Roman thinking was the titular head of all four Catholic dioceses (the western end of the state being picked up by the Sioux City Diocese) in Iowa. There were about 120,000 Catholics in the Davenport Diocese. To Blaine, the account was a small potato, but potatoes nevertheless.

He had picked up the business of the Davenport Diocese when the Sain and Lake firm had gotten into one of its many conflicts of interest, but, as typical, refused to admit it. Blaine had reported the problem to the State Bar, which issued a reprimand. The hard-nosed O'Meara cut them off like a cancerous wart and chose Blaine because of the "courage it took to report your old firm." That statement told him a lot about O'Meara's proclivity to misjudge people's motives and also his willingness to take strong action.

On the occasions that he had worked with O'Meara, he saw that the man was remarkably close-minded and precipitous in judgment. O'Meara's Chancellor, and top advisor, Monsignor George Duncan, seemed to have marginal impact on his Bishop's mind. But creep Duncan was another story in itself. Blaine had learned to await O'Meara's quick judgment and then work from there in either agreeing with him or spending the time trying to tum around this disjunctive Irishman.

He pulled into the Diocesan Center at St. Vincent's in midtown Davenport. "Kim," he looked directly into the attractive blue eyes of his second, ''just observe in this instance. Try to make a good impression on these celibates. Oh, and by the way," he smiled with an ever so slight leer, "keep your legs together, and for God's sake, don't bend down to pick up a pen or something. That blouse does rather open." He patted her knee and noted a slight blush on her cheeks but, and it was only a perhaps, also an apparent appreciation that he noticed. She was definitely a project.

St. Vincent's was a three-story, red brick building that was erected in 1910. It had served several functions for the Diocese-an orphanage and an old age home-but in 1962 it was designated as the Chancery, and it was where O'Meara held court during the day, with his residence in the near southwest part of the city about three miles away.

"Bishop O'Meara and Monsignor Duncan, allow me to introduce Kim Rice who will be second chair in the Father Taylor case. She is one of our most gifted attorneys." Blaine noted that the Bishop and his Chancellor were somewhat ill-at-ease with Rice. Her beauty would help them over it-well at least O'Meara. As to Duncan, maybe he'd bring a cute guy the next time for him.

"Bishop O'Meara, how's Father Taylor doing with the Trappists?" Blaine asked.

"Well," he spoke with a noticeable brogue, a lyric tone of extended vowels but offset by the unexpected and unpredictable brusque stress on a consonant, "he's there. What else can I say? His car was taken from him, and he's in for the long haul, you know." O'Meara was a handsome man by anyone's reckoning. He stood about 6 feet 2 inches, had pitch black hair, and was in athletic condition, weighing about 180 pounds. He had an unusually long face, with ears to match. His intense brown eyes and slightly sullen mouth gave no sign of humor. Blaine, in the years that he had known him, had never heard him laugh; a smile, maybe a halting chuckle, at best, is what you'd get from this tight and austere man.

"Bishop, the last time I met with you, you were going to do some checking around with his fellow priests. Do you have anything for us?"

"Well, I'll be leaving that report to Monsignor Duncan. Father, if you would." He nodded to Duncan.

Blaine always felt disgust toward Duncan, a supercilious little creep who reminded him of Uriah Heep-oily, self-regarding, and untrustworthy. He calculated that he was shrewd enough to determine O'Meara's opinion (hardly a big puzzle) and then go out and manufacture a reality to support the opinion. It was a bad omen for the Church that this strange duo was at the top of the heap.

Duncan was a round man. There wasn't a sharp point anywhere around his average height, round pot belly, and round, porcine face. Blaine, a practiced poker player, knew that Duncan had no idea as to how he was perceived by him.

The Chancellor cleared his voice and spoke softly, "Well, Chip, I talked with just about every priest in the Diocese. We had a Priest Retreat and it was a mandatory attendance situation. We have 102 priests in the Diocese, and I tried to get around as the Bishop had ordered. I particularly talked with those who were 45 and up who could touch into that era when Father Taylor was, shall we say, perhaps-sexually active." Blaine thought that this was a bad piece of science. He could see priests in their forties, fifties, and sixties – he knew enough of them from his Diocesan work – a somewhat hard, acerbic, independent, and crusty lot – telling this little queen to fuck off because it was obvious that O'Meara and Duncan had made up their mind that Taylor was guilty, and the priests wouldn't like one of their own to be given to the dogs.

"Well," Duncan continued, "Father Taylor enjoys a lot of good will. They all to a man support him, and it became obvious that they are blinded by loyalty. It seems, also, that Father Taylor has a reputation among them for being an extremely spiritual man. But, as we know, who's to know?" He smiled at his play on words, and the Bishop seemed to crack a smile, grudgingly. Maybe the play on words was raucously funny for the humorless Bishop. Blaine gave Duncan a full hypocritical smile, and he noticed that Kim Rice smiled only after perceiving that he had manufactured one, a smart and cute little duckling following the leader.

Duncan went on, "It appears that Father Taylor is a bit of a cult figure to that generation and that he can do no wrong. Perhaps that mystique explains how he could have done what he did. I mean, of course, may have done." He looked at the Bishop for reassurance and was given a nod.

"So, it sounds as though you came up empty on that rung of the inquiry?"

"Well, yes, in terms of finding any indication that Father Taylor was a pedophile." He spat the last word out like it was a bad plug of chewing tobacco. "I did a total analysis of his personnel file, especially sensitive to criticism and correspondence between him and the Diocese. I'm sorry to report that the worst I could find is an angry letter from a father for whose daughter's wedding Father Taylor was two hours late. The bottom line was that he had witnessed an accident on the way to the church and had administered Extreme Unction." Duncan looked at Kim Rice and saw a look of puzzlement, "Last rites in popular parlance, and then stayed to counsel a bereaved man. No matter how bad he is, I guess you couldn't fault him. But he should have called. It was a rural parish out in the boondocks. We had another from a woman, who for penance after her confession, had to make up with her mother. She didn't think that was any of Father Taylor's business. As you can see, these are pretty standard things in any priest's folder. I guess what I'm saying is that he's pretty covert about this other life he may have had."

"Is there anything else, Monsignor?"

"No, Chip. I regret to say that we've been unable to find anything that corroborates the grounds of the lawsuit."

"And yet, Monsignor, I sense in your words a healthy suspicion." Blaine looked closely at him to see how he'd respond and then tried to catch the Bishop's face when Duncan answered.

"Well, to be frank," he looked studiously at longish nails, "I never did buy Father Taylor. He was always <u>too</u> holy, and when I see that, I see a man dealing with guilt. It's as if he was atoning for something from his past. This charge does explain a lot about him. It completes the new Gestalt as it were. I don't mean to be uncharitable, but you asked me for my opinion. I understand that this Youngquist is a bit of a rogue, but, present company excepted of course, aren't most lawyers?" He smiled cutely.

Blaine noted that the Bishop was nodding in agreement. They had talked this through. "Well, that understood, what is the intent of the Diocese?"

The Bishop responded, "I don't know what we can do. When I spoke with him, he said he wasn't guilty but that he'd have no further comment on the matter. What in God's name are we supposed to do when he won't talk? He just says, 'I never touched that boy.' And then I tell him that the suit will be filed within 48 hours unless we agree to a monetary settlement of a quarter of a million dollars." The Bishop was becoming visibly angry, "and what does he say, 'It must be God's will that this happen to him'? And I remind him of the harm to the Diocese, and he says, 'I'm not guilty. What else can I say, Bishop?' Now how's that for a hell of a situation? And you, Mr. Blaine, had no better luck."

Blaine had called Father Taylor the minute Youngquist had faxed his office of his intent to file. He had asked him point blank – "Did you sexually abuse a boy by the name of John Antle?" His answer was an almost bemused 'no.' When he was told of a pending lawsuit, he said that God's will manifests itself in many ways, and he hung up. From then on Blaine had dealt with the Diocese through O'Meara's orders.

Taylor's two weeks in the Trappist Monastery had changed nothing except that Taylor had missed the savagery of watching his name and reputation being destroyed by an all-too-willing media.

"Well," the Bishop remonstrated, "I'll say this to you, Mr. Blaine. If I had it to do again, I'd settle. The damage is just terrible, and when this man is not willing to go out and clear his name, it leaves us all looking bad."

"I can explore that, Bishop, with Youngquist."

"Well, perhaps you should. But I think a visit to Father Taylor is warranted. I am sending Monsignor Duncan to the monastery tomorrow morning, and we will be in touch with you as to what occurs. After that, I would think that it would be wise to bring him here to the office for a meeting with you and me together. How does that sound?"

"It sounds fine to me. In the meantime, I'll give Youngquist a call and see what we can come up with."

"Very well then. We'll keep in touch. Miss Rice, nice meeting you." And with that insincere comment the Bishop had closed down the meeting.

On the drive back, Blaine asked Kim Rice, "What's your take on this meeting?"

She answered, "Something doesn't seem to fit. I hate to say this, but I think they know something they're not sharing or else they're not terribly loyal to this Father Taylor. It certainly doesn't seem as though there's any love or support for him from those two."

Blaine didn't respond, although his analysis wasn't far off from Kim Rice's. What he didn't want say at this point was that Taylor's response to him when he called sounded like that of a man who was guiltier than hell. "God's will my ass," was Blaine's exact comment to himself.

The Vatican, July 1996

Bishop Scarzi was called by Monsignor Brezinski, personal secretary to Pope John Paul II, "His Holiness wishes to have lunch with you in his private apartment. He mentioned the file on Father Billy Taylor, to please bring it along. He'll be ready at 1:00 p.m. Thank you, Bishop." Other than his hello, Scarzi said nothing and wasn't asked for his opinion about his availability. This was the law. When the Pope wants something, it's done. Brezinski had the tact of a Sherman tank. He had thought about bringing it to the Pope's attention but put it aside. The Pontiff had enough pressures and concerns without worrying about his authoritarian secretary, and let it not be forgotten – fellow Pole.

The private apartment of the Pope had a concealed grandeur. The Pope was still in denial of the Church's role in the Renaissance, with all its magnificence and all of its corruption. Off the main dining room, which was immense and used for official Vatican affairs, was an intimate room that the Pope had prepared for himself. The table sat four, although Scarzi figured that, other than his bedroom and bath area, this was a place only for him and an occasional visitor. On a side table, as he entered the room, was a pile of neatly stacked newspapers from all over the world. The multilingual Pope had a firm grasp of the world of current affairs.

Scarzi was only in this room once and then when it was still being worked on. It was the room of a peasant, and it was a manifestation of the Pope's heart and sense of things. Perhaps, it was a reminder to him of how he would have wanted his life to be had he not been called upon by God to become the Supreme Pontiff.

A quiet nun, who met the Canon Law description of a suitable housekeeper/servant, i.e., old and homely, seated him and told him that the Pope would be there momentarily. Would he care for a glass of wine? He demurred.

John Paul had his arm around him before Scarzi was

aware of his presence. "Guillermo. So good to see you, my old friend. Here, let me look at you."

"Oh, your Holiness, excuse me for not standing. I wasn't aware that you were here." With that Scarzi went down on his right knee and kissed the Pope's ring. John Paul reached down and helped Scarzi stand up, all the while looking intently at him with a kind and thoughtful smile.

"Guillermo, I think of our days at the Angelicum with fondness and frequency. I get your reports on priests through Cardinal Pegis, and you do such a good job. But this private letter that you sent me about Billy Taylor is another matter altogether. It is about this that I wish to talk, and I emphasize that what happens in this room stays here. Cardinal Pegis will be out of the loop on this matter, other than your normal reporting on a case such as this. Understood?"

"Of course. It will be as you say, your Holiness."

"Tell me what you have on the matter."

"The Diocese, at my request, sent the lawsuit filing to me. In effect, it claims that Father Taylor seduced a boy of about seven into a number of lascivious acts. Need I elaborate?"

"No," the Pope said sadly.

"Apparently, the boy, now a man of 32, repressed these memories until about two years ago when, under hypnosis, they came into consciousness. He is now said to be suicidal." Scarzi looked at the Pope, whose somber jaw and tight mouth told of his stress in the matter. He continued, "The case got into the hands of a lawyer named Carl Youngquist who has made a fortune representing sexually abused victims of our clergy. I have seen his name often. He is seen to be a hater of the Church."

A lightly tossed pasta salad was served. "Who is the Bishop of the Davenport Diocese and what is his position in the matter?"

"A man named Brendan O'Meara, Irish, all the right credentials. He was appointed Bishop because he seemed conservative and sincere. Unfortunately, he seems to think that Billy is guilty. He appears to be embarrassed or ashamed by Taylor. I should say that I know this Bishop. When I visited Billy in Iowa some five years ago, I had lunch with Bishop O'Meara as a sign of politeness since he seemed to be unhappy about my staying in the rectory with Father Taylor."

"And-what's the point?" the Pope asked quickly.

"Well, I wasn't impressed with him. He seemed to be stiff-necked and, oh, what's a good word? Arrogant. Yes, arrogant."

The Pope responded, "Of all the problems facing the Church in America, I think these child sexual abuse situations are the most lethal. They undermine our clergy and thus, in turn, the Church itself. It is not good that our best and most caring priests are tarnished with this image. Maybe this explains his shame and his giving up on Billy."

"Your Holiness," Scarzi fixed the Pope with a stare, "it is inconceivable that Billy Taylor could do such a thing. I have met many spiritual men over the years. He's the closest to a saint that I have ever met."

The Pope sat back and looked up at the ceiling of the small dining room before closing his eyes. There was no conversation for a period of at least five minutes. Scarzi wondered if he had said the wrong thing in defending Taylor and tacitly attacking O'Meara.

"Guillermo, I agree with you. It is difficult to imagine Billy Taylor doing such a thing. My sadness would be immense if it came to be that it was true. It would be destructive of our persona even if Billy had made his peace with God. After all, that's what confession is all about." He pounded his fist on the table. "But in America where the law has taken the place of God, hell has become the tool of juries and judges. That country, for all its greatness, is an essential aberration! And one day, just as the Soviet Union did, it too will fall from its own stupidity, avarice, and godlessness." He wiped his mouth and threw down his napkin. Suddenly, a sad smile crept over his features. "Guillermo, you didn't come here for a sermon. Forgive me, my brother."

"Your Holiness, please don't. I love talking with you." The Pope waved at him to stop.

Shortly, the Pope pulled out from under his white sleeve a letter that he passed across the table to Bishop Scarzi. He said, "Guillermo, read this letter and then seal it, and make sure it ends up in the hands of Bishop O'Meara. Furthermore, I want you to be involved and I want reports. Perhaps we can do this again. I must go." He stood up and caught Bishop Scarzi as he was bending his knee-"You've done enough of that at your age-no more!" He patted Scarzi's shoulder and left. Scarzi didn't open the unsealed letter. It could wait. But he was very curious as he headed back to his office.

CHAPTER THREE

New York City, July 1996

Bill McAbee looked out his window at his stunning view of Central Park, the Hudson River, the upper reaches of Manhattan before being interfered with by a quickly moving cloud cover that was heading toward mid Manhattan. The city needed a good storm to clear out all the crap in the environment. In the best of worlds, he conjectured, such a storm could also sweep away half the population, that half which was composed of hustlers, cheaters, obnoxious asses, and assorted other crap in this toxic population.

He was the head of the McAbee Agency, which, by design, sounded innocent enough. In fact, it was one of the most efficient and feared private investigation operations in the world. There was probably no government in the world that hadn't in one way or another run into its tentacles. It was known for its discretion and ability to get things done without leaving a trace. His was a global company long before it became the thing to be. It was at lunch that very day that he had delivered the final details of the extraordinary private capture of a Palestinian terrorist to the Israeli Mossad

Bureau Chief in the U.S.A. McAbee's agency had run him down in Gibraltar of all places. The terrorist was delivered at Haifa yesterday, and the luncheon was a celebration of sorts. As usual, he made a big show of burning the proffered check of David Salter. It had now become a ritual between the two of them.

Of the many beliefs he had hardwired into his brain, the one that stood out the most in his dealings, particularly with the Israelis and Americans, was "always leave them owing you." And what he got from them was information, cooperation, and access. His check-burning costs would be borne by his many corporate and individual clients, which was where the money was when it came down to brass tactics.

Two days previous, Bishop Guillermo Scarzi had called from the Vatican. He had been referred by Cardinal Lepanto, the Secretary of State of the Vatican. He wanted an immediate appointment concerning a problem in Davenport, Iowa. He wanted a consultation and a contract that would lead to a full-blown investigation about what are, in all likelihood, false charges against a priest. The meeting was scheduled for 4:00p.m. today.

True to form, McAbee called Cardinal Lepanto for two reasons. He wanted to confirm the legitimacy of Bishop Scarzi and, in turn, remind the Cardinal that still another favor was being extended to the Vatican. Lepanto, in his judgment, had always been niggardly with information and one had to drive home on him the nature of favors, one of the oldest bonds in the book of life – quid pro quo. And what a mass of information the Vatican had if you could only pry it loose!

His call to Lepanto was on secure lines that McAbee had vetted regularly. Even then, there was always subtlety underlying all messages. Lepanto made one comment that caught his ear: "The superior is on this one, so we are hopeful of a first class effort, Bill."

Bill McAbee had met the Pope twice. The first time he had spent two hours with him detailing a delicate situation with the Bank of Italy, the Vatican, the Mafia, and the CIA. He found the Pope to be as tough as nails. He should have been a general. He would have no hesitancy to send you to your death if he thought that it would help the cause.

On the second occasion, which lasted three days, it dealt more specifically with the death of Communism. Again, the general in him came out, and it was a general who took no prisoners. This was a Pope who would spit at Joseph Stalin's comment: "How many divisions does the Pope have?" When they tried to murder him, the Communists had declared war, and now the Pope could respond to Stalin, and he did it by putting a drill into the cavity that was his native Poland. In those three days, he saw another side of the Pope, the sportsman. He saw the absolute joy of the man as he filleted and cleared the slithering fish of Communism. It was his trophy. If he could put Lenin's head over his fireplace, this Pope would do it. This Pope could be one mean bastard. Those who knew McAbee's way around words knew that this was a very high compliment from a fellow mean bastard.

At the end of his conversation with Leponto, he added that he was working on something and would appreciate some help. Leponto got the message: "Send your man. I'll do what I can."

The McAbee Agency was very careful in its hiring procedure. He made it clear that he would rather give up a job than to hire someone who would do poorly, cause embarrassment, or whatever else bad hires can do to you. He chose across two levels: the diplomatic corps and the special forces corps. Not that everyone came from those ranks, but those were the streets that he worked. Whomever he hired, though, he demanded absolute loyalty and a mindset that saw the world for what it was--dangerous, vicious, and mean spirited. It didn't mean you had to be that way to get hired, but you did have to appreciate those qualities in the world to play the game effectively. In other words, his agency was not for Pollyannas, Boy Scouts, and all that ilk.

Three assassinations had been attempted on Bill McAbee over the years, and he knew that it was perhaps only a matter of time before some son-of-a-bitch would get him, but he wouldn't make it easy. He was a crack shot, his Browning automatic a constant companion, a Derringer over his left ankle, and a cane that with the push of a button became a 12-inch stainless steel bayonet. His car was armor plated and his house in Riverdale was under constant watch. It was a requirement that even his secretarial staff be trained in the martial arts and that in their desks were guns that they knew how to use. True to his makeup, however, he always had one surprise that no one knew of, not even his wife of 30 years, who had long ago said to him that underneath all the suspicion and secrecy was a man who would willingly die a thousand deaths than to fail his family. He knew that she had him down.

When his younger brother Bertrand, the unorthodox classics professor, had left academia because of some of the rotten characters he had run across, Bill had done something that he at the time thought was a decision of the heart and therefore stupid. But he did it anyway. He helped set up Bertrand with his own agency in none other than Davenport, Iowa. True to his unique way of doing things, his brother called the agency ACJ Investigation Services. The ACJ meaning? Anthony (Saint), patron of lost objects; Christopher (Saint), patron of travel and safety; and Jude (Saint), patron of lost causes. When he heard about the name, Bill asked, "So, Bertrand, you're such a religious guy? When was the last time you were in church? So, what gives with the saint stuff?" Bill would be the first to admit to his sarcastic ways. "Bill," Bertrand said incisively, "since when is it a matter of belief? It's a question of symbolism, and that escapes your literalist mind."

What he feared most of Bertrand's entry into the game was that Bertrand wasn't sufficiently paranoid. Although Bertrand knew what the enemy was, he didn't realize the enormity of having a hater or a killer on your tail. At least, not until recently when against all odds, he captured a serial killer, probably largely due to his damn dog – Aries, Scorpio; or some such horoscope nonsense. But that's another story.

At any rate, Bertrand was due in at 3:00 p.m. for a preliminary meeting before sitting in with Bill and Bishop Scarzi. He didn't know how Bertrand would breathe the air of this meeting. It was one thing to handle some dumb farmer in Iowa, quite another-a Vatican Bishop.

He sat down and began to read the work of his research department. It looked as though the only major controversy to happen in the Diocese of Davenport was a sexual abuse charge against a minor by a priest named William Taylor.

He figured that this was what Scarzi was coming about, although he had never said. Buy why was the Pope interested in this? Cases like these were flying hot and heavy all over the U.S.A.

The University of Iowa Medical Center, the Nineties

Dr. Margaret Aaron, a staff psychiatrist and Assistant Professor at the University of Iowa Medical School and Hospitals was hooked hard on depressants. It happened the way it happens all too often in the medical community-fatigue, anxiety, and the occasional sleeping pill. The grueling residency at the Mayo Clinic in Rochester, Minnesota, which everyone knew was ridiculous with its long and exacerbating schedule, had simply worn her down. And she'd be the first to grant that behind her in-control and rigid persona was a very insecure, hurting, and searching woman. So the medical establishment and the medical school deans all knew it was bullshit to wear people down, bad for the doctor, bad for patient care, bad for the staff people, but they did it anyway-bastards! As if it wasn't bad enough coming out of the rat race of high performance in high school, college, and then medical school at Northwestern in Evanston, Illinois, no, they continued the repeating shaftings right through the training process.

She figured that academia-at least when you're not on the receiving end of its shaft-would give her the lifestyle she needed to repair herself. And she found some respite at the University of Iowa, but not all that much. There was the constant pressure to do research and to publish, besides her student load and teaching a seminar at the medical school. She decided to specialize in the field of child sexual abuse and had already published one interesting article in the *Journal of American Psychiatry* on incest and its relationship to other forms of sexual abuse by non-family members. It was a brilliant piece, in fact, and it put her on a fast track to the promised land-tenure.

But beneath it all lurked some monsters in her own soul. She felt that some terrible wall stood between her and mental health and now that she had time to reflect on herself, she could feel a presence of evil in her. She knew that she wouldn't be happy without exorcizing it, and when she couldn't get at it by her own devices, she sought help.

She started informal therapy (no record would be kept) with Dr. Anne Magee, an Associate Professor of Psychiatry at the University. Magee only worked with women patients, and there was an apparent affinity between her and Aaron. But after the fourth session with Magee, it was over. She remembered it distinctly.

Dr. Magee told her to sit down across the circular table in her office. She said, "Margaret, I do agree with you. You do have a problem that is haunting you, and it's not the fact that you are drug dependent. .."

Margaret flew back from her leaning position and protested sharply, "How dare you say this. I have no dependency problem. I can't believe that you're saying this, Anne. How incredible. I don't need this crap from you. Why would you say such an outrageous thing to me?"

Anne Magee was good all right. She just sat there gazing deeply into Margaret Aaron's eyes, who herself could feel a deep flush coming over her features. Aaron knew that she was right but was really angry that it had been figured out. Dr. Magee said in a very quiet and intense way, "Margaret, I have no reason to hurt you. You came to me, not vice versa. Let's make one thing clear. You asked for my thoughts about you. In my judgment you have a drug problem, and you better get it fixed. I'm not going to report you because of the doctor/client privilege, but I believe you do have a big-time problem. I get paid to observe. I don't think that you are impaired, strictly speaking, but it's just a matter of time."

"Why are you saying this?"

"Oh, it's in your patterns of speech. I didn't tape our conversations, but it was so clear to me. It's just a matter of time, however, before it does affect you, and when it becomes clear, believe me, you'll be on a career-ending hit list."

Margaret Aaron fell silent, absorbing the terror from the fact that this all too astute colleague had her figured out. She was scared and decided to stick to her guns. "It's just not the case."

Anne Magee dropped another silence into the conversation. Finally she said, "Listen, Margaret, you're in a state of denial. Our sessions have been informal, so I'm not going to report you. But I don't work with the chemically dependent-nothing personal." Anne Magee, in her late thirties, had a round and not particularly attractive face, but she was not the kind of woman to back down from anyone; that was so evident to Margaret. Magee continued, "Furthermore, I do agree with you. You have a deep-seated problem coursing through your psyche. It's probably ... but here I'm only guessing ... a childhood repression. That's usually a sexual thing and your choice of speciality lends some support to this. You might be a candidate for hypnosis and repressed memory work. I'm hesitant to recommend this because of all the controversy around it, but it does have its merits if it's used correctly."

Aaron saw the opening. There was a way to avoid the drug dependency situation but get in with someone else about her problem, someone who might be more willing to deal with the real issue.

"Well, Anne, I know that you mean well. Let's call it moot in the drug issue, but do give me a name on the therapy issue."

Magee did as asked and the drug issue fell between the cracks as Anne Magee stayed true to her word. After all, in Aaron's view, no admissions were even made, and thus there was never any incontrovertible proof of drug dependency. Legally, therefore, Magee was in the clear and in modem medicine, that was always the prime consideration.

It was then, acting on Magee's advice, that Aaron came under the influence of a visiting Professor of Psychiatry from the University of London, Edward Nelson. By the third session with him, Dr. Margaret Aaron was forced to confront the staggering realization that her father committed incest with her repeatedly between her tenth and eleventh year of life before he had an aneurism and was dead before he hit the floor at the high school where he taught. Upon his death, an extraordinary process of repression had set in and all was forgotten except for the feeling of guilt and anger that paralyzed parts of Dr. Margaret Aaron's personality. Nelson never picked up on her drug dependency, which in her denial mode proved that she wasn't drug dependent. She just had become a disciple of Nelson's and soon she herself learned the art of hypnosis and the articulation of repressed memory syndrome with this art. But late in the two-year span, her relationship with Nelson started to rupture, his final words before separation being: "Doctor, in my judgment, you have been conquered by a process and now you are using the process to delude yourself and your patients. In fact, sexual exploitation of children is a relatively rare phenomenon in this country, but as I hear you speak, it has become the centerpiece of virtually every patient's problem. It appears that when you hear the presenting problem in a patient, you immediately gravitate to incest or pederasty as the cause of the problem. In fact, I believe this to be as rare as you believe it to be common. Repressed memories are easily given to therapeutic manipulation, especially when the therapist is looking for the phenomenon. Don't you see the problem here?"

"Yes, I do see the problem, and it's you. I think that you are committing a form of incest right now. We had the semblance of a father-daughter relationship, and now, for some reason, you're raping me just like my real father. Your work with this method is an unconscious attempt on your part to discover the incestuous part of you, and I will not allow you to victimize me anymore. Our relationship is terminated."

Aaron knew enough about the Englishman to know that he wouldn't pursue the matter with her colleagues. He was going back to England in six months and didn't need his reputation sullied. So still another colleague was held in check by her lively and astute game playing. By this time in her career, she was in a massive denial of her drug dependency and an overwhelming acceptance of repressed memory therapy and its grounding in childhood sexual violations.

Minneapolis, 1994

Carl Youngquist, at 35 years of age, was a stunning success story in legal circles. Already a multimillionaire, he had decided to devote his entire life to exposing the fat and corrupt whore –the Roman Catholic Church in America. That it was a whore with deep pockets didn't go unnoticed, either. It was those deep pockets that made him a millionaire.

He was asked once by a reporter from the *Minneapolis Star Tribune* whether he had a hatred for the Church he so regularly took on. His answer was, "There are many good Roman Catholics with whom I have no quarrel. I only pursue the rot in that Church." In truth, he had an obsessive hatred of Catholicism that was burnt into him by an ultraconservative Lutheran father who, as a Lutheran minister, would regularly read from Martin Luther about the Roman whore. His actual take, which he would never say to a reporter, would go like this: "There are some good people who happen to be Catholic in spite of this horrible flaw."

After graduating from the University of Minnesota Law School in 1984 in the bottom 20 percent of his class, he had set up a solo practice in Mankato, about 80 miles south of the Twin Cities. In 1985 he got the case that would make him famous. A 15-year-old boy had been systematically and continuously sexually abused by three priests in the Twin Cities. The boy had kept a diary. This little coven of corrupt priests had passed the boy around between them. It was during the summer, on a stay with his aunt, that the boy had shared his experiences with a cousin, who took it to the aunt, who took it to Youngquist. The publicity and damages had rocked the Church in the Twins. The Church settled for a million dollars; Youngquist took home a $400,000 check and felt great. The whore was stabbed, he was wealthy, and the 16-year-old boy had enough money to get therapy for the rest of his screwed up life.

His reputation grew and so did his business. By 1994 he centered on only one facet of the law-damages done by hypocritical celibates. He had four associates and two full-time investigators. Business was good for this stoop-shouldered man whose sickly white face and rat-like features became one of the most feared figures for the Catholic Church. The whores called him a scourge and a bigot, and when they did that, it just pressed his resolve still further. He felt that he had a spear and knew where the Achilles heel of the whore was. His deceased father and Martin Luther would be pleased.

But the practice of law was a business first and foremost. Access was based on the principles of business, especially when you were in the kind of law he practiced. He had his staffs regularly peruse journals' dealing with counseling and therapy for articles pertinent to what he was doing. It was with interest that he read an article in the *American Journal of Therapeutic Intervention* by a Dr. Margaret Aaron. It was entitled *Repressed Memory Therapy and Realizations of Sexual Misconduct.* One thing was clear to Youngquist after he read the article-this was a bitch we need to cultivate since she specifically mentioned crimes done by clerical figures.

He sent his best investigator, Herb Scannell, down to Iowa City, which was five hours south by car. Scannell had been a detective for the Minneapolis Police Department and had all the cynicism that Youngquist liked to see in his colleagues.

Three days later, Scannell called him in his downtown Minneapolis penthouse. "Got some interesting stuff on this psychiatrist. Are you free?"

"Yeah. Hold on a minute." Youngquist put his hand over the phone, but he wanted Scannell to overhear. He was proud of his image. "Doris, I need some privacy. There's a bathrobe on the stand over there." He was sure that Scannell not only heard those comments, but he also heard the playful slap on Doris' ass and her too false laugh that followed it. When she was gone from the bedroom, and he made sure she had closed the door, he came back to Scannell. "Sorry, Herb, just attending to an item here." He smiled at his little joke, wondering what Scannell was thinking.

Scannell responded, giving nothing away, a trait that Youngquist admired and feared. "Dr. Margaret Aaron has a reputation for being a sort of psycho. Never heard a patient's take on things that she didn't believe, that sort of thing. It sounds like she tries to connect every adult problem to sexual abuse. Sounds to me like she's a Freudian bitch."

"Where are you getting this from?"

"Good sources. I've spent $5,000 already. But I'm not done. Sounds like she hates organized religion, straight up and down, not just a Catholic thing." Youngquist winced.

Although Scannell didn't come right and say it, it sounded like a critique of Youngquist. But Scannell's tone changed, so you could never tell if it were a critique or merely a statement of fact, period.

Herb Scannell continued: "She has a huge clientele; in fact, she resigned from the medical school a year ago. Reading between the lines, could've been forced, but I don't know. At any rate, she's done court stuff as an expert witness, and she's not hurting for money. Got some good photos of her. A nurse who used to work for her thinks she's into drugs-big time."

"0! .. K!" This was great news to Youngquist. If he could compromise the bitch, he could get a steady line of referrals. And if she wasn't working out of the medical school drug supply it will be a problem for her.

"I'm thinking of talking with her," Scannell continued. "I can tell her about you and your heroic efforts to stop abuse and ask her for her cooperation. In return-and I will be as subtle as I can-I'll make it clear that her wish is your desire. What do you say?"

"I love it. But be circumspect. I don't want you getting busted. Herb, this is great news for the firm. Keep me informed, please. Go out and get laid tonight, Herb. You deserve it." Youngquist laughed; Scannell hung up. Youngquist wondered what the hell goes on inside that guy's mind.

CHAPTER FOUR

Iowa, July 1996

Bertrand McAbee was ailing. An obsessive runner and racquetball player, he was plagued by a series of injuries that now sat on his spirit like a one-ton gorilla. First it started out with severe pain in his shoulder which affected his swing in racquetball. His opponents, seeing the grimaces, naturally worked his weakness. About two weeks later, at a game point, he put a little extra into a serve and felt his arm give out. Officially, he had a severe case of tennis elbow and was told to stop playing for a month. It would do his shoulder and elbow good. Meanwhile, he was subjected to a cortisone shot in his shoulder and elbow area. Always a runner, he thought he'd just pick up the pace in the distance on his almost daily runs. This was until he was hit by shin splints on both legs, a bruised right big toe and plantar fasciitis in his right heel. When he first noticed the splints, he was told by his sometime 31-year-old running companion to get a new pair of running shoes and just run through it. He did as suggested and now he was a walking-only medical case. The orthopedist, who was cortisone happy, was avoided on the leg injuries as he went to a recommended chiropractor at the Palmer Clinics in Davenport. His foot was adjusted regularly, his shin splints were massaged, and he was beginning to feel a glimmer of hope. But all in all, it was a pretty lousy summer for the 56-year-old McAbee.

Not only did he gain 10 pounds, but Scorpio, his 100-pound, white German Shepherd, was also suffering from this catastrophe. The four-year-old dog had been in tiptop shape because he regularly ran with McAbee as they set out on rural Scott County roads in the early morning. McAbee was saddened to see him pick up a few pounds, but Scorpio also seemed to lose his mental sharpness and became a little edgier with frustration. And yet, McAbee felt that Scorpio realized that he was hurting, what with the ice packs, the stretching, and the hand weights used to strengthen his right arm. Scorpio was an observant dog.

It was near midnight when his brother Bill called from New York City. Bill, the never sleeping, all-vigilant older brother ran an international agency that freely skirted every law in the book in the shadowy world of surveillance, terrorism, and protection. Bertrand never could get the proper take on Bill as to what actually motivated him, except for perhaps his overwhelming need for order. And he knew what created that: the dysfunctional and chaotic family structure in which Bertrand, Bill, and two other brothers were brought up. Whether that was the case or not, it struck Bertrand that the turmoil was so bad that order became its antidote. It would be a vast understatement to call Bill an ultraconservative. Rush Limbaugh was probably a flaming Commie to Bill, and Senator Joe McCarthy probably a defamed hero for putting the screws to the filthy bastards who flirted with the likes of Joseph Stalin and his mass murderers.

"Bertrand, you awake?" He was just barely awake. Bill rarely identified himself. Only a fool wouldn't realize that it was his majesty.

"Bill, I'm wide awake. I never sleep. I just wait for your calls. Is something wrong?"

"No, not with the family if that's what you mean." Bertrand knew that was the irreducible to Bill. Ultimately, the way to destroy Bill would be through his family, not some shakedown of the world order. Bill had worked his whole life to make sure that the chaos he had lived through would never come to his family-Mary and the three pampered kids-who had turned out well even with the material spoilage. Bill continued, "But there's a problem out there in Shitsville, and I need your help." Shitsville was Bill's name for the Quad Cities, an amalgam of four main cities on either side of the Mississippi River, two in Illinois (Moline and Rock Island) and two in Iowa (Davenport and Bettendorf). The greater metro area had a population of about 375,000-but Shitsville nonetheless to Bill.

"Bill, we never have problems out here in the heartland. What's the matter?"

"Do you recall hearing or seeing something about a priest named William Taylor who is being sued for hitting on a little boy years ago?"

"Yes. It's a big story out here. I know him. I met him a few times. A very engaging man. It's hard to believe this one, but every time I see such a charge, it makes me wonder. I thought the Cardinal Bernardin thing would put the brakes on some of this. And you know the now-retired Bishop of the Davenport Diocese was brought through similar stuff by two women. Ultimately, they were shown to be psychos looking for hush money to save him from embarrassment. There seem to be a lot of toss-ups in these things." Scorpio had now jumped on the bed and forced McAbee's left hand to pet him. Late calls like this were highly unusual, and Scorpio probably wanted reassurance that everything was OK. Scorpio and Bill were both order freaks, Bertrand thought ruefully. "So, what's this got to do with your calling me at midnight? Are you hard up for conversation?"

"I need you out here tomorrow at 3:00p.m. There's a United Express out of Moline at 9:00, into Chicago at 10:00; a United out of Chicago at 10:45, into La Guardia at 1:45 where you'll be met. Look for a sign with your name on it, and presto you'll be in my office at 3:00. Just go to the ticket counter in Moline. It's all taken care of."

"Bill, what if I have other plans?"

"Cancel them. This is a big, big deal, Bertrand. You're going to be dealing with the right hand of God at 4:00. Oh, and Bertrand, a few other things. See if you can bring the newspaper articles on this, don't dress like a college prof, and don't bring that mutt Aries, or whatever his name is."

"Bill, it's Scorpio, you half-wit. I will be there because I owe you a favor, and I'll dress as I always dress. If you don't like it, you can go straight to hell."

Bill laughed and said, "Looking forward to seeing you, Bertrand." For all of his gruffness and single-mindedness, he still had a sense of humor. If he didn't, he'd be impossible.

McAbee turned his light off and shoved a knee into the supine Scorpio who tended to take up three quarters of the bed. Grudgingly and with a low sigh, the dog moved at least three inches. It was enough; McAbee slept well.

Iowa, July 1996

Father Edward didn't know what to make of Father William Taylor. If he heard Bishop O'Meara of the Davenport Diocese correctly, Taylor was a sexual predator of children. There were no children on these grounds; therefore, he allowed Taylor to stay here and even stay in the cloister with the monks. He had been at the game of assessing suitability and personality for more than 15 years, and he had seen all sorts come and go in the monastic setting. Sometimes one day in the cloister was enough for some. He recalled the young man from Des Moines who arrived on Saturday at 1:00 p.m. with two car loads of friends and relatives, whose tear-filled handkerchiefs would lead one to surmise that a funeral was going on, rather than the joyous calling to the monastic life. At any rate, he was gone by 11:00 a.m. the next morning as a beeping car with his friends tore out of the grounds.

He had yet to speak with Taylor and there were two weeks gone by. From the indirect conversations that he had with senior monks, who were also no one's fools at character perception, they had respect and goodwill toward Taylor. For even though oral communications were virtually banned except for necessary exchanges, the silent language of body movement, posture, and so on, spoke volumes to these discerning monks.

In fact, two of the monks thought that he would make

a fine addition to the monastery. His closest confidante, Father Hubert, who when told of Taylor's alleged crime, opined that he doubted it, but even still that's what this pilgrimage on earth is all about-sin and redemption, and, if in fact, it was the case, the man had obviously repented and that was all that was to be said. Father Hubert went on rhetorically about how many people are walking around this earth who are free from grievous crimes against others. In assent, Father Edward could only nod his head in agreement at this observation, as he watched Hubert's arced fingers make a zero.

Brother Joseph, forever the snoop, was another story and brought a different level of analysis to the question. It was hard to put something over on him. That was why he was in charge of guests at the monastery. Every once in a while, an alcoholic would arrive to supposedly get his life back in order, or a gay couple would show up with the intention of developing a newly found sexual abstinence. Within a few hours, scandal would be occurring as the drunk tipped into his hidden stash of booze or the gay couple discovered the meaning of Augustine's lament: "Chastity, but not now Lord." Brother Joseph handled these kinds of problems with a sure hand and kept the monastery on an even keel, what with the dangerous mix of always seriously religious men and sometimes seriously sinful men. If there was anything to know out there, Brother Joseph knew it. He was the caregiver of the grapevine, and Father Edward, a one-time executive with IBM, knew what that gave to him in terms of influence and power.

But this was the day for Father Edward to meet Taylor.

"Brother Joseph, before you get Father Taylor, tell me your observations."

Brother Joseph said, "By all outward signs, and that's all that we have after all, he's a very saintly man. I've kept a close eye on him at your request. Usually, after two weeks, there are things for me to report, but I have none of the negative stripes. It's as though he has been here all his life. As to positives, he never misses a service, he eats sparingly, he maintains silence, and when he does speak, it's to the point. He's no jabberer, Father Edward." This meant to Father Edward that Brother Joseph was hitting a stone wall with his prying approaches. Good for Taylor, because he was sure that the jabberer in Brother Joseph had made a run at him.

"Well, Brother, why don't you go and get him and tell him I wish to speak with him." Within minutes Father Taylor knocked at the half-open door of Father Edward's office.

"Oh, Father Taylor, please ... please come in." He extended his hand and received back a firm but smallish hand in return from Taylor. He showed him to a seat in front of his desk and they both sat.

"So, Father, how is it for you up here?"

"I'm elated to be here. These two weeks have been good for me, especially given the circumstances that have brought me here."

"You mean the lawsuit of John Antle?" There was nothing to be gained from playing ignorant.

"Yes, but, of course, that charge carries a great deal of baggage with it."

"I'm sure that it's staggering, Father."

Father Taylor didn't respond and Father Edward saw no

foothold to further progress in this gentle inquiry. It really was not his business.

"The Diocese called me last night about you, Father. Their intent is to send up a priest by the name of Monsignor George Duncan. He is expected to arrive on the grounds at 10:00 a.m. I'll have Brother Joseph reserve a meeting room for the two of you." Taylor gave no reaction to the announcement. Monsignor George Duncan could be a Satan or Jesus and Taylor would never let you in on which.

Father Edward had perfected the power of silence in conversation. By just laying in out there, people would open up and tell you things that they sometimes wish they hadn't. Silence, however, was about as effective with Taylor as it would be in changing the landscape of the Grand Canyon.

He pressed him, "Is there any assistance I can give you, Father? Do you need anything for this meeting?" Father Edward was beginning to feel awkward, if not a bit seedy, at about this point.

Father Taylor fixed him with his eyes and said, "Father Edward, you've been most kind to me. Everyone has been sensitive and good, but I assure that I can take care of myself in this matter because of one simple thing-I'm innocent. I feel that this is a purification process sent to me by God. If you remember what I just said and I remember to keep everything in that perspective, then whatever happens is of no significance."

It was a warning growl of sorts from this small and extraordinarily intense man. And yet, as the man in charge, he found it obligatory to come at Taylor one more time.

"Father, I honor your feelings and thoughts on all this,

but I would be remiss if I didn't offer you an ear, either of myself or anyone you might choose here."

Taylor merely responded with a blunt, "Thanks."

They spoke then about accommodations at the Monastery, the schedule, the chores, the routine, the reading materials, and in each instance, Taylor promoted himself as being happy. The one request that he did make was that his car be routinely started and driven a short distance every week or so.

When he left, Father Edward wrote a brief note:

> Talked with Father Taylor this morning. I realize that he's in his seventies and that what appears to be the case today is predictably quite different from what it might have been 25 years ago. But at this point, I can only concur with the prevailing opinion here: he has his life in order and is quite impressive.

Iowa, May 1994

Scannell had long ago given up any pretensions about the goodness of people. He was a social Darwinian in a world he construed to be amoral. The law was the only thing between outright anarchy and civilization for what it was.

His take on Youngquist was without illusion. He was a vicious, meanspirited, money- grabbing bastard who paid well and gave Scannell the cloak of attorney privilege. He had met his share of scum when he was with the

Minneapolis Police Department, and Youngquist was just as disgusting as the meanest contract killer or the biggest heroin-dealing pimp that he could recall. The difference was that Youngquist was featured in the *Minneapolis Star Tribune* as one of the 50 most up and coming leaders in the Twin Cities. Why? Because he knew how to sodomize the Catholic Church with its terribly big pockets. But the pay was good and when it's all done, who really gives a damn in this insane world?

He drove to Aaron's office in downtown Iowa City. He was told that the receptionist left at 4:30 each day and that Dr. Aaron stayed on until about 6:00 doing her dictation and revising typed material submitted to her by the receptionist. The nurse stayed until five. She recommended that he just come by at about five. She would leave the door open. What he did then was his affair.

This information had cost him a thousand dollars and a promise not to expose Dr. Margaret Aaron's nurse, Margi. In this instance, he would honor the promise because he figured that he'd probably have to use that pump again if Aaron started to play ball. The nurse would be the unknown monitor of Aaron. He also knew that Aaron was a closet addict, hopelessly hooked on a full range of depressants even while her practice had soared. From Margi he also found out that she had a patient base of about eight who were dealing with church-related sexual assaults, and of those, five were Catholic priest based.

Aaron was getting her drugs in a variety of ways, all of which exposed her to the wrath of the Iowa Board of Medical Examiners based in the capital of Iowa, Des Moines. Her most common method, besides having a regular and legitimate prescription from a classmate, was a pretty subtle form of reversion. She would tell a patient that a depressant was in order, and she would prescribe a rather heavy dosage. She would tell her usually vulnerable and suggestible patient that it was best that the drugs be kept at Aaron's office. This would keep the patient free of overuse, suicide, addiction, and would also guarantee the patient's cooperation in the tough process of therapy. As long as Aaron kept a modest string of about 10 patients in this pseudo treatment modality, she had a marvelous supply line and all of it cloaked under this apparent care-giving and patient-loving psycho nonsense.

When he saw the nurse leave, he went into the one-story office building on Dodge Street. The waiting room was small, and he decided to sit there after he had thrown the door lock. He heard her muffled voice in what had to be her office. It sounded like she was dictating, and she surely did not know that he was there. He thought through his strategy. She'd either launch on him and threaten to call the police or she'd play some game to finesse him out of the office. He decided to open up on her with both barrels blazing the minute she didn't buy the soft line.

He went through the gate and took a turn to the left honing in on the direction of her voice. He put his hand on the door, turning it quietly to make sure that it wasn't locked, and then simultaneously he knocked and opened it wide at the same time.

This somewhat obese woman in her late thirties was aghast. She put her recorder down and demanded: "Who are you? I'm closed! Whom are you looking for?" Her medium cut hair was brushed back severely and lumped in the back.

She had an oval face with an aquiline nose and pouting lips which were now in a stern configuration.

"Please, Dr. Aaron, your door was open. I've come here on a professional matter. I mean you no harm." He spoke quietly, with his hands laid out, pleading as it was but also done with a purpose-to reassure her.

But she would have none of it. "No, I will not do business this way. Either leave or I will call the police. Which is it?" She looked at him with a dare as if to say she was now in control. She had misinterpreted his nonthreatening gestures and voice as a sign of weakness and was seizing the moment.

There was a silence of a few seconds, after which she picked up the telephone. When she did, he said, "You're a drug addict practicing reversion. If you make that call, your license will be suspended in a month. Then we'll see how easy it is to keep up your addiction, Doctor. I just want a few minutes of your time. My name is Herb Scannell."

As he said this, she froze, phone midway suspended between her ear and the cradle, but more importantly her face went white and the standing authoritarian woman sank back down into her chair. The power had changed again, and now it was time to flatten her. She put the phone back into the cradle and asked in an unsure voice, "What are you talking about?"

"Doctor, listen. This can go on for hours or it can end in a few minutes. I have a business proposal where all the forces of good win and a terrible force of evil loses. Would you listen?" This statement, of course, was pure nonsense, but perhaps it would work on her. After all, she was treed and they both knew it. She nodded in assent. "I work for a very dedicated attorney in Minneapolis. He specializes in personal injury, but especially in sexual abuse that was done to children and young adults by Roman Catholic clergy."

"So what? What is this to me?" She was trying to make a comeback in the force game. He pressed, "Believe me, Doctor, it's not so what, it's how can I help? Are you going to listen?" She sat back resignedly, realizing that anything she could do would have to be done when he said his piece. "This attorney came upon your most recent article on therapy, and he feels that you are two kindred souls in your battle against sexual predators. Very simply, Doctor, he wants to use you as an expert witness, and he wants referrals from you anytime a Catholic priest is implicated in a sexual crime against children."

"That's dishonest. I don't make referrals to lawyers."

"Well, that's what we'd like you to consider. To help you in this deliberation, I have some goodwill gestures. One, for every client you send his way who has a viable case, you will be given $10,000 cash. Two, we will gladly remove you from the reversion problem you have. We will become your supplier. As a sign of our goodwill and ability to deliver, allow me to present these to you." He handed over a small duffel bag. "You don't need to open this in my presence in case you think that I'm a cop or this is some form of entrapment. I will call you at nine sharp tomorrow morning. Please have me sent through to you and just answer yes or no. Here's my card. I will visit with you on occasion. You are never to have any contact with Mr. Youngquist. We would expect at least one or two referrals a year. Questions?"

"No ... no. Please leave now." He noted the tears in her eyes.

He left. When she finally did open the bag, she would

find enough depressant to last a deeply addicted person three months. They had been FedExed to him a day ago by a Youngquist intermediary. He drove away with one thought-'Yuppie scum!'

The next morning he was put through at nine.

She said, "Yes, I'll be in touch." He was heading north on Interstate 380 ten minutes later.

CHAPTER FIVE

Iowa, July 1996

Bertrand McAbee was up at 6:00 a.m. He took a long walk with Scorpio on a rural road just a bit north of his house. The com was unusually high, the soy beans a lush green, and all was good for Iowa agriculture. Scorpio rambled along as if he was the overseer of a huge plantation, his long tail wagging, black eyes darting back and forth, and his black nose searching for scents.

When they arrived back at the house, McAbee took him into his dog run, filled up his bowl with fresh, cold water, and put food into his canister. Scorpio normally would have put on a barking and running protest, but now that he was falling out of shape like his owner, he just went into the unit with his head bowed down. McAbee felt a stab of pain at this. He always understood his protests at being left alone and didn't like to see this resignation.

He went across to his neighbor, Gloria, who was the unofficial worrier about McAbee. Since his recent divorce, she had become just a bit too overprotective. Gloria, unwittingly, had saved McAbee's life when a serial killer had made an effort to kill him at his home, and in the process she had taken a vicious blow to her jaw, which was broken in several places. She was one of only a handful whom Scorpio accepted and obeyed. When McAbee went on trips or would be gone late into the night, this gracious woman would keep an eye on Scorpio.

"Gloria, guess what?"

"I wonder if Scorpio needs looking after-guess what?"

"You're right. I'm going to New York City and won't be back until quite late, probably 11:00 or so. His dinner is inside the back door. Just go in and get it and perhaps talk with him for a few minutes."

"How're your legs doing?"

"Yeah ... OK. I think I'll start to make some effort next week to get back into things. We'll see. How are you?"

"Oh, fine, Bertrand. Now you watch yourself in New York. That mayor is always talking about how safe it is, but the rest of America knows it's a snow job."

"It's a deal, Gloria. Thanks."

New York City, July 1996

Jan Canton had worked for Bill McAbee for five years. She was a gofer, the kind of gofer who managed details. It was in those details that Bill McAbee separated himself from others. His agency was never late for plane pickups, hotel reservations were checked and doubled checked, fruit baskets and flowers were always in the rooms, dinner reservations made, all under the guardianship of Jan Canton who also kept a vigilant eye on any client or associate of

Bill McAbee's. The innocent-appearing and low-keyed Jan Canton was psychology degreed from New York University.

She had met Bertrand once but only for about 20 minutes as she successfully purchased a pair of tickets to the Met for a performance of *The Marriage of Figaro.* That was when he was married to that brittle lawyer. The family physical resemblance between Bill and Bertrand jolted her at first, but his voice, mannerisms, and MO were quite different from Bill's. She had the impression that Bertrand looked at people as enigmas and the world as a puzzle and would probably die that way. His mind seemed open to possibilities and nuances whereas his brother was the most disjunctive, focused, and narrow person she had ever met. They were so opposite that even after a few minutes, she was surprised at the gulf that separated the two.

She stood at Gate B-17 with a sign that read Dr. McAbee; she knew that he had been a classics professor at a small liberal arts college in Iowa. When she saw him, she felt that he had aged around the eyes, had lost even more hair on the top of his head, had gained a bit of weight, and perhaps there was a touch of sadness in him, an aura. Even though she knew what he looked like, it was a rule of Bill's that a sign always be held out to demonstrate attention. Only on three occasions was she told not to do it, and on five occasions a false name was used.

He observed the sign and came over to her and smiled. "Hi. I'm Dr. McAbee ... Bertrand. I know you from the tickets to the Met, but I'm sorry, I forget your name."

"Jan Canton. Our car is right outside. Can I give you a hand with the bag?"

"No, thanks. This is all I have with me. I'm leaving again tonight."

He was carrying a small bag, the kind professors always seem to attach themselves to. They went to the Thunderbird that was parked by the curb. She had given $20 to the cop. He tipped his hat when he saw her and cleared a lane for her with his outstretched hand.

"How was the trip, Bertrand?"

"No problems, perfect. It's easy to fly in July as long as there are no thunderstorms. So how's work going?"

"We're so busy, and as you can imagine, your brother thrives on it. I've met so many interesting people over the years."

"Where did you graduate from?" That comment caught her. Everyone just assumed that she was some sort of GED or high school person. In fact, few ever spoke with her, many preferring to look at the sights, hit their cellular phones or tie into their PCS. She noticed that the question could still imply only high school. So she responded, "George Washington High School in upper Manhattan."

"No, I meant college."

"NYU."

"Major?"

"Psychology."

He had an open face with a broad nose, razor-thin lips, and gray eyes that more often than not were unfocused, as if they were weighing things. Then suddenly, the eyes would focus, and she felt intimidated in the sense that he was in her soul somewhere. Maybe that was the difference between the two brothers; the one, Bill, was always focused, while Bertrand left you unguarded for the most part. But when he did focus, he was a laser beam. Maybe this was so because of the contrast, but perhaps because he went much deeper than Bill. Bertrand seemed to be a soul piercer.

She got him into Bill's office at 2:55 p.m. and promised to have him at La Guardia at 7:15 p.m.

New York City, July 1996

Bertrand McAbee never did have that meeting at 3:00 p.m. with his brother Bill. An emergency had sprung up, and it was only at 3:55 that he saw his brother's door open and three spooks exit the building. They had to be either CIA or some such equivalent, and it looked as though two of them were guarding the third. They all wore sun-sensitive glasses and exited Bill's office with their uptight, quick strides-looking right and left for assassins or whatever.

Nor did his brother follow them from his office. This was very unusual. If Bill said 3:00p.m., it would be 3:00 p.m., unless some hellish situation occurred. He went back to reading *Architectural Digest* when a smallish man entered the outer room to Bill's office. He wore a Roman collar and had on a bishop's cross across his chest. He guessed him to be in his late sixties or early seventies. The man moved with a quiet elegance. Bertrand saw him as either Italian or, perhaps, French. He wore wire-rimmed, bifocal glasses, had thinning white hair, and he had a look of peaceful efficiency about him. Bertrand figured this was the right hand of God that Bill had alluded to last night. He knew, also, that you didn't get into this room before being vetted by a six-foot-tall, blonde secretary who looked to be a cross between an aerobics instructor, basketball player, and model. He figured that somewhere on that awesome body she was packing.

At 4:00p.m. sharp, the door to Bill's office opened and he came out. Bill had graying hair, blue eyes, and a thin mouth line. He was, as ever, dressed in a $3,000 suit, and true to one of his pet theories, wore a tie with a bit of red in it. If Bertrand had been Scarzi and had been made to wait, Bill would be offering excuses and begging forgiveness, but not so a blood relative. All of his family knew that business was business and not to expect any apologies. He did what he had to do and that was it.

Scarzi and Bertrand were introduced to each other and led into Bill's mahogany-dominated office where heavy drapes and tall bookshelves leant an air of calm. Only small sectors of natural light were allowed into the room as Scarzi and Bertrand were led to a table at the far end of the office.

Bill said, "Bishop, I brought in my brother, Bertrand, who lives in the Davenport Diocese and is aware of the matter about which you'll speak. He has committed himself and his people to get after this problem, but I thought you'd want to explain the situation as you know of it."

Scarzi, in free-flowing and eloquently Italian accented English, spoke for 45 minutes. He detailed his friendship with Billy Taylor, the nature of the charges, the Minneapolis attorney, the Trappist Monastery where Taylor was staying, and lastly gave a brutally unflattering assessment of Bishop O'Meara.

At the conclusion of his presentation, Bertrand asked, "How can you be so sure that he is innocent, Bishop?"

"If you are asking could I be wrong, the answer is yes. I have not hovered over Father Taylor all of these years. Could he be a secret sinner like this? I answer yes, of course. All of us are cursed. But if you're asking me for my assessment of the man-would he have done this-the answer is no. As you will undoubtedly find, he is a man of supreme spirituality. That Bishop O'Meara has, perhaps, given up on him is sad, but it is conclusive only of his views on life, and these are not to be respected. Because your brother has been such a good and trusted friend of the Vatican and the Church, I am entrusting a letter to you to be given to Bishop O'Meara. I do not want copies made of it, and I prefer that it be delivered tomorrow if possible. I have already called Bishop O'Meara, and he is awaiting your call and visit." He handed Bertrand a wax-sealed letter and then took from his briefcase a Xeroxed copy and handed it to Bertrand. "Please read this and then I will take it back. It is what Bishop O'Meara will read tomorrow, hopefully."

It was written in extremely small but meticulous penmanship. It read:

> Dear Brother In Christ- Bishop O'Meara:
>
> The travails of Father Taylor have come to our ears. Our personal knowledge of him suggests nothing but innocence. We have availed ourselves of the personal attention of Bishop Scarzi. Please give to the bearer of this envelope every cooperation, since he represents Bishop Scarzi. Bishop Scarzi is to be informed at all turns on this matter. Father Taylor was and remains a close friend.
>
> In Christ,
> Pope John Paul II

Bertrand was taken aback. This wasn't the vice president of the local savings and loan worried about theft in Davenport, Iowa, or some husband who was worried about his kleptomaniac wife in Rock Island, Illinois.

He pressed Scarzi, "Bishop, you said the Pope knew him some 50 years ago. But I take it, from what you said, that except for two other subsequent brief encounters, Father Taylor and the Pope haven't met, yet the Pope seems so sure of himself on the matter. That strikes me."

"The Pope is a shrewd judge of character. He has gotten to be where he is by trusting his instincts on people. He doesn't make many mistakes. You know in classical theology, Bertrand, such a talent is a gift of the Holy Spirit. The Pope simply trusts that he has it." He smiled gently.

"And yourself?"

"Ah, that's another matter. I deal day after day with errant priests and nuns. Too much of that and you lose your footing in sure judgment, but I still believe that in this case Father Taylor is innocent. But I do not pretend to be blessed with the gift of the Holy Spirit. Just everyday prudence, I hope. The Pope ... he comes at matters with God's light. But I look at you as I speak, and I see incredulity?"

"Well, somewhat, Bishop. But I don't hold myself out as a religious man, so what can you expect?"

Scarzi looked at Bill and then Bertrand and said with dead seriousness, "I expect only one thing. That you will get to the bottom of this matter and hopefully assist in exonerating Father Taylor. It is not necessary that you be a religious man. But it is necessary that you have the ability to work yourself through the maze of interests and cross-interests that abound in this matter." He looked at his watch and said, "And now, gentlemen, I have an appointment with your Cardinal, another one of these Irishmen of the set opinions." He left.

Bill looked at Bertrand and said, "How do you feel about this?"

"Well, you weren't kidding about the right hand of God. I'll give it my best, Bill, of course. But question. Why were you so quiet during this session? You hardly said a word during the entire hour."

"It's going to involve you and Scarzi. It was important that you develop a relationship with him. Oh, he seems to like you, but I think that he has given up on your soul. You know, guys like Scarzi make judgments real quickly. He probably sees you as quite intelligent but another example of American Catholicism, skeptical and faithless."

"So, Bill, tell me your expectations in this."

"It's your kind of case, Bertrand. It's not a murder story. There are no bodies, there are no serial killers, and so on. So, I don't worry for your safety, since you don't seem to take me seriously about it anyway."

"Bill ... hold on." Bertrand put his hands up in the air. There were several things going on. He didn't like his brother's tone. He was uptight and his judgment had a shrew-like quality to it, not the typical sarcasm that invited repartee. He wondered about the meeting that had taken place while he was in the outer room. "You're right. I don't intend to lead my life behind bulletproof autos, wired fences, and all the other things that you do and call it life. On the other hand, I do take precautions when it's necessary. And, yes, Bill, I do own a gun and I know how to use it. So, back off. On the other hand, you seem to be really tight. Is this something that's a result of your meeting just before Bishop Scarzi got here?"

Bill hesitated before answering. "Yeah, I'll admit it, Bertrand. Some really bad things are coming out about Switzerland and Luxembourg during World War II. The Israeli government is fully engaged, the Swiss, the Austrians, Jewish organizations, and so on. You should realize the OSS, now CIA, was in the middle of document securing processes, for former Nazis. So, it's with suspicion, in a way, that I have to face the goddamn CIA. So, yes, Bertrand, I don't have time to be gracious."

"Well, don't worry. I never looked for that quality in you."

Bill laughed. "No, I guess not."

"OK. I stay in touch with the Bishop, and I call you once in a while. Just who is paying the bill for this work, which might get complicated when it's all said and done?"

"Just send it to me. I'll reimburse everything. My payment from the Vatican will be in-kind. Corporate America will virtually pay for this operation. But before you go, tell me about what's going on in your life? Beth . . .?"

He was referring to Bertrand's recent divorce which had sent him reeling. "She's a done deal, Bill. I see her about once every six months on some matter of business, but that's it."

"Is there anyone in the picture?"

"Uh . . . no . . . not really. I don't know if I have the psychological energy to get into another situation. Let's just leave it at that."

"And David? Still in Europe?"

"Still there. God knows where. I get a letter from him about once a month. Just wandering." David was Bertrand

McAbee's son by a first disastrous and short-lived marriage. David was restless of spirit from the word go and had a mind of his own. He shared his father's love of the classics and graduated magna cum laude from Dartmouth in 1990 and then proceeded to leave for Europe on a one-year adventure. He wanted to trace the route of Hannibal's invasion of Italy, to Thucydides' Peloponnesian Wars, to Herodotus' Persian Wars, to the bombing of Monta Cassino, and so on. Bertrand saw that his list had 312 entries and grew each year by about 50 entries. It was 1996 and David was still in Europe completing his list and surely adding to it. He supported himself by odd jobs and was writing journals of his adventures. He never shared them with his father. Bertrand knew that Bill didn't approve of this idyll, but there was nothing that could be done. It was David's life after all.

Jan Canton's presence was announced. It was time to take Bertrand to La Guardia for his flight to Moline, Illinois. The brothers parted. Bill was preoccupied more so than Bertrand had seen for some time. He wondered what the CIA was doing in the matter of the Swiss gold. And he wondered what he was walking into in this Father Taylor matter. A lawsuit is filed and suddenly a variety of players are put into play. He could never accept that an unseen hand was at play, but he sympathized with those who did. It was easy to draw that conclusion.

Iowa, August 1994

Eric Paulsen, M.D., was a family practitioner in Iowa City. It was his recommendation that brought John Antle to Margaret Aaron's office. Aaron's nurse, Margi, had handed her a file with only one note written by Margi when the phone call had come in directly from Dr. Paulsen. "Mr. Antle is very distressed. He refers to childhood trauma, but Dr. Paulsen chooses not to get involved. He's sure it's heavy stuff. It's not his game. He thinks John would benefit immensely from some therapy."

Aaron looked at the freshly filled-out patient record sheet. Antle was 30 years old, single, and was an assistant manager at a McDonald's in Coralville, Iowa, a smallish town just west of Iowa City. There was nothing unusual in the man as she went out to meet him.

Antle was wiry, about five-foot-ten-inches, had wheat-colored hair, and very pale blue eyes. His face was gaunt and his eyes were skitterish. He couldn't hold a look. They were like water in a paper bag; attention leaked away from them.

"My name is Dr. Aaron, Mr. Antle." They shook hands; his were soaked in sweat. Aaron used a long, comfortable couch and suggested that Antle lie back in a full prone position. He did, but his eyes darted to everywhere in the room except onto Aaron, whom he avoided. Aaron had been in the practice of psychiatry long enough not to let it disturb her. She sat at the equivalent of his chest, in a rocking chair.

"Do you mind if I call you John?"

"No ... no, it's OK."

Aaron was very deliberate in her approach and tried to create an environment of calmness and peace.

"Dr. Paulsen seems to think it might be good for you to talk with me?" Aaron had perfected the technique of making a statement but hooking a question into it. She also would not speak again until he responded.

"Yeah. I guess so ... look, I'm pretty nervous. I probably don't show it, but I am."

"Lots or people are nervous when they come to a psychiatrist. They're afraid that when they say something, they'll be judged as being bad or something like that. Does that ring a bell?"

After a long pause: "A bit. Yeah, I guess."

"You know, sometimes it takes multiple sessions to break through. But there are some short cuts if you'd care to discuss them. I guess you don't need too many of these sessions?" She smiled at him, inviting an inquiry.

"Yeah. That would be good. I'm not sure what to expect. Dr. Paulsen told me to follow your lead."

"Some therapists use mild drugs to relax their patients. That's not a preferred approach of mine. Personally, I've had good results from hypnotherapy. Have you ever head of that?"

"Yeah, but I don't think that you could hypnotize me. I think that I'd be real nervous."

"I'm sure that you would be. But you'd be surprised at how many patients are like that. Usually, the smarter the person, the easier it is to hypnotize." Aaron had read that often and knew the research data behind the conclusion. She thought it simplisitic and didn't think hypnosis had anything to do with intelligence. But, since most patients liked to be perceived as being smart, she had no problem nudging along the unwilling or resistant with the observation.

After a minute, Antle said, "I'm sorry. Am I supposed to say something?"

"I'm waiting for you to decide how you want to go about getting things on the table?" Aaron responded gently.

"Well, if you can hypnotize me, and it would be good, I'm OK with it. But I warned you." He smiled shyly. His vulnerability was marked.

"Do you see that clock directly across the room? The second hand ... focus on it. Just keep staring at it as it goes around and let me take you away. It's easy now to watch it go around. We're going to relax and take a trip, and we're starting to feel real secure. We're ...." She stopped for about 30 seconds and asked, "John, can you hear me?"

"Yeah." She knew the monotone immediately in his voice.

"I want you to scratch your left ear with your right hand. That's the way. You're to do what I ask. It's for your good. Do you understand me?"

"Yeah."

She turned on her tape machine at this point, whispering into one of three mikes: "John Antle, August 4, 1994." She would tape the first few sessions on the possibility that she just might be able to use the material for a case study in a journal. It never hurt to have a full transcript.

"So Dr. Paulsen seems to think that some things are bothering you. He's right?"

"Yeah. Some things bother me, like they come in dreams, and I'm scared of the dark. I keep a light on."

"It's important, John, that we try to get that out in the open. I'm going to need all of your help. So, try to help me?"

"OK."

"What was the best thing to ever happen to you in childhood, let's say up to 14 years of age?"

"Little league. I hit a home run in the title game. My dad was so proud of me; everybody really liked me."

"It's nice to be liked?"

"Yeah."

Aaron kept him moving through the pleasant areas of his childhood, keeping him focused on the positive until she decided to make the shift to the area where she felt almost all hurt came from-the betrayal of innocence.

"Sometimes people like you in the wrong way?"

His face showed pain before he responded. "Yeah, I know."

"I'm sure you have some examples, John?" She noticed that his body tightened and he frowned. There was plenty of pain in this guy, and it was childhood stuff. The 45 minutes were drawing close, but she wanted a testimony.

"Hands ... touching me."

"But everyone is touched, John ... like when you hit the home run. I'll bet lots of people touched you, patted your back, slapped your arms and your rump?"

"No." He was firm. "It's not the same, this touching me. Things that weren't to be touched by another person. No, not by friends either. No one!"

"Daddy or mommy?" Aaron asked.

"That's what they taught me."

"When did daddy or mommy touch you that way?" She went to the direct question, pressing to uncover incest if it was there.

"No, no! Not dad or mom! They never touched me that way."

"Others?"

"Yes ...." He started to perspire, his upper lip and forehead were soaked, and she noticed that his tee shirt was getting moist around the armpits and chest area. His face became twisted. He was a person in torment. It wasn't incest, but someone had had their way with John Antle; that was for the next session. She spun him away from the dangers of his bad memories and had him dwell on the little league game and his home run. She told him that he'd feel great and that this session was well done, that he should be proud of himself. Then she took him out of the hypnotic state.

"See, I told you I'd be hard to hypnotize." His eyes caught the clock and then he realized that he had been in a state of hypnosis for about 35 minutes. "Wow! You did get me, didn't you?"

"You were terrific, John. I told you it's consistent with high intelligence; you're very cooperative, and that's a good sign."

CHAPTER SIX

Iowa, July 1996

Monsignor George Duncan sat in his burgundy BMW 735. He loved that car even though he knew that it was controversial. As he never tired of telling the priests of the Diocese it was a gift from his mother; that usually stopped their querulous looks, because everyone knew that his family was loaded, and since diocesan priests didn't take the vow of poverty, it was none of their damn business anyway. His father, in fact, had built a mini-empire in the road construction business all through Iowa and everywhere in Illinois except Chicago, which, as everyone knew, was in an orbit of its own. He left the running of the business up to his father and his two brothers and a sister. In fact, he wanted nothing to do with the situation except to draw checks.

Nor was his lifestyle frugal. He had developed a highly cultivated set of tastes, and as a consequence, he spent the money lavishly but covertly. His wine cellar probably had no peer in Iowa. He had a staff of devoted and skilled workers who assisted in food preparation, maid service, gardening, and all those assorted arts that impact impressions. The mansion in which he lived overlooked the Mississippi River, but the paper on the mansion was held in the name of his father and mother. His cover story was that he was the caretaker of the property.

Although his position of Chancellor was secured by a $3 million endowment to the Diocese by the Duncan family, it also was kept under a veil of secrecy. It was listed as an anonymous gift. O'Meara had just been consecrated Bishop of the Davenport Diocese in 1988. The Duncan family, with George sitting out quietly, had placed an all-out assault on O'Meara to appoint George Chancellor and had clinched it with the $3 million gift. At the time, George was only 32 years old and had been a parish priest in Bettendorf for three years, since graduating from North American Seminary in Rome and receiving his J.C.D. (Juris Canonis Doctor-Doctor of Canon Law) from the 'Alphonseonum' in Rome.

It was clear to George that his mother had groomed him for the Church and from early on had associated him with supportive priests and nuns who would reinforce her decision. He figured that she knew he was gay from an early age, probably in part by the fact that his totalitarian and crude father backed away from him as if he was a walking sore of some sort.

George was the master of discretion and had learned early on that the Church had no quarrel with homosexuality as long as the homosexual remained celibate, and furthermore, in the case of priests, stayed in the closet in terms of public proclamations of such. It wasn't all that dissimilar to its stance on adulterers, thieves, etc. He had his experiences in high school and college, and yes, and very much so in the seminary. He had an on/off relationship with a fellow priest, but only when he was drunk and then he would be quick to renounce it. After all, people are weak, and Christ came to Earth to redeem us and wash away our faults, and like anyone else, he had his faults.

George had learned to work with the Bishop, a thickheaded Mick who thought he knew everything. He was out of the 19th century with his ideas on Marian worship, the rosary, prudishness, and particularly – authoritarianism. That O'Meara could end Duncan's cozy lifestyle and send him off to some remote parish in the sticks of Iowa was never far from his mind; therefore, he handled the Bishop with kid gloves. O'Meara was the kind of person who would hurl back the $3 million endowment if it got down to a matter of principle. He had never run into single – mindedness as he had found in this arch-conservative prelate. As for Irish wit and sense of humor, the joke was that there wasn't one ounce of it in his soul. O'Meara, he'd say to his intimates, belonged in some Green Beret unit.

O'Meara, he thought also, knew that he was socially maladroit, and Monsignor George Duncan, profusely elegant, gave him a sense of security. Duncan would advise him on how to say things, remind him of people's names, and sort out social sites for this all too backward Bishop. Accordingly, they had settled into a professional relationship which both of them saw as an advantage.

George Duncan had likened himself to a Florentine prince or churchman during the Renaissance. He built up around himself a style of life that had panache and yet which was understated due to the politics of the matter. He also had an immediate, longstanding, and visceral hatred of Father Billy Taylor who represented another aspect of the Church-the guilt-ridden, driven, fatalistic, somber, and prayer-fixated screwballism. Taylor never explicitly judged Duncan, but he could see the disrespect that was in his eyes. And now, after all of these years, to find out that this pious fraud was a kid – banger – well, maybe, a kid banger.

He knew that O'Meara had no love for Taylor either, but it wasn't based on a lifestyle thing, because there actually were a few points of similarity between the Bishop and Billy Taylor. No, in the case of the Bishop, it was a social thing. When that Bishop from Rome, Scarzi, stayed with Taylor rather than with O'Meara, O'Meara was greatly offended and laid it at the feet of Taylor. Even Duncan thought that the Bishop had overreacted, but he could give a damn about Taylor.

His drive to the Trappist monastery took him on Route 67, which was an alternating two- and four-lane road that stretched from St. Louis all the way to Minneapolis. Duncan played a CD of Renaissance music as he yawned lazily at the profuseness of the rich farm soil of Iowa.

He parked and went into the building that said "Guest Services." On the desk he saw a name plate that read "Brother Joseph," who looked a little like Andy Rooney; a grizzled kind of guy who would probably present no problem as long as you didn't cross him in some way. But, he thought, in these monasteries with all of their seclusion, quiet and non-communication, it was probably pretty easy to piss off someone without knowing it. Furthermore, with his elegant way, he generally didn't care for grizzled types unless they knew their place.

"Can I help you, Father?"

"Yes." He was grizzly all right. Duncan took out his card case, deliberately removed one, and handed it to Brother Joseph, and said, "Brother, I have come on diocesan business to see a Father Taylor. Am I in the right place?"

Brother Joseph's eyes squinted a bit, and he hunched his shoulders just slightly. Duncan thought, don't tell me this old monk is going to be protective of Taylor. Maybe he doesn't know that Taylor is a pederast. He looked over the card as though he was some kind of cop checking IDs. Duncan was glad that monasteries were closing. They manufactured idiots like this.

"You're expected, Monsignor. I'll show you the visitor's room." He looked pointedly in Duncan's direction and said, "You know all of the monks are very impressed with Father Taylor. He is an extraordinarily spiritual man."

Not "seems" or "appears" but "is," Duncan noted with annoyance. He decided not to even grace the Brother's irrelevant comment with a reply. In the world's caste system, the two of them were on different continents.

Billy Taylor came to the open doorway of the visiting room and stood there until Duncan waved him in. They shook hands, and Taylor said quietly, "Monsignor."

Duncan said to himself, 'The usual glib and personable Billy Taylor.'

"Father Taylor, I'm here at the request of Bishop O'Meara and Chip Blaine, the Diocesan attorney." Don't think I'm here out of any concern for you.

"I see ... and what can I do for you, Monsignor?"

Taylor was dressed in a black cotton pair of Dockers pants, a plain white tee shirt, white running shoes and socks. He had developed a nice tan from all his walking and actually looked better today than he had for years. A 75-year-old man who looked no older than 50 was Duncan's take. His eyes looked so young and bright, also. Duncan became self-conscious of his own roundness and flaccidity.

"Well, we are beginning to think of our vulnerability in this case, Father."

"Yes, I know. That's a concern for sure."

"Well, yes ... yes ..., but there is some considerable consternation about you ... that you're not cooperating ... that you don't seem to care." Duncan said this in a halting way hoping to diminish the real anger he felt toward this fraud, a fraud who was endangering the financial health of the Diocese.

Taylor sat there for about a minute staring at Duncan, who looked away after a ten-second interlude but who could feel the laser-like eyes of Taylor. Finally, Taylor said, "Monsignor, I have devoted my adult life to the work of the Davenport Diocese. I have taken every assignment with equanimity, I have tried to be true to my calling as a priest, and I have endeavored to remain celibate during all of these years. I am not a drunk, I have not been an embarrassment and I am totally innocent of these charges. My lustful thoughts, and I certainly have had them, are not toward boys, and ...," he stopped and let the pause hang in the air,... "they are not toward men. On the other hand, I do have thoughts and dreams that are focused on women, curiosities and yearnings, but even these I have learned to deal with. I don't say this as a matter of boasting or out of pride, but simply to let you know that I do live my promises as a priest of God."

Why do I feel so uncomfortable and gross, Duncan

asked himself. This little bastard was aware of some things and was trying to turn the tables. He wondered just exactly what did Taylor know about him. He could feel his face reddening as Taylor spoke and as each statement appeared to be an indictment of his own life. And in full duplicity, he responded to Taylor, trying to rattle and hurt him, "You know, Father, I spoke with numerous priests at the annual retreat, and with few exceptions, they were not surprised by the charges." He knew his voice had now taken on a harsh edge.

Taylor never moved his fingers, which were cupped to his uncrossed hands. Nor did he respond immediately; he was a paced and controlled individual. "I am sorry that so many of my peers think this of me. I can only revert to the scriptures and recall that Christ himself was also seen to be a bad person by many. But like so many things in life, Monsignor, it is beyond my control."

"I suppose you would call this cooperation, Father Taylor?"

"I wouldn't call it anything except my attempt at communicating with you. What else do you want from me, Monsignor? Would you be pleased if I said that I did this terrible thing?"

Taylor never took his eyes off him, and Duncan felt that whatever else he had from his authority and his association with the Bishop and Blaine was gone, beaten out of him by this man's personal inner strength and its face off with his own standing and values. In fact, he felt that he was getting his newly whitened, glistening teeth kicked down his throat. Grabbing for anything, he kept repeating to himself-pederast, pederast, pederast. "Well, to be frank with you, yes, because personally, Father, and this is just between us, I do think that you are guilty. What do you think of that?" Duncan knew that he had gone too far once he said it, but he was caught in his desire to hurt this man, to shake him out of his serenity.

"Well, Monsignor, you are no friend of mine as we both know. I've been candid with you, but it appears that whatever I tell you is not what you want to hear."

Duncan decided to end the meeting. "Father Taylor, this is getting us nowhere. But there are other things I have to say. You will be summoned down to Davenport shortly to meet with the Bishop and Chip Blaine. You are permitted to drive your own car." He was finally feeling in control again. He was flailing on this bastard, and he had it coming. "But you are to return immediately to these premises, and you are to surrender your keys forthwith. Am I clear?"

"Yes. Quite."

"Lastly, the Bishop sends his regards and wishes to know how you are being treated."

"Monsignor, I couldn't ask to be treated better. This monastery is a delight, a jewel in the Church's crown. Please thank the Bishop for his solicitude."

"Yes ... well ... it's his job to be concerned for all, even sinners. Is there anything you wish to convey to Bishop O'Meara?"

Taylor thought for a bit (it was these kinds of deliberations that irked Duncan) before saying, "Yes, one thing. Please tell him that I am aware that he has stewardship over diocesan funds and that I understand his concern for any jeopardy that these funds may be exposed to. It is a hard job to be a steward and also be supportive of your priests." He said this without apparent irony. "But please tell him again, I am totally innocent of these charges."

Iowa, September 1994

Dr. Margaret Aaron had had three sessions with John Antle and was scrutinizing her dictation. The actual tapes of the sessions were kept in a wall safe in her home, since John Antle knew nothing of them, and she knew she was in a first-degree ethics violation. If she published on this case, she intended to ask him for permission, but only in a general manner, never revealing the taping itself.

It was clear to her that Antle had been sexually abused as a child, apparently on a number of occasions during his seventh and eighth years. It was in his parish church. Aaron reflected that of all the congregations and groups, Catholicism was most out of the mainstream. It carried within it 20 centuries of varying forms of insanity and perversion and had a number of institutions that fostered practices that, to say the least, were un-American. The Church was like an ostrich racing in a horse race. It might keep up in the race, but it was out of kilter and it just didn't fit.

If it was merely a matter of being an anomaly or being eccentric, Aaron could care less. However, the Institution, in all of its haughty arrogance, repressiveness, and stealthiness, had done much damage to lives. She had read of its clandestine dealings with the Mafia, the Nazis, and a variety of other subhuman entities that the Church had readily slept with over the years.

She had heard the horror stories of seasoned psychiatrists, both within and outside of medical school, who spoke of suicidal Catholics dealing with the great sins of homosexuality, masturbation, abortion, birth control, and whatever other critical piece of moralistic nonsense that the Church would use to threaten its adherents with hell and eternal damnation.

Thus, on the patient intake form, she carefully scrutinized religion and, in fact, created two categories: Current Religious Preference:, Religion of Childhood: _ Catholics always set off a warning buzzer in her mind. She recalled the nasty exchange with a Jesuit priest psychiatrist from Loyola University in Chicago. They were both on a panel dealing with sexual abuse of minors, and she opined that Catholic patients had extra baggage when dealing with sexual abuse. The Jesuit snapped back that her predisposition on the matter probably led her to a manipulative and heavy-handed therapy laced with prejudicial assumptions. It brought down the house and was the buzz of the American Psychiatric Association's meeting in Chicago. Her retort to the Jesuit, as both of them were gavelled to silence, was that he was in a state of denial and probably himself was a sexually abused person, perhaps continuing the crime as an adult pedophile. Her supporters (she thought a vast majority) thought that she had gone just a bit too far, but then so did he.

When she took on cases such as Antle's, she felt that she had to show extra prudence since these cases proved the point that she had been making in Chicago. The more that Antle spoke and revealed, the more enthusiastic Aaron became. It was like reeling in some gigantic game fish – the ever present and ever dangerous Church.

At each session, Antle was more relaxed and more trusting as he settled back on the couch. His vulnerability continued to cause anger in Aaron. That some hard up priest would take advantage of a lamb such as he was revolting.

"John, today I think we can put the final pieces together and then we can begin the mending process. How does that feel?"

"Yeah, OK. I've been getting more and more dreams."

"Dreams are important?"

"I'm being chased and cornered by men dressed in black. They have scissors and they keep snipping and stabbing them at me. I'm trying to run, but I keep falling. My mother is in a locked room far away. She's having coffee and laughing. I'm screaming her name, but she doesn't hear me. When I wake up, I'm soaked. It's really scary."

"The people chasing you?"

"They're dressed in black."

"Dressed in black?"

"Cassocks ... you might not know what that means. Long robes worn by altar boys and priests."

"Cassocks?"

"Yeah. It's like they're altar boys or priests."

"Altar boys are usually young?"

"Yeah. These are older men. One has a beard. Priests. Priests are what they are."

Aaron stopped at this point. She hadn't taken him into hypnosis yet, and she decided that the material of the dream was best pursued at that level.

He was under in 30 seconds, and within five minutes she had taken him back to his childhood. He was still calm as she focused on the little league. And then she dove in.

"Churches have interesting names sometimes?"

"Yes. Mine was kinda normal, I guess. St. Anne's."

"Sounds Roman Catholic?" She was intent on getting confirmation details that could be checked out and confirmed. Perhaps this case could get her some more medication. She was already relieved at ending the practice of storing the pills in her office. She had simply had her nurse call the patients and indicate to them that Dr. Aaron was a bit concerned about how the situation would look to outsiders, even though she still thought it to be a good practice. In the meantime, she hoarded Scannell's contribution, always worried that the supply would dry up.

"Oh, yeah. We're real Catholics. My dad was in the seminary for a while when he was young."

"St. Anne's in ... ?"

"Iowa ... Scott County ... Long Grove."

"Sounds like a small church in the country?"

"Yeah. It was only open on Saturday nights and Sundays and holy days. I was an altar boy. There were masses on Sunday mornings at eight and eleven. I would stay and do both."

"You'd get there before mass?"

"Mom would drop me off at 7:45, and then she'd leave to take care of my grandfather who was in a home. She didn't like me to go to the home because it was pretty bad. He had had a stroke and could be pretty ornery."

"So, it sounds like you were free between nine and eleven?"

"Yeah."

"Was it then, John, that you were touched?" She departed from her usual indirect technique and now went straight to the matter.

"Yeah ... yeah."

"Tell me about it. You were finished with mass, then what?"

"There was a room, a small room for the altar boys. The man would come and help me unbutton the cassock." He was concentrating and becoming visibly pained at this memory. "He'd brush his fingers on me ... around my zipper. It felt good. He knew just where to touch me. He'd smile and tell me that it was OK." Tears swelled in his eyes.

"Go ahead, John. It's important for us to remember this?"

"He'd kneel in front of me and say that this was OK; it was good to show how grown up I am. He'd loosen my belt and my pants would fall to my ankles." And now he cried copiously.

Aaron's heart was a mixture of grief and hatred as she heard this man speak of this insidious crime and violation.

"Go ahead, John?"

"He'd take my underpants down to my knees and them he'd touch me until I ... I ... could no longer think of anything except what was happening to me. And then ... he'd stand and put my hand on his penis and together we would pull on each other-Oh, my god, this is terrible. It's so bad. . . every Sunday ... week after week ... until we moved into Davenport to be closer to my grandfather."

Aaron clenched her teeth. She let his soft sobs hang in the air. "John, who was this priest?"

"Father Billy. Father Billy Taylor was the priest."

She found it to be unnecessary to pursue the nightmare that he had been having, their messages so clear and distinct. So, another priest and another victim! Par for the course! She wondered how many other children this monster had compromised in the altar boys' dressing room. And did the Diocese of Davenport know about it?

She brought John away from the scene of seduction, and eventually she pulled him away from the state of hypnosis. When John was returned to his normal conscious state, he said, "I was crying, wasn't I? I don't feel good like the other times I've been down. What happened?"

"John, you have a lot of things that you've repressed. You laid a heavy black blanket over some pretty bad experiences. I'm peeking under that blanket, and when it's hypnotherapy, we both look under that blanket. Some things that we talked about today were double tough. Next week I'll have some specific recommendations. Let me dwell on what happened and make an appointment for next week, same time, Wednesday at eleven. I think that we're about to make a big-time breakthrough. How does that sound? Are you ready for that?"

When Antle left the room, she called Herb Scannell in Minneapolis. "Herb. I think that I'm getting a case squared up for you."

"Great."

"Why don't you bring another delivery as a show of support." "I think that can be arranged."

84

CHAPTER SEVEN

Iowa, July 1996

They knew he was coming. The minute he mentioned his name, Bertrand McAbee was afforded the courtesy of choosing his time. The Bishop would be happy to accommodate. Scarzi or some higher force had prevailed, and he hadn't even shown the letter yet.

On the flight back from New York City, McAbee reflected that in this case, at least, there was no apparent danger. It was a puzzlement. Did this ostensibly holy priest-William Taylor-sexually molest a little boy? It certainly seemed that there wouldn't be any need to bring out the heavy guns of Jack Scholz, a shadowy ex-military colonel who now operated a sort of soldier-of-fortune network of psychopaths, whom Bertrand would occasionally employ in extreme cases. Nor would there be a need for his computer and research man, Barry Fisk, the five-foot-two hunchback whom McAbee maintained could tap into any computer network he chose, and one of the most brilliant men McAbee had ever met.

But McAbee had a mind that rarely accepted the

obvious. And if he did err and buy into the obvious, he had been kicked in the face enough to catch himself from falling off that cliff. So, as he drove to St. Vincent's Center for his 10:00 a.m. appointment with Bishop O'Meara, he caught himself from oversimplifying the matter. He was working to discover the truth and not to help some kind of obvious criminal and his sleazy lawyer. And if he found compelling evidence against Taylor, he would call his brother Bill and pronounce the case closed. Scarzi, the Pope, and his brother may not like it, but that's the way he saw it.

The tall athletic-looking man came forward to meet him. He wore a black cassock with red buttons down the front of it and a red skullcap. His handshake was brisk, firm, and dry. There was no apparent nervousness in the man. He requested McAbee to sit across from his desk, as he himself sat in an ornate desk chair with a high back and seat. McAbee couldn't help but notice that his own chair seat was set low, so that the Bishop's sight-line was angling down toward him. Under these circumstances, the only way to tum disadvantage to advantage was by maintaining a cool self possession that told the authoritative Bishop that intimidation was impossible. In his heart, though, he lost respect for game players like the Bishop who tried to use furniture to establish personal power.

"Doctor McAbee ... it is Doctor? You were a classics professor and philosopher at St. Anselm College?" The Bishop had done some quick checking.

"Classics. Yes. Philosophy was more faute de mieux, but as long as I stayed with the ancients, the Medievalists, and the Renaissance, I felt pretty comfortable. But you're from Ireland?"

"Indeed I am." He smiled grudgingly. "I am from County Waterford in southeastern Free Ireland where by God's grace, there is a plethora of priests; or there was. But now Ireland has some new troubles and vocations are falling."

"What would those be?"

"Well, for starters, the economy is good. When people are doing well, they often forget the giver–God– and turn their backs on Him to choose the things of the world. Consequently, their morals have slipped. The old days of obedience to the Church of God has diminished, and I'll add one other thing, and I'll lay it right at our own door-the scandals around our clergy-child abuse, bishops fathering illegitimate children – the outrage!" He looked at McAbee intensely and accusatorially

McAbee's impression of all this was that the Bishop was an angry man who, if he had his way, would wield his crozier like a billy club. As calmly as he could, McAbee said, "Bishop O'Meara, as you seem to be aware, I've been asked to look into the Father Taylor matter."

"Out of curiosity, how would I be knowing that?" he asked coyly.

"Because when I called this morning at eight for an appointment, I was told by your secretary that your schedule would accommodate any time I chose. To the best of my knowledge, you and your secretary have no knowledge of me, and therefore I find it odd that I would be given such a privilege from a cold call and with an unknown agenda."

"Yes ... yes. We're not that subtle, are we? In fact, I'd have to say, the Irish have no business being subtle. We just don't do it well. Now the Italians ... that's another matter. But, yes,

I was called by Bishop Guillermo Scarzi last night, and I was told in no uncertain terms to make myself available to you. The conversation was short, and the only other thing that was said was that it referred to the Taylor matter."

"I have a letter for you. I think we should start there." McAbee took the wax-sealed letter from his inside jacket pocket and handed it across the desk. He figured that O'Meara would never think that he had personally seen the contents. He watched the Bishop take a letter opener from his desk and slice across the top and thus not disturb the seal. He removed the Pope's letter and read it, by McAbee's estimation, at least three times before looking away from it and gazing at McAbee.

"This letter is from a very high personage that I am bound to obey. It says I am to give you every cooperation. It is against my better judgment to do so, but I will." He then proceeded to take from the bottom of his desk a large ashtray and a matchbook. He held the letter out and set it afire and didn't look anywhere but at the ashes that started their inevitable collapse into the receptacle.

"Bishop O'Meara, I'm in pursuit of the truth about this matter. I met Father Taylor on several occasions at social functions, but I don't ever think that he'd recognize me. So I have no vested interest in the matter. I will not be beholden to some defense lawyer. When I make my determination, I will forward my report to New York and that in turn will be sent to Rome."

"Do I get a copy?"

"It's not in my directions, so, no."

"Well, let me tell you a few things, Dr. McAbee. In this Diocese we do not play the police game of protecting our own. I've told my priests that they must lead unimpeachable lives and I expect it. Father Taylor, in my estimation, is probably guilty, and, if he's not, he's guilty of even allowing this charge to be filed."

"That's a tough standard."

"Well, that's the way it must be!" He pounded his fist on the desk. "In Ireland they pushed these sins under the rug. They'd get complaints and wink the thing away, and when that's done and it finally comes out, they lose all of their authority and standing. It's as if they were right there abusing the children themselves. Don't you see what I'm saying? It's zero tolerance!"

"It's still a tough standard, because you're saying that the priest is responsible just by the fact of being charged. Someone could forth tomorrow and sue you for sexual abuse. By your standard, you're responsible."

"That's true, and with the exception of my 67-year-old secretary, I am never in the presence of boys or girls or women without a witness. I just will not get myself in these straits. Everyone knows my position." His mouth was set in a firm and unyielding position.

McAbee recalled a conversation with a priest sociologist many years ago who maintained that many Irish priests from the 17th century had been sent to France for their major seminary training. There, they came into touch with an extreme right wing and puritanical vision of the world, including a harsh and disgusted hatred for sexuality. The world became a very black and white place in that French movement called Jansenism, and it came to haunt the modem Catholic Church in Ireland. McAbee, raised a Catholic, was very familiar with the tenets but rarely ever heard them articulated in the 1990s. Just maybe, he thought, O'Meara was a living example.

Of course there were some who argued that this same Jansenism overwhelmed the Catholic Church in America because of the dominance of the Irish. O'Meara wouldn't be that far removed from the great French philosopher and mathematician, Blaise Pascal, who was associated with the movement. This gave McAbee pause in his outright criticism of Jansenism and its center in Port Royal. He had great respect for Pascal.

"But Bishop? What if a female came to you and wanted to confess?"

"I would do it in a confessional, but in a public place, never in my office or house."

"So Father Taylor is guilty one way or another?"

"So to speak, yes. But there is guilty and there is guilty, if you see my meaning." He spread his hands apart and made a papal-like magnanimous gesture, as his hands made a slight lifting gesture.

"Bishop O'Meara, will the diocese offer a vigorous defense for Father Taylor?"

"I'll leave that to our attorney, Mr. Blaine."

McAbee groaned within himself. He had dealings with Blaine before and had concluded that the man was duplicitous, unreliable, and dangerous precisely because he was a very capable, and he put on a good performance. Bertrand's recently divorced attorney-wife Beth had also recounted some stories that disturbed him, including Blaine's efforts to bed her at a conference in Des Moines. In fact, she felt that he may have put something into her drink, but she was rescued by a member of her firm, much to Blaine's anger, because he did everything he could do to slight her for the next three years until he had to deal with her at a public event. With the divorce, he imagined that he had renewed his efforts. "Chip Blaine. I know him, Bishop. I didn't know he represented the Diocese."

"Ah, yes. And a good Catholic man he is."

McAbee observed that this Bishop, with his tremendously impressive presence and thoughtful disposition, had this gaping hole in his analysis of people. The Bishop had a strong dose of naivete. Thinking of Blaine, how many times had Bertrand heard, "He's a good Baptist or a good Catholic or a good Jew or a good Moslem," only to find the said jerk to be an absolute crook.

"So, Dr. McAbee, what is it you need from me?"

"I need to see all your records pertaining to Father Taylor, raw stuff, etcetera. I need a public letter to the priests of the Diocese that will tell them of my role, because I do intend to talk with some of them, especially his contemporaries and near-contemporaries. And I need to have access to Mr. Blaine's depositions and whatever else he has relative to this case."

"I think that this can be arranged. Oh, and you might want to speak with Monsignor Duncan, my Chancellor, who visited with Father Taylor just the other day."

"Yes. That would be good. Did he have anything to report by the way?"

"Why, yes. He thinks that Father Taylor is as adamant in denial as he is mired in guilt. But I don't want to prejudice you, sir."

"And, of course, most important, Bishop, I'll need to spend some time with Father Taylor."

"That can be arranged through Monsignor Duncan. It's

almost a truism that when you speak with him, you speak with me."

McAbee left. The Bishop, by a telephone call to McAbee's office, would confirm the steps that he had taken by the end of the day.

Iowa, February 1995

Scannell got the call from Aaron to inform him that she finally had a man who was potential material for a lawsuit. She had been treating him over a series of sessions; it was clear to Aaron that a priest had sexually molested him. For the past month, she had introduced the potential of a lawsuit, and he appeared to be open to it, but only after considerable discussion. He was very anxious about his name not appearing in the newspapers. He was a very hurt and shy man, and she wanted assurance that his case would be treated with care.

"We usually just have to bring the papers to a diocese and their lawyers and threaten to file the suit. That usually does the trick. There's no publicity or anything. A settlement is negotiated, and he gets two thirds of the settlement, less expenses, and we get a third. We do our homework so carefully that when we present our threat of petition, we have the goddamn offenders caught with their pants down." He laughed but noticed that Aaron didn't. So much for humor with this fat, hard up, druggie, neurotic bitch.

"And what happens if the diocese says no?" She asked in this telephone discussion, which Scannell was secretly taping, as he did with phone calls like these.

"Then we press the point, but only with the consent of the victim," he said disingenuously. He did not add that the client was now in debt to the firm for expenses by usually $10,000 to $20,000, largely due to the efforts of Scannell or other investigators. So, if the victim tried to pull out, the firm would bring down the debt hammer on him. And since these matters were almost exclusively secret, no one really knew how rough it could get in this legal shakedown business. Aaron probably didn't hear his comment or chose not to pursue it that the client got two thirds less expenses. In fact, the client typically would be lucky to get 50 percent. Yet it was still quite a payday for all concerned with settlements ranging anywhere from $100,000 when the cases were really thin to up to $3 million when it was a clear win. Youngquist preferred not to go to court if he could get a settlement, because, in Scannell's view, he was a pretty stupid attorney, albeit a brilliant bluffer and poker player.

"And when it goes to court, what happens to the victim? Is it cathartic?"

Yeah, right. Whatever you need, you rationalizing, druggie bitch. "Oh, yeah. The client comes out of the trial vindicated, a victory is scored over all the rottenness they've had to endure. It's quite a good experience, although, obviously, it can be painful, dredging up all of those terrible memories, as you well know." He said this with all of the candor and sincerity that he could muster, hoping that Aaron didn't pick up on the hardened cynicism that surrounded his world. He was relieved that this was a telephone call.

"Very well, then. Can you come next week? I'll be seeing

him again today, and if that goes well, I'll confirm the time and date. Is Tuesday OK?"

"I'll be there. Just name the time."

"OK. Oh, ... and do you remember the conversation ... you... uh ... ?"

"Yes. After I talk with him and detail it out with Mr. Youngquist, I'll have the money for you." Scannell knew that she wasn't interested in the money. She wanted another pallet of depressants, the bitch.

"No ... well, I mean yes to the money, but do you recall leaving some ... a ... ?"

"Medication?" He'd relieve her of the necessity of saying that she was dependent. She'd appreciate him for that.

"Yes. That would help. It would be a nice touch."

"No problem, Dr. Aaron. It's done!"

Scannell waited in Aaron's office. He saw Margi, the nurse who had compromised her doctor and slipped her a hundred-dollar bill. While there, a slight man in his early thirties came in and sat down. This was probably the stiff, Scannell thought. He saw all sorts of these characters, the X-generation with its tired and inane love affair with the X-Files, celebrity, and purposelessness. This guy had nothing going for him. Sexual abuse by some priest was low on the list of his problems.

Margi came to the little blondish wimp and just said, "John, Doctor will see you now." She turned and winked at Scannell. He gave her his knowing smile, knowing that they were both bastards hitting on the weak.

Twenty minutes later Margi came and said, "Aaron wants you in the holy of holies. Good luck!"

He nodded his head, smirked, and went into the room.

Antle was sitting on the couch facing Aaron, who had placed a chair next to hers. She signaled to Scannell to sit beside her and formally introduced the two men to each other, after which she began:

"John, I've told you about a law firm in Minneapolis that focuses on cases such as yours. Mr. Scannell has consented to speak with you about the process. Anytime you don't feel comfortable, just say so."

Scannell went on to explain the process to Antle, who had a long-practiced look of stupidity on his face. Scannell omitted nothing that was to his favor in convincing Antle to file the case and added nothing that Antle might find to be daunting. He concluded by saying, "I understand from Dr. Aaron that you have been sexually molested by a priest. The chances are that you are one of many children who have been preyed upon by this man. I know that Mr. Youngquist hates these crimes and their perpetrators, and that he has devoted his life to destroying men who do these vicious things. You do agree that they must be stopped?" he said with all of the moral indignation that he could generate.

"John, do you have any questions for Mr. Scannell?" Aaron interjected.

"Well, I guess it scares me. I don't want to be in the newspapers. I think my friends would make fun of me or … or … reject me."

Scannell assured him that the chances of its going public were small, and if it occurred, the potential payoff would have his friends envious. He looked at Aaron and didn't like the look he received when he presented this last argument. He backed off. Antle still hesitated. "You can pull out of this at any time. It's your right." His expenses, however, were occurring right at this time if he signed the forms.

"So, if I sign the forms, what happens?"

"Dr. Aaron can share your records with Mr. Youngquist, who will study them and make an estimate on value and damages. After that, I, personally, will begin an investigation on the Diocese and particularly on the priest. And I want you to note that this is nothing personal. I don't even know the name of this priest, and I might add that I have a lot of respect for priests, my uncle is one, but not for the likes of these vicious offenders," he added with, he hoped, just the right amount of moral righteousness and impartiality.

"And I can pull out at any time?''

"Yes, sir!"

"Oh, well, I guess there is nothing to lose under these circumstances. Where do I sign?"

Aaron butted in. "Now, John, it's important to me ... are you sure you want to go ahead with this?"

Great, Scannell thought. The sale was made and this guilt-ridden bitch throws a cog in it. Antle sat still for a few seconds before saying, "Well, I guess it's OK. I mean you did have Mr. Scannell come here, and you did say that it could have a great therapeutic effect. So, sure. Let's do it!" He smiled wanly.

Scannell produced the four forms that were routinely used by Youngquist. He referred to them as the four forms of the apocalypse. Gratuitously and insincerely he told Antle to read each one carefully, knowing full well that the sale had been made, and this inept character would do no more than scan the incomprehensible. He was right. The forms were returned with all of the Xs signed in the small and bashful signature: John Antle.

He shook hands with Antle and left saying, "Dr. Aaron, I'm sure that you have more business with John. I'll be in your waiting room. If I could have a few minutes of your time?"

Aaron spent no more than ten minutes with Antle when Scannell was summoned, once again, by the winking Margi. Aaron was sitting behind her desk now. She offered him a seat in front of it.

"I hope, Mr. Scannell, that you do well by John. He is unstable to say the least. I worry about him."

"Dr. Aaron, the Youngquist firm is expert in these matters. You'll see. After all, we'd like repeat business also." He now very carefully removed a smaller bag from his large bag and handed it across the desk wordlessly. Their eyes met, nothing needed to be said.

She opened her lower right desk drawer and placed the bag into it and removed a large packet. She locked the drawer carefully. She handed the packet across to Scannell and said, "Here's the complete Xeroxed file on John Antle, excluding today, naturally. I think that you'll find it in good order and highly articulated. But I warn you in advance, it's repressed memory material and some find it to be controversial, and some say it is invalid. Please stay in touch. Thanks for the medication. It will come in handy." She gave him a somber smile and he left.

The process now would involve Youngquist taking the materials to one of his whoring psychologists who would give him a value estimate. After that it would be a wholehearted, no-hold barred investigation on the sinning priest. But even at this stage, Scannell liked something--one look at this miserable bastard Antle and you'd want to be blaming someone for his sorry existence.

CHAPTER EIGHT

Iowa, July 1996

Scorpio decided that it was time for Bertrand McAbee to wake up. As an adept manager of humans, he used a variety of techniques, beginning with the low warning growl at the paperboy, still a block away, and ending with the hellacious barking and rampaging through the house as the paperboy showed the tenacity of delivering the paper to this German Shepherd's house. Use to it by now, McAbee was only dimly aware of this ritual and would rarely react by getting out of bed.

Having successfully saved the house from the villianous paperboy and perhaps, with German Shepherd subtlety, warning McAbee that his sleeping time was adequate, the dog moved to the next level of manipulation. He would jump on the bed and march around, stepping over and between Bertrand's outstretched legs and arms, and yes, occasionally stepping on parts of McAbee that would lead to shoving, pushing, and human growling. In the world of Scorpio, of course, all of this was a positive sign-McAbee was waking up. When the testy edge came into McAbee's voice, he would lie down on the bed and systematically scooch and nudge his back into the now agitated McAbee, who would eventually run out of room avoiding this leviathan, and soon he would be up and doing all the things that servants to dogs should do.

McAbee took a long walk with the pressing and anxious dog and reflected on the case of Father Taylor and decided to start the investigation by visiting Chip Blaine, the diocesan attorney. Blaine might be able to give him a read on Antle's attorney, Youngquist, and whether or not this was a shakedown.

He entered the offices of the Blaine firm which occupied the top two floors of the 10-floor Norwest Bank Building in downtown Davenport. Blaine's office was at the end of the building. It had windows that afforded him spectacular views of the Mississippi River, the Rock Island Arsenal Bridge, which split in its center, bringing traffic to the mammoth federal installation, which was on an island in the middle of the Mississippi River or otherwise moving traffic between Davenport, Iowa, and Rock Island, Illinois. A few hundred yards to the west, he could see the Centennial Bridge which spanned the Mississippi between Rock Island and Davenport. In a few more months the bald eagles would come to settle in the area and provide extraordinary entertainment as they fished the river. Blaine was king of the hill, but it was only a small hill in a world of hills. Regardless, he was someone with whom to reckon. Blaine could give him 15 minutes, and it was made clear to McAbee that this was being done because the Bishop had made a personal plea.

Blaine had picked up weight since Bertrand had last

met him, and he had aged. He was dying his hair. He might have had an eye and jowls job, but he was not winning the fight against age. Kim Rice was another story, and it was apparent to McAbee that she was his acolyte as she hung on his every word and gesture. McAbee figured that she was being groomed for partner and bed at the same time, a dangerous game in a firm so dominated by one man.

Chip had a voice that could be melodious and gentle to one that best resembled a shrill, barking dog. Bertrand was treated to the latter.

"McAbee, what do you want?" He looked at his watch impatiently.

So it was going to be like that. "We're a bit at cross purposes, Mr. Blaine. Different focus-different effort."

"How so?"

"I'm trying to determine the truth. You're trying to defend the Diocese-and secondarily-a man. I don't have an agenda except to determine the truth." McAbee knew this would arouse Blaine.

"Oh, come on! Please! Do you really think you'll ever find that out? That attitude is malarkey, McAbee. I'm surprised at you. In cases like this, it's one word against another. And don't kid yourself. Taylor says he's innocent, and Antle says he's guilty. Do you think Perry Mason is going to come in and shake out a confession from one of them?" He gave an effusive and mocking smile to Kim Rice who awkwardly returned it. Perhaps she still had some kind of belief in truth.

"In answer to your question, I think it's quite possible, but I didn't come here to discuss epistemology with you.

I came to find out what you might know as I set up my investigation."

"Well, I already told you. The priest claims to be innocent. Who the hell knows! The Bishop has pretty much written him off by the way. But let me tell you something else, and this you should know from the outset, Youngquist is a crooked bastard. He has made a fortune screwing dioceses around the country. He faxed the filing to me and said I had 72 hours to offer a settlement."

"That's not all that unusual anymore in your trade," Bertrand fired back at the barking pomposity.

"Hey, listen, McAbee. Are you in here to take shots at me because you couldn't hang onto your wife, who is in the same goddamn trade I am?" McAbee caught himself and repeated within his head the words of the great stoic philosopher, Epictetus, 'You have no control over outside agencies.' It was true that he had no control over Blaine. But the bastard did score on him, and it hurt.

"Hey, Chip, this has nothing to do with my former wife, who, like many others, wanted nothing to do with your hustling and two-timing ways." He felt better.

Blaine was out of his seat as Kim Rice stepped in front of him and said, "Gentlemen, please please. I think we should get back to the case." McAbee respected her for what she did.

Chip said with his forefinger pointing and nodding back and forth, "Don't fuck around with me, McAbee."

She said, "Please, Chip. We were talking about Youngquist."

"So I repeat, Chip. There's really nothing unusual about seeking a settlement before filing."

Blaine stared at him as if waiting for some further clause or word to set him off. McAbee knew that it was the word "trade" that had ignited his temper.

"On a case of this magnitude and with this exposure, it's quite unusual." He stopped, checking to see if McAbee would taunt him again. McAbee saw no reason to say anything and sat there silently. "I cross checked with defense attorneys for the Diocese of St. Paul. They faxed me a scorecard. Kim made a copy for you. He has filed, since 1984, 131 lawsuits against either priests or dioceses or typically both. They figure in St. Paul that he probably has been silenced about 20 percent of the time with immediate offers. Their take on it is that he doesn't like to go to trial because he's not that good an attorney. So he'll settle."

"So why didn't you settle? If the Bishop thinks Taylor is guilty, why not?"

Blaine sat back and took in McAbee and then leaned forward. "I'll share my opinion with you, providing it doesn't go beyond these walls."

"Okay," McAbee said.

"The Bishop is no compromise. His vision of people is very black and white. I don't think that he has any great love for Taylor, and he knew of Youngquist from meetings with other bishops. Believe me. They all know of Youngquist. If the Church had a CIA or a KGB, Youngquist would have been erased a long time ago."

"The point?"

"O'Meara will never compromise with Youngquist unless he feels he's squandering Diocesan funds. He'll fight him to the bitter end, in my judgment. Now, does he sometimes wish that he had settled with the bum? Yes, I'm sure. But deep inside that Irishman there's a goddamn soul of granite."

"I'm confused. If he suspects that Father Taylor is guilty, why fight Youngquist, who has him trapped? Surely the Bishop wouldn't fight a losing cause and expose the Diocese to a massive loss of funds and perhaps expose a fellow priest to a walk through fire. What was the case worth? What would Youngquist take?"

"Father Taylor and his career and reputation mean nothing to O'Meara. So forget that angle. The Bishop thinks that Youngquist has to be raced out, picked on, and worked over every inch of the way. This seems to be the new strategy-pick, hit, slam, and drive the plaintiff's attorney mad. I do it regularly-couldn't think of a bigger scumbag to do it to!"

"And John Antle? What do you know of him?"

"Not much. We're making arrangements for depositions. After that I'll have a better sense of things. Oh, and just one other word. Bishop O'Meara wants Youngquist to know that if he comes into the Diocese again, he'll run into the same resistance. He thinks that some of his fellow bishops have made it too easy for the likes of Youngquist. So part of this is a warning shot."

"You didn't answer my question? What do you think Youngquist would have taken to make it go away?"

"A quarter mill."

McAbee thought about that sum and the fact that there was a lot of money going under the table in suits like this and then remembered that Father Taylor could be innocent. "Are you saying that Youngquist is crooked enough to file a suit if he wasn't convinced that a violation occurred?"

Blaine laughed in about as hollow and empty a way as he could before responding to Bertrand. "I think the bastard would file a suit against his mother if he thought he could make money. Reputations mean nothing to his sort."

McAbee shook his head in wonderment at the rottenness of people before getting up and saying, "I'll be in touch."

As he was leaving, Kim Rice came after him and said, "Oh, Dr. McAbee, here are some materials that Chip had me get for you. Please don't be put out by Chip. He's under a lot of pressure. Oh ... and I have a few friends who had you as a Prof at St. Anselm's College. They really liked you. I'd love to have a drink with you sometime. Here's my card." She left, leaving McAbee to wonder what that was about.

Minneapolis, 1996

Herb Scannell had worked off and on with the Antle matter. Almost immediately after the Antle signing in October of 1994, he was full-timing on a gigantic case against the Milwaukee, Wisconsin Diocese, besides trying to keep ten other investigations under control throughout the United States. In fact, he had to admit that the Antle case had fallen between the proverbial cracks.

Dr. Margaret Aaron had sent along another case that involved the Des Moines Diocese in April of 1995. He didn't think too much of its merits, but he knew that it wouldn't stop Youngquist from filing a lawsuit against the married Deacon and that Diocese. As a reward, he gave Aaron another supply of depressants and noticed that she had picked up a good 20 pounds or so and looked like shit, not that he really gave a damn for her.

He got back to the Antle matter in August of 1995 only to find Antle having second thoughts. "But, John, we've had our psychologists look at the file of your therapy. There is no doubt in their minds that you were assaulted by that filthy priest, and they also think that it would do your soul good to air it out and get paid for all the misery he brought to your life. Our psychologists are the best in the country."

Stupid little Antle gave him that deer-in-the-headlights look and wavered. Scannell gave him a month to think it over and wondered if there was something else in the equation other than Antle's hesitancy about exposure; Aaron said 'no,' but Scannell felt that it just didn't add up.

A month later he found Antle in the same sort of decision-less stupor, at which time he lowered the boom on him, at Youngquist's urging: "Listen, John, you can pull out of this thing, like I told you last October. Just say, 'I'm out.' But remember, you have to cover expenses; you signed that agreement. You owe the firm right now ... let's see ... "he pretended to look in his black book, "$11,380. Mr. Youngquist would hate to have to come after you to recover his out-of-pocket expenses, but he will. And you know what's really bad about this? If he filed against you, he would have to publicly indicate why he was doing so, including the fact that you had indicated that you had been sexually molested by Father Taylor. So ... you see ... one way or another, this is kind of a public thing anyway. Do you see?"

A long time ago, before he became a cop, Scannell had worked for a year in a beef slaughtering plant. He always remembered what it felt like the first day on the slaughter floor-the smell of blood and shit, the groans, the sound of men yelling, the full cacophony of the slaughter. He stayed awake all night and vomited a few times at the cruelty of the whole thing. He asked an old timer at lunch the next day how he did it. The old bastard looked at him like he was crazy and said, "He, kid. It's like picking a tomato-after a while, you don't even realize that it's going on. Life's there; life's gone." After a few weeks, he could relate to what the old geezer said, and it was true. He'd smile when he'd walk into the fancy Byerly's grocery store in Edina, Minnesota, and see some lush display of fresh red meat-the consumer protected from the horrid butchery that brought it there-and he'd think to himself, 'If you only knew.'

The slaughterhouse became a paradigm for him in that he reasoned that reality was based on brutality and viciousness. And when you were forced to be brutal, he likened it to picking a tomato. Only the few know what it is like to be on the slaughterhouse floor.

And when he was drafted and sent to Vietnam, the same realities were confirmed. He was with Army ground intelligence and became an interrogator/translator, not at headquarters, not on the Army base, but in the active battle areas where a long time in breaking a man or a woman meant that you were working on them for no more than ten minutes. He'd always look them in the eyes to gauge fear and came to be able to predict those who were breakable and those who needed time. He remembered once capturing two VC. One of them had an attitude, the other was full of fear. He commandeered a copter and took them up. He asked the one with the attitude what he knew about the VC in the area. The VC yelled, "Fuck you and your mother!"

Scannell snapped at the pilot: "Bring it up to 2000." When he did, Scannell shot the prick in his kneecap and hurled him out of the copter. He could still visualize the shock in the little bastard's face.

He turned to the other one, who was now speechless with fear. Haltingly and through tears and fear, he got the information that he wanted. He then threw him out of the copter. He gave him a break, though; he didn't kneecap him. The information was fed back to the line and it helped the beleaguered Captain. Nobody wanted to know how the information was uncovered. Nobody dared ask. It was like meat at Byerly's grocery store-nobody wanted to know how it got there.

So Antle was up against the wrong person and had signed a pact with Satan. It was too late to pull out. His fear and misgivings meant nothing to Scannell. Antle was a little-hearted man with meaningless feelings standing in the way of making some money. It was like picking a tomato.

Antle cried and remonstrated as best he could before Scannell grabbed him by his scrawny arms, shook him, and growled at him within two inches of his face. "You better wake up and get with it, Mister! You're in the water now-learn to swim." Eventually Antle came around, and Scannell figured that he had moved off that particular square.

He began to collect some data on Billy Taylor, and especially about his time at St. Anne's parish. He concluded that Taylor was extra good at deceit since everyone spoke so highly of him. Scannell pretended to be an advance man for a friend in Rome who wished to honor Taylor with a big surprise party. The hicks in this rural area of Iowa bought it, and he figured that no word of his inquiries got back to

Taylor, and if they did, Taylor might see a blade of truth in the story line about Rome. Youngquist told him not to go any deeper until they actually filed the complaint lest in some way it got out about Youngquist's involvement, and thus they would lose the element of surprise that he had when he threatened the public airing of the lawsuit in three days time if a settlement wasn't agreed to. Youngquist would smile and say that he was like Mike Wallace, except that he practiced ambush law instead of ambush journalism.

Youngquist was starting on the complaint papers in November of 1995 and had summoned John Antle up to Minneapolis. They would fly him up out of Cedar Rapids, Iowa, the hub airport for Iowa City. But he didn't show up, and Scannell waiting at the Minneapolis-St. Paul International Airport was about to leave when he was paged to come to the Northwest Airlines counter as soon as possible. It was Youngquist's office telling him to call Dr. Margaret Aaron ASAP.

He was put right through to her. She said with immense exasperation in her voice: "John tried to suicide last night. He's in University hospitals under 24-hour watch."

"How?"

"How? What do you mean how?" she said bitterly.

"How did he try to do it-gun, pills … what?"

"What in god's name is the relevancy of that question?"

"Will you just answer my question?" he said with that hard edge that toward which prisoners were always attentive.

"He tried to drown himself at Coralville Dam. He was saved by a fisherman who happened to be a wrestler on the University of Iowa wrestling team. If he hadn't been there, it was a sure death. So, are you wondering if he was serious about it?" Before he could answer, she said, "He was! And I think it's time to give him some space. This really worries me. I want you to ask Youngquist to back off for a few more months, Herb."

Scannell tried to picture her before he spoke. She was damaged goods herself, probably as bad as Antle in her own way. It wouldn't do anyone any good to force her at this point. After all she was a source for them and you never knew when she'd hand over a million dollar plum. So he said, "OK, this time. OK."

So they backed away until May of 1996 while Aaron continued to treat Antle. She informed Scannell in March, in between another delivery of drugs, that she might have a barn buster to hand over. Scannell wasn't sure about believing her, knowing that druggies would sell their best friends down the path of lies and distortions. She also continued to deteriorate, her face as pale as white paper and her weight high into obesity.

With a show of force by way of an ultimatum and the threat of a lawsuit, he videotaped John Antle in June of 1996 in the downtown Iowa City Holiday Inn. Scannell asked all of the questions that were given to him by Youngquist. From that, Youngquist prepared the complaint. "We don't want to schedule the little bastard to fly again only to find that he tries to commit suicide again," Youngquist said with a snarling laugh.

In the interview, Scannell reflected back to the first time he had met Antle. He was in worse condition than he had been then. He wondered what Aaron was doing to this little rabbit. This hypnosis crap was dubious in his mind. The question became: "Can we keep him alive in case we have to go to trial," Youngquist argued. "It's much harder to win a case out of a graveyard, especially against a priest with a solid reputation."

Aaron's overdosing was another matter. Five days after the complaint against Father Taylor, was publicized, Aaron was found by paramedics and rushed to the hospital where her guts were pumped out, and she was placed in a drug rehab unit. Dr. Anne Magee came back into the picture, and the stripping down of Dr. Margaret Aaron began. Aaron's nurse, Margi, was sent $2,000, and this provided a continuing chain of information to Scannell about Aaron. After all, Aaron was a key player in any potential trial, and her professional credibility was in serious jeopardy, now and for the rest of her life. Both he and Youngquist had one primary concern about her: What would they do to her head in that rehab unit? And they particularly worried about the deliveries of drugs that were made to her office.

CHAPTER NINE

Iowa, August 1996

Brother Joseph escorted Father Taylor to his car. Taylor appreciated the caring concern of the Brother whom he had come to learn, in brief chats with him, was a veteran and a former Chicago police office. If he had to fault the Brother, it would be about his pestering and prying qualities. Sometimes he would be walking around the spacious grounds and suddenly the good Brother would appear. But, he supposed, he was probably being watched because of the lawsuit, and Brother Joseph, given his background, was the likely choice.

Taylor loved the monastery and its flow. He was pleased to see that this vision of life that went back to the Fourth Century was still part of Catholicism and was still a viable choice in a world that craved polyphasia and constant motion. In fact, he always saw his mission as a priest to be one of providing a backdrop of stability to parishioners programmed to endless searching and spasms of meaninglessness.

After finishing his undergraduate work at the minor

seminary at St. Ambrose College in Davenport, Iowa, he had gone on to St. Paul's Seminary in Minnesota and was then sent to Rome where he received his Ph.D. The Bishop of the Davenport Diocese had told him in the no uncertain terms of the Catholic Church of the fifties that his life was to be fulfilled as a Theology Professor at St. Ambrose. He stayed the course until that bishop died. Many of the priests of the Diocese had learned Scripture, Dogma, Theological Ethics from him. When they would get together at retreats or social occasions, they would joke with him: "We could never get a straight answer out of you, Billy! We used to call you 20-questions Billy behind your back!"

What many didn't know was that he was pursuing a master's degree in Counseling from the University of Iowa. He believed that this would make him a more proficient listener and it did. He became a convinced Rogerian who firmly felt that people knew the answer to their problems, and it was the role of the listener to get them to see it and pronounce it.

Already inclined in that direction, over the years he became a maven of the technique which he contrasted with his education at St. Paul's and the 'Angelicum' in Rome where memorization was equated with Theological brilliance. The Counseling Department at the University of Iowa implored him to pursue a Ph.D., but when he brought the proposal to his Bishop, he was told by the highly opinionated Bishop that, "Therapy and counseling are the Trojan horses of the Modernists and the Secularists. They are meant to replace the central importance of the priest and the confessional. I knew it was a mistake to let her go over there for a master's degree, and now they want to fully destroy your faith. I'll have none of it and neither will you. It is forbidden!"

Taylor fought the tension that rose up within him and took out from his shelf the *Confessiones Sancti Augustinis,* a book that he had translated back in his undergraduate days. He had always considered it to be one of the greatest books ever written. Augustine's wanderings through sin, heresy, and falsity were told in a delicious intensity that he never found in the too intellectual and removed Greeks or with the inconsequential and cynical on the one hand or the sodden and depressed intellectuals on the other hand of the Romans. It bewildered him that he couldn't find another Augustine in Christianity until Martin Luther, where he found someone who came back into sin just as Augustine had left it.

Taylor heard the cries of Augustine's flesh and spirit as he twisted over the fires of truth. At the University of Iowa, he had met a woman, Clare, who if he was in a race, came up on him from nowhere and totally caught him. He fell in love and he wrestled with this Roman Catholic vision of the world and the airiness, beauty, and brilliance of this woman. He found her absorbing his thought process. His efforts at contemplation and fidelity and purpose were collapsing around him, and he spent nights crying and speaking to Christ to free him from the obsession he had for her. But the more he prayed, the more he fell. He was sure his vocation was doomed as the two of them started the precipitous movement to sexual engagement.

But she had her own demons to deal with: a rocky marriage and a daughter with multiple sclerosis. And in an act of the will, she told him on a dark, cold night in the middle of December in Iowa City: "Billy. I love you, but I can't go on. I'm leaving the program here for a while and I'm leaving you forever. I'll never love anyone like you again. You are the gem of my life, but all I see is disaster for both of us. Please ... don't talk ... and don't say anything to me. It's over." With that she kissed his cheek, left his car and trod through the fresh snow toward her car. His tears mingled with the tears that had fallen to her lips and which had streaked his face where she had kissed him. He saw the blue VW Beetle leave the lot and Taylor sat in his car until a security guard rapped at his window and asked him if he was all right. He wasn't. He was a devastated man, not trained and surely not hardened in the affairs of the heart.

But it wasn't over. The *Des Moines Register* reported, in a statewide edition in a small article two mornings later that a multiple car-truck accident had occurred on an icy road near Waterloo, Iowa. The header was emblazoned into his mind-"3 Killed, 5 Hurt On Icy Road." He went by the article only to find something pulling him back to it. When he saw her name among the three dead, he hit the nadir of his life to that point. No one had called him because no one knew of their relationship. If he hadn't read the small article in a paper that relatively few subscribed to in eastern Iowa, he might not have known until after the holidays.

He went to the wake. The casket was closed; there had been a bad fire. He met her husband, a tearful and taciturn man. He offered his condolences and told him he was a student friend of hers. The man said, "I told her not to go to that program. Her place was at home with the girl. Now what?" he asked pleadingly. Taylor found himself uttering the long-practiced nostrums of his religion: "It will work out. It's God's plan."

Standing in front of the casket, he felt the eyes of this Presbyterian family gazing at this man with a Roman collar, and he felt shame. He hurled abuse at himself: 'lf l had only kept her in the car for a few seconds or called out to her, she would have missed the accident.' He felt his prayers and faith to be useless, and when he turned around, he saw an older woman moving a wheelchair through the aisle. In the wheelchair was Clare's eight-year-old daughter, with legs the circumference of a broomstick and arms grizzled with distortion and head permanently alop. But beneath the pain of that visage, he pictured Clare in the casket and a coldness gripped him and froze him in place. He forced himself to sit lest he faint, and the dam broke as his sobs silenced the funeral parlor. The undertaker escorted him to his office and told him to just lie down on his couch. He knew how tough the loss was-"Oh, by the way, how did you know the deceased?"

He never went to the funeral because he didn't trust himself to act appropriately, and he didn't want to have the family wondering any more than they probably did. He did visit her grave over the years whenever he was close to the area. The husband had remarried and the daughter died at the age of 21. There was no way out of the bleak conclusions to the life of this beautiful and brilliant woman, except, as Taylor experienced, an epiphany, through a surrender to God's will.

So it was not hard for Billy Taylor to come back to Augustine a second time around and now understand what the Saint had been through. At this point in his life, he had put on the spirit of Augustine and eventually found peace in his heart. And Clare? She had made the great decision of her life: a reaffirmation of her responsibilities, duties, and love of the family and with that God had taken her, surely to her heavenly reward.

He was taken by Augustine's view that we are sinners and that only through grace and Jesus can we capture salvation. He would argue in his classes that once we made the second conversion, the paradigm changes forever. The model for looking at life was now forever embedded in us and reality would never puzzle us again. There was a reason for everything. Be it ostensibly bad or evil, there is a reason.

He argued that Augustine's theory of divine illumination was an elegant argument for the truth lying within us, as in a darkened closet. Through faith we lit up our inner self as it was and saw the truth. How easy it was for him to place Rogers' theory of counseling into his Augustinian theology.

Finally, with the death of one and the arrival of another bishop, came his permission to go into parish life. From thereon he stayed the course and worked his ministry uninterrupted until John Antle's charge.

And so it was that when he and Brother Joseph walked to his car, he found the car to be spotless.

"Brother, I can't believe my eyes. The car has never looked this good."

"We like to work, Father. It frees the mind to soar to better things; besides, it's to show you our respect. We all think the world of you."

"Well, that's a mutual feeling. I'm awed at all the good that flows through these grounds."

"The keys are in the car, Father. Oh, and when you come

back," he looked narrowly at Taylor, "just park in front of the visitor's door and have the keys in it. I'll pull it around. After these many weeks, it might seem strange to drive at first. You know, Father . . .," he hesitated meaningfully and clearly wanted the effect to last, "we all think that you're innocent." He smiled and left. Taylor got into the car and started toward Davenport and his meeting with Chip Blaine, the Diocesan lawyer.

Iowa, August 1996

Bertrand McAbee arrived at his office ten minutes late. He knew instantly that they had been at each other's throats. In one comer wearing a pair of ugly, medium-brown pants that ended at the top of his ankles and an unmatching, dark-blue shirt was Barry Fisk, and in the other comer was Pat Trump wearing an elegant blue suit, beige blouse, accessorized with pearls. McAbee was not totally convinced that they hated each other, a small voice whispering to him that beneath all of the rancor, they respected and cared for each other, not that they'd ever show it in this lifetime.

When McAbee had left academia 15 years previous, he had hired Pat as his secretary and assistant, a decision he never looked back on. Petite, red haired, chain smoker, and loyal to her core, she was a main support for him. He feared losing her since she was maintaining a weekend marriage with her husband Ray, who had been transferred to Indianapolis, but so far, so good. He had no idea how he could replace her if it came down to that.

Fisk was another story altogether. He was a 5-foot,

0-inch hunchback with a doctorate in American History from Yale. Driven out of an Illinois college because of his impossibly high standard of scholarship and equally low social skills, he had taken to the occupation of private researcher where all of his skills flowered in the pursuit of information. Armed with his computer, there was hardly a system around that he couldn't successfully raid. He was a preeminent hacker. McAbee had used him on many cases, and in his momentous serial killer case, Fisk was indispensable. But Fisk could be a trial. Pat Trump was the only person who seemed to have the skills to silence him or strike some kind of fear in him. For that reason, of course, Fisk resented her and would all too often test her mettle only to be crushed still again by her. He could feel the atmospheric venom that hung between the two of them.

"Pat, Barry, good morning."

"Good morning, Doc. Your nine o'clock appointment is here, as you can see," she said with just a slight hint of sarcasm.

Barry rejoindered, looking at his watch and tapping it with his forefinger, "It is 9:10, McAbee, and the billing started with my leaving my house at 8:45." Barry referred to just about everyone by their last name. First names were, perhaps, far too intimate.

"I know, Barry, I know. Let's go into my office." He showed Barry through the door and saw Pat raise her eyes to the ceiling. He winked at her and smiled for a split second. If Barry had caught any of that exchange, there would be hell to pay.

Barry moved with quick, small steps, but McAbee thought Barry's head was tilted just a little farther to the left and wondered what secret pains this spirited little intellectual bore in his heart. He had long ago given up any attempt at penetrating Barry's steel veil. It was unwelcome. They sat across from each other at a small circular table.

"So, Barry, how's everything going for you?"

"Is this a social visit or business?" Fisk shot back.

McAbee looked ever so closely at him, trying to detect the slightest trace of humor. There was none in that taut face with its pointy ears and squinty eyes, lips that Gillette might want to patent for their thinness, his almost non-existent chin, and the oddness of a full nose.

"No ... no, Barry, it's business. I'm just trying to soften you up for a smaller bill," he said with a humorous cast to his eyes.

"Yes, we'll see about that," both of them knowing that McAbee had gratuitously shared several bonuses with him, bringing Fisk's home computer system to a level that would be hard to match. McAbee had even had a "thanks" from him in reference to these gifts.

Bertrand explained the case to Fisk, omitting few details, because Fisk thrived on detail and needed them to "feel" the case.

"So, right now what I need, Barry, is a full rundown on this John Antle, his attorney Martin Youngquist, and any peripheral play you can find in the mix; for example, I'd like to know if there's a psychologist or psychiatrist involved. In the complaint," he handed Fisk a copy of it, "is the address of Antle and the business address of Youngquist. Oh, and why not run something on the priest, William Taylor. Right now I don't know what to think."

"Well you may not know how to think about the whole thing, but the whole edifice is made from trash found in dreams and fairy tales."

"Meaning what, Barry?"

"All the way through this you have posturers and liars, beginning with the priest, the Church, Jesus Christ, and God. It's all make believe. Think of Mickey Mouse. He started out of some barely recognizable piece of an idea in the mind of a cartoonist and now, he/it, whatever, has become a church, complete with shrines in France, California, and Florida. You have the high priest, Michael Eisner, keeping the faith alive as he's threatened with boycotts by fundamentalists, Catholics, homosexuals, and you name it. The only difference between Mickey Mouse and Jesus is that Mickey didn't need to be crucified to become God. Otherwise the overlay is quite stunning." His eyes glared at McAbee. He wanted an argument, but Bertrand was too busy to do so. He just sat there listening to Fisk.

"Then you attach the shyster element in the legal profession and the self-pitying psycho babblers who find themselves abused in their childhood and use that to explain their failed lives then you have a bonafide Barnum & Bailey Circus. Like everything else I run into-it's bullshit! But I'll start the digging, and I'm sure you'll separate out the malicious ones from the beneficial ones, but what you won't sort out, because you just don't want to see it, is the sheer wall of deceit behind it all." He thumped his hand down on the table, his speech finished.

McAbee thought to himself that some of what Fisk said was true, but the personal cost to Fisk of the whole package was an anarchistic nihilism that made him miserable. He seemed to be a person who lived with hatred and disdain as his companion, a life that McAbee wanted nothing of.

When Barry had left, McAbee looked out his window at

downtown Davenport, a miniature, deserted canyon. Raised a Catholic, he was hardly one now, his visits to church only for occasions when it was socially necessary. And yet he was highly compatible with many of its current moral teachings about social justice, fairness, kindness to the unfortunate, and soon. The absurdity of its position in human sexuality he considered only a minor blemish on its typically solid instincts. Of course, if one took those sexuality prescriptions seriously, then they could be life-wrecking.

It all came down to the enigmatic Taylor. Was he this secret sinner who preyed on little kids? And John Antle? Was he some zero who was trying to make a fast buck, allied to Martin Youngquist who had a history of church bashing?

He went out to the office foyer. Pat looked up from her computer and said, "Boy, am I glad you got here. He was particularly ornery today. It's too bad he's not 6-foot, 5-inches and 300 pounds. He could go out onto the football field and hammer out his aggressions. He's like a little boy who thinks he's a professional linebacker. On the other hand, I'm sort of glad that God didn't give him a powerful physique."

"You always handle him well, Pat." "Yeah ... well ... he was getting to me this morning. He was chopping on you, a new approach to get under my skin." She smiled exasperatingly. "How so?" "Oh ... what's a classics prof doing running an investigation agency? Instead of reading Aristotle and Plato, you, the poor chump, are reading trash like *Modern Detection, Surveillance Inc.,* and a bunch of other titles that he was spitting out. You have become an intellectual pygmy because of the people you have to work with, and then, get this, he gives me this accusatory look, like I'm one of these horrible people."

"What did you say?" She hesitated, but then said, "I reminded him of all of the good things you did for him, and then he screeches: 'That's not the point ... that's not the point!' Then I went below the belt. I shouldn't be telling you this. You'll be mad at me. I told him that he was one of the pygmies who came to my mind when he used the word 'pygmy'. Boy, did that hit!" "What did he say?" "Nothing. He just sat there and glared at me, all five feet of him. About two minutes of pretty intense silence and then you walked in. Thank God. I hope you don't mind. He really does need an old-fashioned spanking."

"Honestly, Pat, do you like him?"

She thought for a minute. "The way I assess that is, if he died, would I be unhappy or sad? And you know, I would, because beneath all of that piss and vinegar is a fragile little boy. So, yes, he touches my limited maternal instincts." She smiled.

"Well, he was on the attack universally today. If I had let him go, the entire substructure of western civilization would have been dismantled. So I don't think that it was personal. He was just plain mean today. But like you, I'm attached to him in an odd way. I can't explain it."

CHAPTER TEN

Iowa, August 1996

"Kim, come down to my office," Blaine barked into her phone. No hello, no good morning-just plain all-male arrogance.

Kim Rice was at the Blaine firm because of advice she received from Professor Theodore Goldberg at the University of Iowa. Goldberg was her mentor and was one of the most respected profs in the Law School. He was a specialist in Iowa law, and it was to that field that Kim was most drawn to, probably because her father had been driven into near bankruptcy by a fraudulent S&L bank in the grim early 80s when the Iowa farm economy was virtually gutted. She never forgot the searing experience that she went through as a little girl or the brutal personal toll that it took on her family. So, the farm girl from Carroll, Iowa, about 75 miles west/northwest of Des Moines, saw law school as being part of a mission to not let Iowa's little people get legally murdered by the "big-uns," as her father referred to the banks and their attorneys. Goldberg pretty much saw the world through those lenses also.

"Kim," Goldberg said to her when she came to her office with 31 bonafide offers from all over the country, "it appears to me that it might be best not to stay in Iowa. You have offers from five excellent firms. Interview them."

She did and she'd now have to admit that Chip Blaine overwhelmed her. He had all the spit and polish of a real pro, but he also had a sense of the little guy and did pro bono work. She went back to Goldberg, "I'm drawn to Blaine. He seems honest, and he's clearly well connected. He's into the ABA and the Iowa Bar. Have you met him?"

Goldberg responded, "He has the hottest firm in Iowa. He's come out of nowhere and has taken the number one spot in the Quad Cities, which has about a large population base. His written work is efficient and on point, but by no means brilliant, and his oral skills are superb. You could learn a lot." On the basis of her perceptions and Goldberg's advice, she signed on with Blaine.

The day she left the Iowa Law School for keeps, Goldberg took her arm and said, "Kim, just a word of advice. For the first three years, smile, watch, and do what you're told. It's an apprenticeship. Don't make enemies in the firm and keep Blaine happy. Ok? And by the way, your beauty will open all sorts of doors, but it will also be a curse. Be really cautious. It's like carrying around an elephant gun. It can really draw attention, but if you fire it, you might throw out your shoulder permanently."

Chip Blaine had many attractive personal characteristics. He moved gracefully through every social circle. He was perceptive, and he did take a high interest in her career. But he was also into touching, ogling, intimacies, and she sensed that one of these days, he'd make a move on her. She did everything she could to win his confidence and support, even though she winced in her heart at the thigh pat, or the arm around the shoulder, or the distasteful jokes. So she felt that she was between a rock and a hard place, wanting to learn from this master and being repelled by his sexism and insensitivity.

When she met with her former classmates, they would talk about the occurrences that they would experience, and she'd mention some of these things but conceal Blaine's name by referring to attorneys on the other side of the issue, as if they were the perpetrators. There would be the question: "What did you do?" and she'd say: "Nothing." And they'd jump down her throat: "Nothing? I can't believe it. Tell him you'll bring him before the bar. You can't allow this."

So, she continued to waver on the issue, and she knew that she was part of the problem because she was making a pragmatic decision to put learning ahead of the sexist environment. Furthermore, she hoped that Blaine's behavior would never go beyond where it was. That he sometimes treated her like a slave and ordered her to meetings didn't bother her. She knew that it was part of the apprenticeship. Most of the time Blaine had no idea of how horrid he could sound.

It was, then, on his command that she picked up her pad and file and walked dutifully to Blaine's office.

"Are you ready for the good Father Taylor?" he asked with a hint of meanness. She had noticed that streak in him was becoming more evident as her knowledge of him advanced. Perhaps he was no longer trying to impress her, or perhaps worse still, he thought that was the way to charm her.

"Yes, I am, Chip. What do you expect to come from this?"

"Who knows? At this stage of the game, they're usually still whining about how innocent and good they are. So I expect a lot of denial and anger."

"Have you ever met him?"

"No, can't say I have." He looked at her legs, which she proceeded to uncross. Did she observe just the slightest hint of a smile in his face when she did that? "I'm going to bat him around a little and see how he reacts. You know the Bishop and the fairy princess, Duncan, have already written him off. They probably know something that we'll never find out. Goddamn clergy! They operate behind seven veils of secrecy, especially as in the case of these two; they studied in Rome. It's like the Romans are grooming every one of them to become a diplomat."

"So, you think it's a foregone conclusion that he's guilty?" Kim asked.

"Well, look at it this way. My primary client is the Diocese, not the obscure priest. The Diocese has pretty much written him off. Hell, they've shipped him off to Siberia, the fucking Trappist monastery. How would you like to spend a weekend up there, Kim? They'd show you how to keep your legs clamped together." He laughed heartily at his joke. She smiled and cursed herself, blushing crimson. He had noticed the uncrossing of her legs and seized on her self-consciousness, the son-of-a-bitch. She knew what her friends would say: "Don't smile. Don't reward the behavior. He'll just keep it up." He continued, "So the diocese has written him off, and I've come pretty much to the same conclusion. The psychiatrist was a former prof at the Medical Center! So we're not dealing with some broken-down drunk trying to make a few fast bucks. It's just not the kind of product they put out up there. So, in effect, I have the damn medical school validating this abuse. Lastly, let's face it. I'm representing the Diocese. Sure ... I know ... I'm representing the pervert too. But my real interest in this is the chief client-the Bishop! And it seems to me that he wouldn't shed a tear if we strung Taylor up by the balls!"

"And what do you make of Dr. McAbee?"

He paused as if his convenient world view had suffered a blow. "Who knows what to think of him. I'm always leery of people who go around saying they're trying to discover the truth. We'll let him float around out there. On the street they say he's good. Apparently his wife didn't think much of him." Again, that suggestive leer came on his face. For once, she ignored it by looking down at her notes.

The buzz caught his attention. "Father Taylor is here" the speaker squawked. It was a peculiar thing about Blaine. He kept around him the machinery and things of the 70s and 80s, the voice box just one of many.

"Send him in."

Father Taylor was an elegant looking man. The Roman collar and black suit set off the contrast with his white hair and tanned face. His deep brown eyes were intense and his smile was deep and sincere as he shook hands with Blaine and while shaking hands with Kim, bowed slightly. Her notes said that he was 75, but he looked no older than a man in his fifties. She had only a passing and slight acquaintance with priests until this case had come to Blaine. The difference between this man and the Bishop and the foppish Duncan was huge. This guy bespoke holiness, and if he wasn't so, he was the best actor that Kim had ever run into. She sensed that he was the kind of person you could tell anything to and he'd handle it. She figured that it wasn't hard for him to be with the silent Trappists.

After they sat, Blaine began: "So how are the Trappists treating you, Father?"

"It's extraordinary. They're an incredible group. I admire them, their dedication." He spoke very slowly and deliberately.

"Well, good. It seems as though it has been good for your soul. I'm sure the Bishop will be pleased." Taylor didn't respond. He wasn't the type to waste words.

"Tell me, Father, do you recall John Antle?"

"Yes, I do. He was an altar boy at St. Anne's back in the 70s, for a year or two. His family then moved into the Quad Cities. He was a very shy but good little boy."

"Father, when his attorney called me with the threat to file, he told me that the boy had full reign over the church and the rectory every Sunday; that, in fact, he was given a privileged place in the rectory. Does that make sense?"

"Well ... no ... not really. I've tried to think about this thing, and I do recall his being around there. We had two masses and his mother would go into town and the boy would serve at both masses. So, in a way, he was given some freedom, I suppose. But he was a good kid. I had no problem with that. He wasn't into the wine supply, if that's what you mean."

"No, that's not what I mean. If that was the problem, we wouldn't be here today. I'm talking about opportunity. There was clear opportunity for you to have at this kid!" he said, staring harshly at Taylor.

"Opportunity? Mr. Blaine, if I am to be accused based on opportunity, then there's no end to what I can be charged with. I never touched this boy, and if I did, it would be a pat on the shoulder for a good job. He was a very dutiful boy. Perhaps this is where the confusion is. Somehow an encouraging pat on the shoulder is seen to be a sexual act."

Kim liked Taylor from the outset, and as he went on with Blaine, she liked him even more. She thought of Bertrand McAbee and saw something common to the two of them, something she didn't see in attorneys, an uncommon quality, hard to pin down. But it was there, a thoughtfulness, a sense of genuineness, a sense of Socrates' old saying: "Know thyself." Blaine was interested in appearance, always measuring potential effects on juries or outsiders. Not this man. Nor from what she could tell, but in a less evident way, was McAbee, who seemed to be significantly more indirect and subtle than Taylor.

Blaine and Taylor went through the entire matter in about half an hour. As Blaine pressed and cajoled, Taylor became more relaxed and powerful. Blaine was frustrated and ended the meeting in a despairing tone. "Father, I hope that you go back to the Trappists and find a way to the truth, because, right now, it doesn't look good."

Father Taylor responded, "I'll think more on the matter. But, again, I'll tell you. I never have practiced pedophilia. I'm a sinful man, but that's not one of my sins."

When Taylor had left, Blaine looked at Kim and said, "That little pious fraud is guiltier than Hitler!"

Kim said nothing. She was puzzled because she knew that Blaine had good case judgment about the probity and convincibility of a witness. Could it be that Father Taylor, deep down, was a liar and a pervert?

Iowa, August 1996

For three weeks, Dr. Margaret Aaron had been relentlessly pounded in the rehab unit at the University of Iowa. The process of withdrawal had been intensely difficult, but for the first time in years, she was beginning to feel her life coming back into view. Between the coke heads, acid heads, and drunks, she felt that she was sitting suspended in a dunk tank, and those sure-handed addict bastards never missed a throw that would plunk her into the water. She had said this in group therapy and both she and the group had laughed uproariously. She admitted that she needed a good kick up the ass and her newly found friends complied.

Within a week she asked an old adversary to speak with her. It was Dr. Anne Magee who had fingered her addiction but who had told her she didn't treat addicts per se. It wasn't her game. In fact, however, Magee's visage had troubled her ever since that time. Deep down, somewhere in her gut, she knew that Magee had her pegged, and she knew that this big-faced woman was strong enough to face her down.

Magee came and told Aaron she would work with her but not referential to her drug problem, but rather to the area where they had left off from, the terrible sexual abuse that she was put through by her father. At first, fighting and rationalizing, it wasn't long before Aaron came to grips with what had occurred and what she had to do to get past it. She and Magee were connecting on all cylinders within a week;

two quite brilliant women synergistically and momentarily, as life spans went, focused on one issue.

Magee then pressed Aaron to speak of her negative experience with the English psychiatrist Edward Nelson and guided Aaron over the coals of that difficult situation. Aaron knew that Magee was onto something and gave herself completely to the ministrations of Magee.

"And exactly why did you and Dr. Nelson part ways, Margaret?" Magee queried.

"Well, his complaint was that I was too stressed out by my own life, that I was taking my experience with my father and was trying to turn all of life into that prism."

"And ... did he have a point?"

"Anne, this is hard for me. If I say 'no,' my gut tells me I'm lying, and If I say 'yes,' my mind tells me I'm repudiating all of the work that I've been into, all of my patients, the center of my point of view, that I've been wrong. Oh, Jesus!" And she cried a well. But Magee didn't judge her.

She just listened and asked Aaron for more insight and more courage. And for that short period of time there seemed to be no end to the self-discovery that Aaron was coming to.

By now, Aaron was no longer concealing anything. She felt that she had opened a dark pit, and Magee was shining a brilliant light down into it. Every part of her was exposed, and she was amazingly jubilant. The drunks and cokeheads were astounded by her continued honesty and efforts. At this point, Magee came at her from a new angle. She asked about her drug supplies and her supplier. The rehab types hadn't gotten to that yet and yet Magee was landing on that sensitive soil. Her stomach constricted. She knew that

Magee was getting close to the one area that even she, with all of her candor and lucidity, wasn't ready to reveal.

She responded lightly to Magee's thrust, "Anne, I thought you didn't treat addicts and their addictions."

"Why are you defensive, Margaret?"

"I'm not defensive, goddam it," she snapped at Anne.

Anne didn't have to say anything. She just sat there looking at Margaret, the truth of her comment proven in Aaron's hostility.

Finally, Margaret responded, hesitatingly and fearfully, because she knew where this ugly path would take her-into the violation of patients for the purpose of supporting her addiction. It was the ultimate truth that she had to face. It was one thing to damage herself but another thing to use patients for these ends.

"I was into reversion, Anne. I would talk my patients into giving me their supplies, and I would skim them."

"Did any druggists know this?"

"No. Just my nurse, Margi."

"Was that the extent of this?"

"How do you mean?" And then she felt stupid. "I'm sorry, Anne. I know what you mean. About two years ago I got some drugs from an investigator for a lawyer who was into repressed memories and liability."

"Meaning ... ?

"Meaning ... Goddamn it. I'm so ashamed ... meaning drugs for clients." And she cried again as the somber face of Magee gazed at her with neither sadness nor sympathy. She was the agent of realism, Margaret knew.

"So tell me, Margaret, what happened in your therapy? Were you finding truth or were you using suggestion?"

"I'm not sure anymore. I just don't know anymore. It sounds like I was a charlatan. It's incredible. I can't believe I went so low. Can you?"

"Going low is not the issue here, Margaret. Recovering is what this is all about."

Magee plowed this ground for some time, pressing Margaret into recognition, forcing her to realize that she had compromised the field of psychiatry and that even the barest of medical ethics could not stand the test by which she assaulted them.

"So, Margaret, did you give them someone?"

"I ... think so. I mean, I'm sure that he was abused. I don't think that I had that wrong, but it's the details that can go wrong in this therapy. I don't know if I was diligent. I may have led him into what I thought should be heard. At any rate, I gave over his name and they began the process. He tried to suicide and something in me cracked. He didn't want to sue. I told him it was therapeutically good. I forced him, Anne, and now he's a wounded man, worse for my intervention, I think, than when he came to me. The negative harm principle. You know. Don't cause more harm than was there when you start out. I did it, I think. John is definitely hurt. That broke me some, that and all the rest of my problems. It got to be too much. He's such a lamb and I'm a bitch of a wolf. He didn't stand a chance. More than anything else, that's why I'm here right now."

Magee again said nothing.

A day later Aaron called Margi, her nurse, and asked her to come to the hospital over lunch hour.

"Margi, I'm going to be pretty short about some things. I'm experiencing a new view of myself. I've been a rotten person. I've hurt my patients to serve my addiction, and I've hurt you. I made you an accomplice in my reversion game. I've been telling a lot of things to my therapist, Anne Magee. We think that I should speak with the Attorney General's office about what I have done. I'm going to implicate Scannell."

"Are you sure this is the way to go? It will devastate your reputation," Margi was quite defensive.

"My reputation isn't important. How many people are getting hurt by these characters is what is important. On Friday I'm coming to the office at 5:00 p.m. to get my Antle file and a few others where I think my addiction may have caused harm. Will you be kind enough to be there?"

"Of course. Anything else?"

"No. I've got to come back here. I feel like a little girl going on her first bicycle solo. They're going to give me two hours! Can you believe?"

"I think it's great, Dr. Aaron, but will you ever practice again?"

"Anne says yes. That she will be going to the Board of Medical Examiners to argue my case. She is sure that she will prevail. But I've got to be totally honest with myself and with her. It's my only chance, and truthfully speaking, the only way I could go back to helping people. Margi, I've really changed. It's been the best and worst three weeks of my life. By the way, have you heard anything about John Antle?"

"Yes. He called. He didn't sound all that good. I told him you were sick and would be back soon. At least he's alive, I guess."

"Yes ... well ... I've got to talk with him about Scannell

and that whole thing. I was wrong. I feel terrible about this thing. I think that I may have caused that attempted suicide. I've got to right this wrong, Margi. I just have to, believe me."

CHAPTER ELEVEN

Minneapolis, August 1996

Scannell gazed at the number flashing on his telephone ID system. The call was from Margi Hayslitt, Margaret Aaron's nurse. "Hello," he said tentatively. "Herb Scannell?"

"Yeah," he pretended not to know her.

"Herb, this is Margi Hayslitt from Dr. Aaron's office in Iowa City."

"Oh, yeah. Hi, Margi. Wow! What time is it?-10:30 p.m. I don't usually get calls from beautiful women at this time of night." He was trying to conceal the tension in his voice. She rarely called him at home, and never this late. He knew it couldn't be good news.

"There's a big problem here, and I think you should be aware of it."

"Shoot."

"You know that Dr. Aaron has been in the drug program. Well, she's finding Jesus or something, and I don't like it. She had me come to the rehab unit today to meet with her. She wanted me to pull the files on Antle and a few others; also the other one your firm was given. I forget the man right now ... uh...."

"That's OK, Margi. Don't worry about that detail. What's the story behind this?" She'd clearly been drinking; not drunk but a bit tipsy.

"Well, she's coming over to the office the day after tomorrow. She's ... it's incredible .. she's in a frenzy, like she sounds like ... you know ... she's trying to ... repudiate. Yeah, repudiate her past life. At any rate, she's going to look at or take the files and then talk with the Attorney General's office. It's like she's surrendering everything ... like ... total confession. I'm afraid that I'll get into trouble. Give me some advice."

Scannell's mind was raging through choices midway into Margi's outpouring, and by the end, he had made a decision, and if all the stars were in place, it would happen.

"Now, Margi. Don't you worry. These addicts can say something one day and the next day they're saying just the opposite. She's just getting one side of the issue too. The druggie programs all beat the hell out of them ... brainwash is a better word ... and when they get out, they see what happened. That's why so many go back to their drugs of choice." He laughed consolingly.

"No, Herb. You don't know her. Yeah, she may be screwed up because of what they did to her, but I know her. When she gets an idea into her head ... you know ... it's her way ... there's no compromise in her, believe me. And she mentioned you, also"

"What if I talked with her?"

"I don't know. I think that ... that ... I know she sees you as a problem. I don't know what you gave her, but I'm no fool. You come around and suddenly she's not dipping into patient supplies so much anymore."

He laughed, as sincerely as he could. "Why, Margi. You're a perceptive woman. Tell me. When is she coming over to the office? Oh, and before that, is she out of rehab often?"

"No. They're letting her out for a few hours. She mentioned it. She said she felt like a little girl on her first solo. She's coming at five. She doesn't want to see any patients. She asked me to stay around for a while to help her."

"Margi, do me a favor. Leave the door unlatched. I might be able to just happen by. Don't worry. I won't implicate you. Maybe I can talk some sense into her. What do you think? Is that OK?"

She paused and then said, "Yeah ... yeah, I guess so. Just keep me out of it."

The next morning Scannell went to see Martin Youngquist. Several years previous they had agreed to a code between them that when something potentially illegal was in the works, they would signal each other by a finger to the lips and proceed to walk outside the building around a small but noisy fountain. Youngquist felt that he was always in danger from the forces of the Vatican, even suggesting that the Mafia might put out a hit on him or that he might be secretly taped by the Justice Department or the Minnesota Attorney Discipline Committee. In his prism, the world was without scruples.

Scannell explained the situation in Iowa City.

Youngquist said, "Can they tie you to the drugs you left there?"

"No. I always handled the bag gingerly and with a

handkerchief or gloves. She never noticed that, but I did it just in case. The packets I got from ....”

“It doesn’t matter. I don’t want to talk about that. You’re clean is the conclusion.”

“Yes.”

Scannell didn’t care for Youngquist, but he admired the way he covered his ass and thought ahead. The bond between them was very tight when it came to covering trails.

“But Antle is another matter?”

“Well, yes and no. I, officially, went down there to question her about her availability as a potential expert witness, but she knows who I am and whom I represent, and if she goes to the cops, she could make it very hard on us. Too many forces could combine against us. So, I have an idea-$50,000 cash.”

“Yeah. I’m listening.”

“I know a guy, no connection to you. He takes out trash.”

Scannell looked at Youngquist who, he observed, was looking around. “And?”

“Tomorrow night the trash ... two of them ... will be together, poised as it were, to break down our doors. I can put out a feeler. It can be done.”

“What happens then?” Youngquist inquired.

“The trail ends. I’m going to be a big presence tomorrow at the Casino, Mystic Lake. There’s no tie in. There’ll be blood thrown on the records. She works with psychos. The cops, if they reach out for my name, will have nothing. The trail ends there. You’re so removed from the thing that it’s not even close.”

“This ... the only way?”

"If we want to stay firmly in business, yes."

"I'll give you the money in a half hour. Gloves ... gloves." He patted Scannell in the back and went into the building.

Scannell knew Toby AKA "The Princess" Leonard from his days with the Minneapolis Police Department. A series of four assassinations over ten years occurring around a trucking firm had perplexed him. They had been professional hits. A two-bullet hit, always to the head; the second bullet always behind the left ear. He used a silencer and he seemed to be a man of disguises, or at least he was so nondescript that Scannell could never get a make on him. Was he from out of town, flown in for the purpose, or was he locally grown?

Scannell had concluded that a fifth hit made sense and did some stalking of his own around that potential victim. Three times within two weeks he saw the same man, dressed in a tan outfit and a baseball cap. He carried a bag with him. It seemed that he was into repairs of some sort. Scannell got his license, and when Leonard was in a nearby building, he put a homing device under his car. The man, Toby Leonard, lived in a grand area and in a grand house in Edina, a suburb of Minneapolis. Scannell watched him and noticed that Toby Leonard dressed impeccably, spent a lot of time at a nearby golf club, and frequented a gay transvestite bar. Further surveillance showed that he called himself an antique dealer. What exactly that meant was anyone's guess, since the sign on his small shop said: "Open when I'm here." From the window, Scannell judged his stock to be quite thin. Two days later the fifth person was dead, a frontal bullet to the head and one behind the left ear. The Minneapolis PD tracked two people who had been nearby and nothing was noticed. Privately, Scannell visited with the one he thought was the brightest and probed him some more. He mentioned the tan outfit. Bingo! "Yeah, I did see someone like that."

Within the week Scannell found out that Toby Leonard was a steady-attending Episcopalian, an active member of the Democratic Party, and an active member of the Sierra Club. He was also queerer than a three-dollar bill. Mister middle-class suburbia with no visible means of support. Toby Leonard was an assassin, an extraordinary hit man whose cover was ordinariness in outfit while doing his murders.

When Scannell first approached him, Leonard put up the normal defense "Moi?" Scannell maintained a presence in the Edina neighborhood, and he and Leonard became friendly adversaries. Scannell never opened a file on him, seeing a potential bonanza with this man as an ally. The five murdered victims? Who gave a damn? They were all crooks anyway. Good riddance.

Scannell had a girlfriend who had a sister being stalked by a threatening maniac who had been released by the liberal state authorities from the security hospital in St. Peter, Minnesota. There was no stopping the maniac, and he probably would kill her one day if he wasn't stopped. But the authorities sat on their hands, talking, at best, of a restraining order. "I could forget everything that I know and we could become future business partners if you paid one of your visits to this maniac." The maniac was found dead three days later, shot between the eyes and taking another bullet behind his left ear. The Minneapolis PD tried to figure out the maniac's relationship with the trucking firm.

Scannell figured they were still trying to figure it out these many years later.

He drove to Edina and picked up The Princess, as he was known in gay clubs. "Fifty thou for this one. It's a twofer. Here's a bag of blood. Toss it on the files. Make it look like a patient went crazy ... all of that. Kill both of those bitches. But how about altering your technique? We don't need this going back to Minneapolis."

Leonard said, in his lisping, but strangely flat and professional voice, "You know, Herb, this is short-order cooking. I don't like it ... lots of risks. But the fifty thou is needed, and you're a good friend. Let me put it this way. There's a 90 percent chance I'll do it. I'll go down. I'll be there. I'll scope it out. If I see something, though that I don't like, I'm backing away."

"Understood." Scannell knew that this was a universal caveat in the world of hit men, like, don't get your hopes up until it's done. He had no doubt that Toby Leonard would deliver and that Dr. Margaret Aaron and Nurse Margi Hayslitt would be corpses by tomorrow night.

Iowa, August 1996

Scorpio was devouring his breakfast while McAbee was reading the *Quad City Times,* whose cover story referred to a baby of less than two weeks of age who was found dead in the Mississippi River. What miserable set of consequences brought this on? Now some self-righteous prosecutor would set his sights on probably some teenage girl who broke down under the stress and try to pin a life sentence on her.

Scorpio wandered over and put his head on McAbee's lap, but he also eyed the unfinished piece of toast on the plate. Absentmindedly he patted Scorpio's large white head and then looked down at him and saw the intense eyes. "Scorpio, it isn't love and affection that inspires you, you big creep." He took the toast and Scorpio's ears went back as he sat awaiting the small gift. McAbee gave it to him wondering if they'd ever get back of the conditioning they had before his injuries. They were both acting like two middle-aged fatsos.

The phone rang and Bertrand picked it up. "Dr. McAbee? This is your brother Bill's office. He wants to speak with you. Can you hold please?" Bertrand had no real choice since she didn't even wait for his answer. Of course, he could hang up in protest, but to what end?

"Bertrand? Bill here. What's going on with this Taylor thing? I have a call from Bishop Scarzi and before I return it, is there any news?"

"Good morning, Bill. How are you?"

"Hey. Don't give me this crap. Are you trying to make me feel guilty or something?"

"No. I'd just like to see a semblance of politeness, of human discourse. You know?"

"Sure, sure. I'm fine. I hope you're fine. Now, what's up?" Bill was into one of his high moment days.

"I'm trying to get the thing in my head, Bill. I talked with the local Bishop, O'Meara, and the diocesan lawyer. They've written off Taylor. They'd sacrifice him to the gods if they could. I've got Fisk doing the detail work and hopefully I'll get to Iowa City today and do some probing."

"Fisk? Is that the little bastard who made me use a chip on that horse trainer case?"

"The same." Bertrand remembered this too well. The FBI had caught Fisk red handed hacking at some top security investigation files. Bill had to lay out a big IOU to spring Fisk, who had no sense of gratitude in any part of his being. This lack of gratitude was probably the most horrendous sin one could commit in Bill McAbee's book of social no-nos. And, of course, Bertrand had to pay the price as his brother ranted and raved about the kind of people that his younger brother employed. When Bertrand had pushed Fisk to send a note to Bill thanking him for the intervention, the note said: "I know that you think you did me a big favor. Thanks!" The note was FedXed to Bertrand with these words scrawled across it: "Next time the little midget will burn!"

"I can't believe you use cretins like that. He wouldn't last two minutes out here. Is the talent pool so thin out there in Shitsville?" His voice was quite agitated. There was a thin line between Bill's acerbic humor and out and out brutal attack. The trick in dealing with him was to keep him reined in and away from that brutality zone.

"Scorpio says hello. He's listening to my end of the conversation."

There was a ten-second delay before Bill relented and laughed, conceding thereby the overreaction. "Ok ... OK ... go on," he said with a sense of humorous exasperation.

"He's doing some research for me, especially about John Antle, and then I"ll head up to Iowa City and poke around. Bill, there's nothing to tell Bishop Scarzi at the moment. After I speak with Antle, if he'll speak to me, I intend to see Father Taylor, who, by the way, is meeting with the Diocesan attorney today, if I'm right."

"Fair enough, Bertrand. Oh, by the way, are you packing?"

"Of course not. This case isn't exactly dangerous you know."

"Yeah … well, when you think that, you're in the biggest danger of your life. But there's no sense talking with you. You know, that oversized mutt of yours gives you false readings about the safety of your environment. Keep your eyes open. See you." Bertrand hoped that Bill was wrong about danger. He didn't care for a world when obsessing with fear dictated life's choices.

When he arrived at his office, there was a message to call Barry Fisk. "Barry, good morning. What's up?"

"A $300 bill." Fisk charged his research at $30 an hour. Bertrand thought that Fisk's skills were worth $300 an hour, but he couldn't and wouldn't tell him so. Fisk, forever distrustful, still seemed to think, apparently, that Bertrand would stiff him on the bill. He just shook his head in dismay.

"Barry, just submit it … fax it … E-mail us. I'll make sure that Pat pays it today! Now, what do you have?"

"John Antle is 32 years old. He was born in Des Moines. Parents divorced when he was three. Mother moved to Long Grove, Iowa, when he was seven, and they moved to Davenport when he was about ten. He graduated from Davenport schools, Central High his last stop. Work record is spotty; a lot of jobs: Kmart, Walgreens, Younkers Department Store. He was there for five years, his longest, and he ended up in Coralville, Highway 6, as the Assistant Manager of McDonald's."

"Married ... kids?"

"No. Neither. Probably gay. Has some credit activity at the gay bars in Iowa City and one in Rock Island." He gave McAbee the addresses of the gay bars and Antle's address and phone numbers at work and home.

"What else?"

"Well, he's scheduled to leave work today at 4:30."

"And how do you know this?"

"They have a stinking old Mac in the place that a baby could get into." He laughed in a way that sounded like a series of distinct kicks against a door.

"But there's more news here. He's being treated by a Dr. Margaret Aaron, a psychiatrist in Iowa City. Thank you Blue Cross/Shield of Iowa."

"Files?"

"No, and Aaron's office doesn't put them on a computer. The Blues never asked for a detailed set of records. That leads me to think that Aaron has a good rep.But the petition for payment verification form specifically says that Antle was being treated for sexual trauma from an early age incident."

"So, there are some walls around this one." McAbee could tell from the slight tremor in Fisk's voice that there was more and that some of it was interesting. Fisk loved to hold his best stuff until the end, the artist in him. Bill McAbee would put all of this down to a mean streak in Fisk, a kind of Toulouse-Lautrec of the PC. Bertrand, on the other hand, always played the straight man and let Fisk weave his story.

"Antle was hospitalized a few months ago, an apparent suicide attempt." He flung this datum out.

"God ... incredible. Does anyone know this?"

"Yeah."

He let it stay. McAbee was supposed to bite. "Who, Barry?"

"His psychiatrist. None other than Margaret Aaron who-listen up-almost ODed from depressants a few weeks ago."

McAbee, who had been standing idly looking at traffic flow in downtown Davenport, sat down and tried to absorb all of this. He wondered if Chip Blaine had this information and didn't pass it on. And then he wondered whether or not there was an association between the two suicide events. "More?" McAbee asked suspiciously.

"A little."

That was it. McAbee was going to have to ask. "What?"

"The lawsuit has outed Antle, and as far as I can see, McDonald's is behaving itself. Aaron is another matter. She's in the drug rehab program and has been there since she ODed. I can only tell you that she's being treated in the drug dependency program-that says something-and she's also doing psychiatry stuff with a Dr. Anne Magee who's known internationally for work in female psychiatry. Right now, that's it."

"How about the characters in Minnesota?"

"Just getting into it. That's going to be more complicated."

"Good work, Barry. I'll head out to Iowa City this afternoon and see if I can track down Antle at least. Stay in touch."

McAbee drove west on Interstate 80. He knew where the McDonald's was in Coralville, just a bit north of Highway 6. While he drove, his mind wandered back and forth. He wasn't sure just what the significance of the two suicide attempts was. His trained mind stayed clear of seizing on cause-and-effect relations when there was possibly only coincidence.

He went into the McDonald's at 4:20p.m. and went to the counter where he ordered a cup of coffee. His gaze found the one most likely to be Antle, a smallish, sandy-haired man with blue, darting eyes; a thin mustache and a face that appeared to be frightened of something or someone. This was not a strong man. But there was nothing about him that he perceived to be nasty or sinister. Antle looked to be what he was-an open book of insecurity.

McAbee went back to his car, which he had parked next to Antle's, the tag number given to him by Barry Fisk. He sat in his Explorer, drinking the coffee and wondering if Antle would deal with him. There was nothing to lose, after all.

Antle came out from the back door and immediately took off the McDonald's baseball cap and moved quickly to his car. He didn't notice McAbee, who now left his truck and moved to face Antle who now eyed him with every possible suspicion.

"John Antle? My name is Bertrand McAbee." Antle stopped and looked back at the door from which he had just egressed. "Please, John, just give me a few minutes. I mean you no harm, and I'll leave the minute you tell me to. Fair?"

Antle now looked at him with a wondering visage. "I'm sorry. I don't know you. What do you want?" He kept his distance to about five yards. McAbee had no intention of breaking the boundary that Antle had set.

"It's about Father Taylor. I don't represent Youngquist, and I don't represent Taylor or the Diocese of Davenport. I'm not a newspaperman. I have a very unique angle here, if you'd hear me out." It was about as direct and yet as nonthreatening as McAbee could make it.

Antle continued to look at him, obviously knowing that he could tell McAbee to get lost, and yet he was wavering. He said, "Look, I know that I'm not supposed to talk to anyone. I mean, they didn't tell me that, but I'm sure that's what they would tell me." He was about to say 'no,' and McAbee tried one more angle.

"John, I represent a very important person. He needs to find out the truth. He has no interest in your case, either helping you or hurting you. Can you just humor me for a few minutes. I won't take notes, and I'm not wired; if you want to search me, please do it." Bertrand held his hands, palms up, in the air, a pleading motion in any language, he conjectured.

Again Antle teetered. He looked at McAbee and then said, "OK, just a minute. What is it that you want to know? And you just stay right there and we'll do it right in this parking lot."

"Your suit speaks of these crimes being committed in Long Grove at St. Anne's."

"Right. And don't think it didn't occur. I can still see him going down in front of me. Look, McAbee, you'd have to experience this to realize how bad this is. I was just a little boy for God's sake. This guy was a 50-year-old priest."

McAbee listened to Antle and heard his pain. It sent shivers up his spine. At that moment, Bertrand had no doubt that Antle meant what he said. Perhaps it didn't really happen, perhaps he was confusing it with something else, perhaps it was some other person violating him, but in John Antle's mind he had been violated by Father William Taylor.

He was no fraud. The pain in his eyes was just too real. For better or for worse, John Antle had been violated and would carry the pain of that perception to his grave.

"From my heart, John, I can see that you are sincere. I don't doubt you. My question is Father Taylor. Everyone I speak with says he's a saint, a man of extraordinary religious sensibility. To his friends, it's inconceivable. I've got to ask this. Are you sure it was he, and not another priest?"

"Taylor was the only priest! I remember him grabbing me, all the time touching me, leading me into his office or the altar boy's change room. I can see it and feel it, mister. You had to be there. Listen, I'm not in good shape. I'm hurting. This hasn't been easy. Dr. Margaret made me realize all of this. I'm going to come through all of this, believe me." He had tears in his eyes. McAbee ached as he watched this thin, smallish man recount the terror of his childhood.

"John, I know of Dr. Aaron. Are you aware that she's sick, that she had a drug collapse, that she's a very sick woman?"

"Yes. They told me ... Nurse Margi. But her situation is different from mine. Margi told me to stand firm and I will. And Herb? He's been real good."

The name of Margi, probably the office nurse, and Herb meant nothing to McAbee, but he filed them away.

"John, I don't want to pick you up on any of this. Father Taylor ... that's my concern. Did you like him as a boy?"

"Of course. Everybody liked him ... loved him. But he hid behind that damn collar. Look. I'm done. I probably shouldn't have talked with you at all. If Herb finds out . . . . Oh, well, that's it."

"One more thing, John. Here's my card. If you ever want to talk or you remember anything, please feel free to call me."

Antle took the card and went to his car. Bertrand McAbee stood by as he drove away. Antle had made an impact. He was telling the truth as he knew it. There may be fraud, but Antle probably wasn't part of it.

Five-thirty p.m. on a Friday in Iowa City recalled happenings in the mind of McAbee. He had courted his second wife Beth in this university town that housed the University of Iowa. The old law school building was now being used by the Communications Department, and the new law school was quite the edifice. He recalled the many trips to Iowa City, the waiting for her to come out of the building, the pizzas, the worries, the strains, the exaltations, the love making, the proposal and the marriage and its recent collapse that had staggered McAbee to his foundation. On the off chance of finding someone there, he decided to visit Dr. Margaret Aaron's office.

He arrived at 5:45 p.m. and walked toward the office, which was located in a small, one-story building in downtown Iowa City. As he neared the building, a tall, thin woman in a UPS outfit opened the door of the building. She jumped as McAbee put his foot on the curbing in front of the building. Her eyes registered fear almost, and she lisped, "Sorry, you scared me." She looked down, tipped her hat, and left hurriedly. McAbee thought nothing of it, still preoccupied with his conversation with Antle.

Aaron's office was at the back of the small building and to the left. He went to the office door and knocked. No answer. So what's new, he thought. Why did he even bother. He turned to leave, and just as a matter of habit, he turned the knob to the right. The door opened an inch and reshut. He was surprised. He hesitated for a second, and then decided to enter.

CHAPTER TWELVE

The smell caught him first. It was odd. It had a sulfurous component and also a raw odor. Gunpowder? Blood? He couldn't describe it. He went to the desk and looked over the counter. Nothing. He yelled, "Hello? Hello? Anybody here?" He went through the doorway into a hallway and saw another door, ajar again by a few inches. He tapped at it. "Hello?" He opened it. The blinds were drawn and his eyes needed to adjust. He first saw a row of five file cabinets, each with four doors. They were opened in a haphazard way, and there was a red liquid ... blood? ... dripping from them. He looked more closely across the room and saw the bottom of a white nurse's skirt and white stockings lying oddly across the carpet. As he looked closer, he saw the blood flow and streaks. He ran to her and felt her pulse-dead. He looked behind the desk and saw another woman. He went to her body-she, too, was dead. Blood was everywhere, as he became adjusted to the setting. It had been a fresh kill, he knew.

These two were probably Margi and Dr. Margaret Aaron.

McAbee struggled to keep his emotions in check. He was in the game of investigation and detection, but he didn't really have the stomach for violence. He knew his brother was correct in asserting that violence was a blood relative to many of the facets of the business. He liked the puzzle, the adventure of discovery, the sense of completion, but the violence was for other people. It wasn't a matter of courage or fear. It was simply a question of symmetry and perhaps his inner karma.

His first response was to call 911, but response-immediacy would not help these two victims. There was a chair in the far corner of the room. He sat. The room had the aura of a settling or descending peace after some cataclysmic occurrence. He wondered about Kubler-Ross's work. Was there anything to it? Were the spirits of the two still in the room, gazing at him, watching over the death scene, grappling with the loss of life? He listened closely to the environment and heard the ticking clock on Margaret Aaron's bookshelf, the low whirling noise as the clock sounded 6:00 p.m.-six gongs-and then, again, the low whirl as the clock prepared for the next movement. He didn't know these people, but he wanted to cry over the loss. He reflected on their parents, their friends, their accomplishments, the grueling process that had brought Aaron her M.D., and surely the difficult tasks faced by the nurse; how life had betrayed them at the hands of a murderer.

He got up and wandered through the office suite. He opened each door in the office and looked under every desk, and seeing no one, he locked the front door of the suite. He went back to the killing room and started to browse, for nothing in particular. On Aaron's desk was a red file folder. He noticed the name-Antle. With hand shaking, he opened it. There was a stack of papers, about 20 pages in all, and in the back of the folder a lone microcassette. He scanned the papers. They were summaries of the therapy given to John Antle. He noticed that the copy machine was still on. He copied them. The clock chimed. It was 6:15.

The microcassette was another issue. He could not duplicate it without jeopardizing himself relative to time sequence. He made a decision that Bill, his brother, would applaud, but one about which he was terribly uneasy. He found a small mailer in the receptionist's desk drawer, along with a roll of stamps. He addressed the package to Pat Trump's home address, placed five stamps on it, unlatched the door, and walked a block to a mailbox and posted the package, trying to be as . nondescript as possible. He was pleased to see that last mail pickup was at 7:00p.m.

He went back to the office and called 911. Because Pat Trump was already on her way to Indianapolis to meet her husband, he called Augusta Satin whom he often used as an independent contractor in cases. He said, "Augusta? I only have a minute. I'm working on an investigation and I'm in Iowa City. I've come onto two murders. I just called 911. Please call Mike Melnick and inform him."

There was about a five-second delay. McAbee realized that meant that she had figured out how tense he was. Augusta was a former detective for the Rock Island, Illinois, Police Department. She was a gritty, divorced African-American who was incredibly perceptive and for whom McAbee had the greatest regard.

She said, "Were these two victims adversaries to your case?"

"Yeah, in all likelihood."

"I'll be up there, and I'll try to get Melnick if I can. They're going to put you through a ringer, Bertrand. Try to drink a coke or something. Don't let them wear you down. Bye."

He went out to the waiting room. He heard car doors slamming and the clock chiming at 6:30p.m.

The Iowa City Police Department brought in the Iowa Bureau of Investigation. By the time they got to McAbee, it was 7:00p.m. He told them that he was working a case and had come to the office on the off chance that Dr. Aaron would be there.

"What time was this?" He was a fat, gruff man in his mid-forties by the name of Johnson. McAbee wasn't sure if he was Iowa City or IBI.

"About 5:40 or thereabouts." He knew that they'd check out his story, but he felt secure in giving himself a ten-minute safety valve.

Johnson looked at his watch and then looked at McAbee. "So what the fuck did you do for 50 minutes, McAbee? What the hell's going on here?"

McAbee said, "I was surprised that the door was open. I was in Iowa City for another purpose...."

"And what would that be?" the contemptuous fat man queried.

"A client."

"Gee. You're really forthcoming, aren't you?"

"Look. Do you want me to finish this story or not?"

McAbee shot back, irritated by this man whom he knew was trying to get under his skin.

"Yeah, as long as it's not a fictional story, sure. But don't fuck around with me, mister! And, by the way, where's your Iowa P.I. license?"

McAbee showed it to him. Johnson grabbed it out of his hands, studied it, and gave it back. He looked at McAbee. "Well go ahead. Let's hear it."

"The door was open and I carne in. There was no one at the receptionist's desk. I said 'hello' a few times, but I didn't yell or anything like that?"

"Why?"

"It's a psychiatrist's office. I thought that she was probably working with a client, so I picked up a magazine and read through it. I read the paper, but I just waited. I didn't feel right about interrupting a session, because if I did, she'd probably hurl me out of here."

"What magazine? What paper?"

McAbee saw the *New Yorker* from last week. He had read an article on Bosnia at his home a few days ago. "There was an article on Bosnia."

"Hold it." Johnson picked up the magazine and started to thumb through it with the grace of a rhino. "Where the fuck is the table of contents in this fag publication?"

"If you give it to me, I'll show it to you." He threw it at McAbee's chest. McAbee found the index easily and showed the article to Johnson.

Johnson looked at the title and then started to turn the pages. It was long and ranged through about 14 pages. Johnson kept turning and finally said, "Do these fucking articles ever end?"

McAbee said nothing, letting the detective come to grips with the length of the article and the overall tight weave of his false story.

"And the paper?"

"The *Des Moines Register,* but don't ask me about it. I took a brief nap."

"So what time are we at?"

"Oh, about 6:15, 6:20. I took a brief walk down the block. I was sleepy. Then I came back."

"OK. Let's hear this again?" He turned a new page in his notebook. "What time did you leave here for this walk?"

"About 6:15, 6:20. I was back in a few minutes."

"Go ahead," he said resignedly, knowing that the story was holding.

"Well, I guess I thought it was time to be more aggressive, and I went back into the hallway to the left of the receptionist's desk, saw the door to her office ajar, yelled out 'hello,' and entered the office. I called you right away. I then called an associate in the Quad Cities, and I came back out here to wait for you."

"Who's the associate?"

"A private investigator named Augusta Satin."

"Who?"

"Augusta Satin."

"Black babe?" he asked incredulously.

"Yeah," McAbee said tentatively.

"She's not with the Rock Island PD anymore?"

"No. How do you know her?"

"I had a case down there about six or seven years ago. Good woman. So you know her, huh?" Fat boy was impressed.

"Yeah. What about it?" McAbee didn't know where he was going with this piece of information.

"Well it tells me that you're probably not as bad as I think you are." He smiled caustically, stood up and hitched his pants up, and walked away.

Two minutes later he came back. "The medicine man says they've been dead for at least an hour and a half. If you didn't kill them, and your times are correct, you just missed the murderer. By the way, did you see anyone around here?"

McAbee reflected on this and remembered the UPS woman, but that was all.

"Well, yes. When I came up the walk there was an UPS driver just leaving, a woman-short blonde hair, tallish, thin."

"Did you see the truck?"

"Not that I can remember. No."

"Do you mind coming down to the Iowa City PD and taking a paraffin test?"

"No. I'll do that. Augusta should be coming up."

"Why's that?"

"I don't know. Maybe she thought she'd see you again," he added cryptically. Johnson glared at him, unsure whether or not this was an insult or a compliment. McAbee left him guessing.

On the way down to the headquarters, McAbee reflected that his story checked out. There was no way a hole could be punched into it unless someone saw him mailing the package. He would have to take his chances, and if push came to shove, claim that he found it on the street and decided to do a charitable deed. He couldn't help but note that Augusta's name had turned Johnson into a more agreeable guy.

Another detective had a go at McAbee at the Iowa City Police Department headquarters. He was less hostile, probably because Johnson had told him to let up. The test took only a few minutes. Then they let him wait. Johnson came back. "Can you assist in a drawing?"

"Of course."

"But here's the problem. The guy can't get here until tomorrow morning. I'd prefer you stay overnight. Problem?"

"I guess not."

"It's on us."

There was a knock on the door. Johnson said, "Yeah. Come in."

It was a uniform. "Can I see you outside for a minute?" the uniform inquired.

Johnson left and stayed gone for about ten minutes. When he came back, he said, "Gus is here. You can leave, but I want you back here tomorrow at 9:00a.m. I made a reservation for you at the Hampton Inn. Oh ... and McAbee ... sorry for the gruffness, but you don't exactly strike me as the investigator type."

"Yes ... well ... whatever that is."

McAbee found Augusta in the waiting room. They shook hands and she hugged him and held him in that embrace for a solid five seconds. She whispered in his ear: "I'm buying supper. Let's split from this place."

She drove him to a small Indian place on Dodge Street; only when they sat down did they begin to speak. She said, "This has to be very hard on you. You don't deal in bodies, do you?"

"No. I was really caught off guard, Augusta. And you're right. You know that I'm having a hard time, don't you?"

"You're no big macho guy, Bertrand. It seems that your work draws you into more and more violence also. Let's face it. Both of us wouldn't be here today if it wasn't for some luck with good old Tommy Lee." It was a case wherein both of them escaped murder by a hair.

"Tell me about it," he said in agreement.

"So, these women were murdered. Do you think it was anything to do with the case you're working on?"

"Don't know what to tell you on that one, Augusta."

"Johnson told me that they think it was some patient. I guess there was a lot of blood tossed. But who knows, could be a deception. They're really interested in your description of the UPS woman. The only UPS truck in that area last night at the time you gave was being driven by a black man. There wasn't any blonde woman. They only have two women drivers who could fit that description, and one of them was off and the other was in Cedar Rapids."

They both ate a pretty simple rice dish with the usual curry overlay. Every time McAbee would try to focus, he'd see the bodies. He knew that Augusta was picking this up. He decided to change the subject. "So, this fat guy, Johnson. He calls you Gus? That's a new one."

She smiled and said, "I know, but what can I say? It's his way of doing things. He says to me ... I was still pretty new as a detective ... a black ... a woman ... young ..., you name it, and this meanspirited bull asks me if it's OK. So I say, 'Sure.' What the hell? He's the only one. Didn't think I'd ever see him again."

"Such a pretty name," McAbee said sarcastically. She laughed and said, "Yeah, right!"

They ate in silence for a while before she said, "Oh,

Bertrand. I spoke with Melnick. He was on his way to the synagogue. I didn't know he was Orthodox. He told me he'd come up if you were arrested. He said to tell you that you don't have to answer anything if you don't want to."

They went out to her car and she drove him back to his car at the Iowa City Police Department. He said, "Well, I guess I'll stay up here. It sounded more like a demand than a request, and in case I need to help, I'd better stay. So, Augusta, how do I say thanks? I really needed a friendly face. You're right. I don't do deaths well."

She looked at him and said, "Bertrand, do you want me to stay with you tonight? I can cover the kids. I'm worried about you."

"Oh, no. That's OK. You've been great."

"Well, OK. I'll be on my way. You know where to find me if there's a problem. Bye." She kissed him on the cheek. He left her car and waved goodbye to her.

He walked toward his car and realized that he had just been kissed by her, and she had offered to stay the night with him. He stopped and looked back. Her car was out of view. He looked up at the sky, put his hand on his hips, and yelled out-"Bertrand! You stupid, stupid son-of a-bitch!"

The oh-so-patient Vietnamese police artist kept working the computer program as McAbee attempted to dictate an image to him. McAbee had only gotten a glance at her, lasting no more than a second at best. She had high cheek bones, watery blue eyes, large lips, and short blonde hair. She wore a cap and had shorts on. Her legs were a bit thick. Her breasts were small, as McAbee tried to free associate about her qualities. The final image was pretty close. It was "the best I can do" he told the small man with the nimble fingers.

The Vietnamese studied the screen image and said, "You know this could be a man."

"No, it was a woman," McAbee said in a puzzled way.

"You don't understand me, sir. This person may have been trying to deceive. If, at the end, we find that the person was a man, would it be inconceivable to you, or just surprising?"

"Well, if you put it that way, surprising, certainly not inconceivable."

McAbee drove to the University of Iowa hospitals and inquired about Dr. Anne Magee. He picked up the phone at the desk after he had been called over by the receptionist.

"Hello?" he said.

"Anne Magee here. What's this about?"

"I'd like to speak with you about Dr. Margaret Aaron-just a few minutes of your time please."

"I'm on the fourth floor, room 404. I have five minutes for you."

Dr. Anne Magee was built large, but she wasn't fat. She wasn't a pretty woman, but there was an attractiveness to her, an attractiveness marked by intelligence, savvy, and ... what was it? ... honesty.

"Look, McAbee. I know she was murdered. I'm very upset about it because she was putting her life into order. She was here for three weeks. We let her out for two hours, and she's murdered. It doesn't add up. Somebody said something somewhere."

"Did she ever talk about John Antle and his case against a priest in Davenport?"

"I'm going to speak to this because she's dead and it might help. You say you're interested in the truth about the priest. She was convinced that John Antle had been molested. Does that answer your question?"

"Well, yes and no. She used recovered memory material."

"Look. She wondered about some of her cases, but not this one."

"And what about her mental status?"

"She had a drug problem and maybe that affected her judgment on some things, but she swore Antle was legit. There was a problem, however, that I'm going to let you in on. She was being worked over by a detective … from Minneapolis. He was feeding her drugs. He worked for the lawyer who's in on the Antle case."

"Youngquist?"

"Yes. That's the name."

"Name of the detective?"

"Scannell. That's all I have."

"And just what do you expect me to do?"

"Let me put it to you in no uncertain psychiatric terms- break his balls! Margaret had enough problems without this drug pusher destroying her. I have to go. Maybe I'll see you again if it's necessary." She gave him a firm handshake and was on her way.

This was one woman he would not want to be compulsing, obsessing, rationalizing, displacing, or whatevering around. She was a tigress.

He was on Interstate 80 heading east toward Davenport. Magee's point was well taken. How is it that someone knew Margaret Aaron would be in her office? There was high improbability here, but even still, maybe it had no association with the Antle case.

Then he thought of Augusta Satin and wondered why he just couldn't, or wouldn't, pursue the status of their relationship. There was no good answer, as he entered his driveway and was besieged by the yelping and barking of Scorpio.

CHAPTER THIRTEEN

Iowa, August 1996

As he drove to Dubuque, Bishop O'Meara prayed as hard as he could for guidance on the Taylor matter. Monsignor George Duncan, with all the grace of his socialite judgment, was also clearly in favor of jettisoning Taylor, and that kind of quick agreement with his position led O'Meara to hesitate, because Duncan had his subtle ways of usurping him on other issues. Duncan was a casuist, a man who would intuit his conclusion and then fit and retrofit all of his premises in support of his position. Morally, therefore, O'Meara had great disdain for him and, to prove the point, suspected him of acting on his obvious gay tendencies.

If it wasn't for the extraordinary clout of his family and Duncan's enablement of access to the makers and shakers of the Diocese, he would have exiled him to the farthest reaches of the Diocese, a tactic he had employed on a member of doctrinal recalcitrants whom he found at the center of his liberal Diocese. But, however he looked at it, he couldn't understand the depth of Duncan's hatred for Taylor.

Blaine, the lawyer, was another matter. He saw him as

capable but hypocritical and had heard enough stories of his drinking and whoring to make him wonder when the fall would occur. A pet theory of O'Meara's was that people collapsed at the apex of their career if their moral values were out of order. Blaine was ready to fall by this standard. He did not appreciate his introduction of the female, Kim Rice, into the case. In fact, he thought the fool was somehow trying to taunt him.

Yet, like Duncan, he served a purpose, and he would be tolerated as long as he continued to produce good results for the business of the Diocese. But, already, the Bishop was keeping an eye open for future representation. He calculated that Blaine had another three years in him.

O'Meara would frequently speculate on careers. He was an avid reader of biographies and likened career management with the running of a successful company. If Blaine was being traded publicly, he was a good candidate for short selling.

So, these two diverse advisors, Duncan and Blaine, both thought Billy Taylor was dead guilty. That, coupled with his own judgment on the matter, made it a 3-0 judgment. Taylor just didn't have any support, and pray as he would, he saw no other answer. As to Scarzi and the Pope, what did they know?

O'Meara had called Father Edward and told him that Monsignor Duncan, Chip Blaine, and he would be at the Trappist monastery at 11:00 a.m. for the purpose of getting Taylor to sign some documents. Kim Rice's presence or absence was of no consequence. He asked Father Edward to be present at the meeting and added that his support would be most appreciated. Father Edward was noncommital, but O'Meara figured that to be a Trappist thing.

Blaine was coming over to the meeting from Chicago; Duncan from Victor, Iowa, where he was assisting a friend (whatever that meant). The plan was to converge on Taylor and force his compliance with a deal that had been worked out by Youngquist in Minneapolis and Blaine in Davenport. According to Blaine, Youngquist had called to inform him that Antle's psychiatrist had been murdered and that Antle's file would be passed on to a team of psychologists regularly employed by Youngquist. Antle, who had attempted suicide some months back, would not be available for depositions for several more weeks, but he did want the Diocese to realize that Antle was a bonafide suicide attempt and was under a watch. The murder of Aaron could be spun in a variety of directions, all suited to Antle's case. Thus, he was offering a one-time settlement of $300,000, a signed admission of guilt by Taylor along with a promise to seek therapy. Antle was quite concerned about this last part, so that Taylor would never again violate children. "So take it or leave it, counselor. It's a one-time offer with a five-day window on a case that might be worth two million or more, given the temper of the times about hypocritical child-screwing pedophile priests." That quote from Youngquist, reported by Blaine, revolted O'Meara, who in his heart agreed with this church hater.

So Taylor, the papal classmate, the Scarzi pal and the big-time liberal who advocated women priests, freedom of conscience, and a general overhaul of the entire Church, that had existed and thrived for 2,000 years because of its discipline and orthodoxy, was also about to take his fall.

Since corning to Davenport, O'Meara had transferred him and humiliated him, but Taylor continued to turn the other cheek. He had to give that to him even though he was a pious fraud. Liberalism could never and did never produce saintliness. Its high-water mark was the destruction of faith and the assimilation of Catholicism into an undifferentiated mass of worthless sects like Episcopalians, Methodists, Presbyterians, liberal Lutherans, and assorted other inane and purposeless groups. In sum, Taylor could be made an example for those who fall by the wayside and also serve as a reminder for the spiritual toughness of the Bishopric.

When he arrived at the monastery, Blaine and Kim Rice, Duncan and Father Edward were already in the visitor's room. All four rose as he entered the room. He was wearing his Bishop's robes. This was as close to a diocesan council as you could get. Father Edward left to get Taylor.

The Bishop said, "So, it's come down to this. Do you have the papers, Chip?"

"I do. Bishop, I'm going to need all the authority that you can muster on this one."

"Well, I'll do the best I can." He noticed that Kim Rice was dressed modestly with a dark blue sport coat, full-necked blouse, and a mid-calf skirt. She also had a quizzical look on her face that O'Meara couldn't quite comprehend.

Duncan said, "Bishop, may I suggest that Chip lay out the situation before Father Taylor. I'll come in then and tell him my opinion and then if there's any trouble, perhaps your authority can bring it across to him as to what's at stake."

"Sounds wise to me. I just don't believe that a Roman-trained priest would resist the call of the Church," O'Meara said, noting that Kim Rice's visage had gone from quizzical to stern.

Part of the strategy was aimed at getting Taylor to sense being overwhelmed and surprised. Blaine had referred to it as a spiritual blitzkrieg, although O'Meara was hard pressed to see the spiritual piece outside of himself and Father Edward. When Taylor walked in behind Father Edward, O'Meara immediately put aside the analogy. Taylor was as calm as he could be, nonplused, taking in each participant with his studious and gentle eyes. He kissed O'Meara's ring, shook hands with Monsignor Duncan and Chip Blaine, and gave a brilliant smile to Kim Rice as he took her hand in both of his. Rice clearly liked the pious fraud, O'Meara noticed, and therein was perhaps the explanation of her odd facial expressions.

O'Meara said, "Please sit, Father Taylor." Taylor bowed his head and sat down. "We've come here for a purpose, Father, and I think it wise for you to listen as Chip lays out our strategy. I think it important, that's why I'm here." Taylor nodded his head but didn't say anything. "Chip . . .," O'Meara said, as he pointed to Blaine.

Chip was now in charge, and he had his ways of getting attention. He brought his beaten-up satchel to the table and brought from it a slender, black folder that was as elegant as his bag was downtrodden. All eyes were upon him, except for Taylor, who peered down at the table. Chip, you're impressing the wrong audience, O'Meara thought.

"Father Taylor. Thanks for coming to this meeting." He had stopped in mid-sentence until Taylor gave him eye contact. "Some things have happened that I wish to convey to you. A change in strategy seems warranted. John Antle, the complainant, attempted suicide some months ago. This isn't his first time, but it is, according to his lawyer ... no angel by the way ... relative to the stress he is feeling from this case. I have no way to find otherwise since Antle will be unavailable to us for depositions for several more weeks."

"I'm very sorry about John Antle. I bear him no bad will, even though I am experiencing new dimensions of personal hell and triumphant heaven," Taylor said with a sad smile.

"Triumphant heaven?" Duncan spurt out.

"Oh, yes, Monsignor. This monastery. I think, sometimes, that I needed this test to reach a new dimension of spirituality."

Duncan didn't respond. No one did. O'Meara knew, however, that they all had their secret thoughts on this matter, and some not particularly charitable.

Taylor looked at Chip Blaine. "Is this what you came to tell me?"

"It's not that simple, Father. John Antle was being treated by a psychiatrist named Margaret Aaron in Iowa City. Of importance to us about this matter is that she, along with her nurse, was brutally murdered last Friday night. There seem to be a number of events conspiring against us on this matter. I get paid, Father, to weigh risk and advise. Thereby, the attempted suicide and the murders do us no good. They only harm us. Do you understand me?"

The room fell into a dead silence, eventually broken by Taylor's quiet response. "I understand what you have just said. But am I supposed to see or hear something else, Mr. Blaine?"

Blaine looked at the end of his upraised right hand and

said, "Perhaps. Perhaps not, Father. The lawyer for John Antle, Martin Youngquist, a man who has made a fortune off the peccadilloes of the Church, called me yesterday and presented me with an offer. I'd like you to listen to it, weigh it, and hopefully accept it. Will you give me a good-faith ear, Father?"

"Of course," Taylor responded quickly.

"There is a reluctance to put Antle through a trial or even depositions. They fear another suicide attempt, and the last one was close. They're willing to withdraw the complaint ... and please hear me out on the whole matter ... providing you publicly admit your guilt, seek counseling, and the Diocese pay $300,000. This is not a bad deal in my judgment. This case has a potential value to Youngquist and Antle of about $3 million. Oh, and by the way, the Bishop has ... and this is charity that shows you where his heart is ... decided to pick up the $300,000 through Diocesan funds, liability insurance, or some combination thereof. In a nutshell, that's it." Chip sat back in his chair and proceeded to draw out of the folder three distinct documents and spread them across the table in front of him.

Taylor's look never changed. Perhaps his mouth tightened a bit, and perhaps his eyes slitted a bit (a tough read for the Bishop). Taylor didn't respond and the Bishop used that lack to give a small nod to Monsignor Duncan.

Duncan said, "Look, Father Taylor, we'll get you into a really good program in Texas; then you can get out and retire. You are 75 after all. Everyone in the room really believes that you're guilty. Maybe you forget that you're up in years after all. Maybe you were having a difficult stage of life back then. If you think about it, what is really at stake is the reputation of the Diocese and the reputation of your fellow priests. Take my word on it. You did it!" He emitted that disgustingly ingratiating smile that the Bishop so detested.

O'Meara had watched everyone during Duncan's plea. When Duncan had said, "you did it," he noticed that Kim Rice and Father Edward stared unbelievingly at Duncan, but as good soldiers, they said nothing. All eyes were now on Billy Taylor.

"Mr. Blaine. There is only one missing piece to this puzzle, and it's this. I never had any sexual relations with that boy or any other boy. You can put the papers away. I have no intention of signing anything." O'Meara observed that he wasn't responding to Duncan

Monsignor Duncan slammed his pudgy hand on the table and yelled, "The nerve of you, Father Taylor! This isn't a game! You're an old man with a sinful past. Why don't you own up to it?"

Taylor looked at Duncan for about five seconds but didn't respond to him. He looked at everyone in the room and said, "Is this all?"

O'Meara arose from his seat and looked down on the white-haired priest and said, "Father Taylor, I order you to sign these documents! Put this pretense away, please! In the name of Jesus!"

"Bishop, I will not lie under orders from anyone, the Pope included. I think I'm done here." He got up and walked out.

Father Edward moved only so minutely. He sat back in a just slightly relaxed manner, and Kim Rice lost the puzzled look all of a sudden. Duncan sat there shaking his head in dismay, or at least feigned dismay. O'Meara wondered whether supercilious Duncan would have signed in like circumstances. Blaine was busy packing his bag. O'Meara felt as though he was the only normal one in this simple room decorated with a crucifix, a picture of the Madonna, a vase of flowers, and a holy water fixture next to the light switch. "Father Edward. Thanks for your presence. I was rather expecting you to say something in support of our position."

"Bishop, with all due respect, I have watched Father Taylor for well over a month. I have seen no reason to condemn him or suspect him." He fixed Duncan with a look of scorn. "He's a very spiritual man as surely you and Monsignor Duncan must be fully aware of, and if on the off chance he has sinned in this manner, he has surely made his peace with God. However, his denial is virtually proof positive to me that he didn't sin against this boy. The civil law means very little to me when it allows for recovered memories of traumatic events from many years past. I held my peace when your Chancellor deigned to speak for me, and I fully intend to report my sin of omission to my brothers. I should never have allowed his comment to go unchallenged." He, again, stared at Duncan in a most untrappist-like way.

"Well," Duncan retorted, "it was a mistake to have you in this room. Your judgment is obviously clouded. You've been tricked by this fraud."

Father Edward didn't vocalize a response. He merely looked at O'Meara in a disgusted way, which made O'Meara cringe. Duncan, after all, showed well in some social circles, but among those clergy who took religion seriously, Duncan was a risky proposition. The Bishop raised his hand and patted the air. "That'll be enough, George. Father Edward. Let us say that there is a serious disagreement on this matter between us. Perhaps eventually you will see it our way," he said to Father Edward in his most ecumenical tone. In his heart he entertained the thought that Father Edward was a simple-minded monk best left to his isolated rural setting. "If we may, I'd like to use this room for a few more minutes to consult with the team." Father Edward nodded his head in assent and left. O'Meara hoped he realized that he was no longer a member of the team and then caught himself wondering whether the monk really cared about such a nuance.

"Now what, Chip?" the Bishop intoned.

"Well, we go to trial if we can't get them to change their demands. I'll start deposing when the psychiatrists OK Antle. But I'm nervous. I don't want the little bas ... uh ... character suiciding on us. That would really expose us to liability. Is there anything else you can do to Taylor? More pressure on his thumbs?"

"Yes. I can suspend him from saying mass and from performing any sacraments. I can move his personal possessions into storage."

"I would suggest doing this forthwith. Perhaps he will weaken. It can't hurt. Is there anything else?"

"Chip. The days of the inquisition are over. Between you and me if I had the opportunity, I would put him to those tests, but alas I don't." As he spoke, he noticed that the quiet Kim Rice had sat back, crossed her arms in a highly defensive posture, and frowned. O'Meara didn't want her here anyway, and certainly not if she was going to be hostile.

He shot a harsh look at her and said, "Miss Rice, you seem upset about something. What is it?" Blaine immediately looked over at her in an unpleasant way.

"Well, Bishop, I'm still stuck on the point of his innocence. And to be quite frank, I. ..."

Blaine reacted by turning his chair almost full circle. He got within four inches of her face and said brutally, "That's enough of that, Miss Rice. Someday you'll run your own cases, but while I'm in charge, there's only one response-obedience! Do you hear?"

Her face reddened and tears welled up, but she caught herself and said meekly, "Of course. Sorry."

The Bishop was pleased. She had it coming. He glanced at Duncan. He was beaming. At least someone got slapped around today. He wondered what Blaine would say to her when they were alone.

Iowa, August 1996

Barry Fisk's simple house had a basement, two bedrooms, a living room/study, a kitchen, and a bathroom. Except for the FBI agents who busted him for invading their file base awhile ago, a furnace repairman and a plumber on two occasions, no one had ever been in his house since he purchased it three years ago. He rarely used his bedroom, preferring to sleep on his couch; his stove was used to heat the many canned goods he preferred, and the second bedroom was stacked with an incredibly good collection of historical tomes, for although he no longer taught, he was still an active researcher who freelanced articles to a variety of magazines. His doctoral work at Yale focused on the Lewis and Clark expedition. It was Fisk's contention that they were, in fact, spies for an aggressive expansionist, Thomas Jefferson. And although he could pen puff pieces for the sake of a buck, he was at heart an anarchist who deeply resented the federal government.

He had long ago given up any pretense to a normal life of family and friends. His obvious physical abnormality repelled people who looked at him as some sort of sideshow and eventually he became genuinely suspicious of anyone who treated him courteously, or worse still, friendly. Simply, he saw himself as a mean, tenacious, and sullen man who owed nobody anything and expected nothing in return. The only man who had glancing success at breaking this veneer was Bertrand McAbee, who had treated him with generosity and had given him referrals for what was now becoming a mainline business-research. Fisk knew that he was good; in fact, he thought that there were few who could match him at the game of computer surveillance, and he felt that no system was safe from his attacks, although to his chagrin, he had been uncovered by the FBI after invading the upper echelons of their supposed foolproof system. McAbee's bigwig, fascist brother had saved his neck on that one.

Martin Youngquist's system was a joke. Fisk was into his billing records and files in 12 minutes and was downloading anything he thought would be relevant. From that large amount of data, he would prepare the equivalent of an executive report for Bertrand McAbee, the classics scholar, who ironically didn't care much for detail anymore. "Barry, just give me the essence please." There was a barely audible voice in Barry's head that told him McAbee was paying him a high compliment-an implicit trust in Fisk getting things right. But in Barry's world that was hard to accept.

It was clear that Youngquist was a multimillionaire. He had made his fortune off huge awards and settlements by various dioceses around the country. His cut was 30-40 percent of all monetary settlements along with expenses, which usually took him near the 50 percent mark. He copied down the names of his employees and a variety of consultants and private contractors that the firm used. Herb Scannell was one, but he had no reason to note it at this point.

Youngquist's new billing system was begun five years ago in 1992. Calculations showed that the firm had grossed $43 million with about $23 million going back to complainants represented by Youngquist. His payroll expenses, salaries, bonuses, and the like cost him about $5 million, and thus Youngquist grossed in five years, about $18 million. Not a bad living for a lower-end graduate of the University of Minnesota Law School, records of this work, his phone bills, and credit reports, medical records having already been captured. There was no sign of pro bono work by him, and his charitable contributions amounted to about $1,000 a year, mere change for this guy.

It was in the reading of his correspondence that Fisk became aware of the gray tones that hung over Youngquist. With his staff, he always appeared to speak in equivocations and amphibolies as if he suspected that he was being watched. With dioceses, on the other hand, his language was bold, incisive, and taunting. He liked to play chicken with his adversaries. Fisk had one lasting impression of him-a chiseler who had found a racket and who played it for all that it was worth. He felt sympathy for the priest, Father Taylor, both sentiments being unusual for him: sympathy as an emotion and Father Taylor as being anything other than an agent for Vatican imperialism and superstition. He had one other impression from the correspondence-Catholic dioceses did a damn poor job of picking defense counsel. No wonder there was talk of dioceses going bankrupt. On the other hand, they seemed to do a damn poor job of priest selection.

He proceeded to his analysis of all the employees of the firm and all of the contractors and subcontractors that he had discovered in the downloaded files. McAbee was in for a big bill at $30 per hour.

CHAPTER FOURTEEN

Iowa, August 1996

Pat Trump went home for lunch at McAbee's request. She also checked her mailbox, in which she found the mailer sent by McAbee from Iowa City. McAbee told her to hold all calls, as he went about studying the reports made by Dr. Margaret Aaron. He was impressed by her perseverence and by her forcing of John Antle to open up, both within hypnosis and in post hypnosis. But he also suspected that she was leading him to a preordained discovery already very much in her mind.

The 20 pages were a blow-by-blow summary of each and presumably every session that the two of them had. There was considerable pain in the pages, a pain that both patient and doctor shared. Margaret Aaron had a sympathetic ear, and it appeared to him that she had a difficult time maintaining an appropriate boundary for a healer. Did John Antle have sexual relations with Father Taylor? He read the descriptions of the perpetrator-"He was robed. He would pull up his robe and expose himself to me. He would force me to touch his penis, to pull on it. He would catch my hand in his and make me move faster and harder, and he would put a handkerchief in front of it to catch his cum. That was important to him. He didn't want to leave stains on the garments. He told me that ... that people wouldn't understand. He would go down on me, make me feel terribly good, but terribly bad." There were a lot of "he," "him," "himself" words, but specific allusions to the person behind these pronouns were rare. This drew McAbee's concentration because he was pretty convinced that John Antle was in fact violated. But were there other priests, church members, officers, etc., who had access to John Antle?

Explicitly, the physical references isolated by Aaron were:

- "He would say goodbye to people and come back to the church. He was white haired, an old man, but he was the priest, Father Taylor."
- "He, Taylor, had this smarmy way about him. He would come up and hug me, pat me on the head, then press against me. I could feel his hard dick under the robe."
- "It was Taylor, now that you have me focused on this. He had these pudgy fingers and white hair. His complexion always seemed pink to me, but he was God; he was the priest. Mother always told me to obey him. He was a good man. He totally overwhelmed me."

McAbee fixed on the following: "He would say goodbye." "He was white haired," "an old man," "smarmy way," "hug ... pat ... press," "pudgy fingers and white hair," "complexion ... pink." That wasn't much to go on even though he did make a clear and explicit statement that the man was Father

Taylor. All of the statements were made, it appeared from the records, while he was under hypnosis. There were no indications in the 20 pages about what preceded some of these statements and, especially, what Aaron might have suggested to Antle by way of prejudicing him. Her quotes (exact descriptions) of the perpetrator showed that she was familiar with the tort system.

He placed the microcassette in his player. He wondered what this would yield. Apparently, it was Dr. Margaret Aaron dictating her progress on several cases. McAbee couldn't see its relevance to the Antle file but continued to listen. Suddenly, about 25 minutes into the tape, he heard her say alarmingly, "Who are you? I'm closed! What are you looking for?" McAbee sat up sharply and raised the volume on the tape. What it came to be was a recording of Margaret Aaron's meeting with a man named Herb Scannell who represented himself as an agent for Martin Youngquist. He was shocked to hear the explicit offer of $10,000 per viable case and the apparent transmittal of drugs for the now-compromised Margaret Aaron. He heard Scannell leave the office, heard sobs from Aaron, and heard the recorder turned of. Scannell had obviously walked in on her while she was taping and had either failed to notice that the machine had been left on record or perhaps he figured that it didn't matter, because any use by her would bring her down, in effect, neutralizing her. Whatever the case, Scannell was a definite follow through.

He immediately called Barry Fisk.

"Barry. Bertrand here. Question. Has the name Scannell come up anywhere in your investigation of Youngquist?"

"Hold on. Yes ... investigator and on Youngquist's payroll for the five years that I've got in front of me. Why?"

"He's come up elsewhere. Don't want to talk about it on the phone. I'd like you to turn up every piece of information that you can get on him. It's critical."

"OK. I'll be in touch."

So, Dr. Aaron had been turned by Youngquist and Scannell. He backtracked through the dates on the 20 pages and cross compared to the date mentioned by Aaron on the tape. Antle had already implicated Father Taylor, so it wasn't a total act of infidelity on Aaron's part. She didn't manufacture sexual abuse in Antle's mind to gain drug favors from Scannell. Even still, Margaret Aaron was a troubled psychiatrist, deeply involved in ethical quagmires.

Iowa, August 1996

It took McAbee 50 minutes to drive north on 67 and east on 30 to the 20,000 inhabitant town of Clinton, Iowa. To many in Iowa, it was a giant environmental problem, having a number of chemical and processing plants. He was heading for St. Mary's parish in the downtown area. The drive was pleasant enough as he saw the verdant farmland all around him, full crops of com and soybeans bursting toward the light blue, cloudless sky. It had been a virtually perfect growing year as rain, heat, and sun produced almost magical conditions for agriculture.

McAbee had asked the Dean of the Priests Council for a meeting with him and three or four priests representing difficult decades through Taylor's life. The Dean, Monsignor

Patrick McMahon, had selected three priests for the meeting. McAbee was pleased to see that they did cut across the generations with McMahon appearing to be about 70, Father Dan Van de Hyfte somewhere in his mid 50s, Father Joe Smith a 40 something, and Father Phil Spain mid 30s at best. They were a serious crew as McAbee was welcomed into the dining room for lunch.

McMahon, a large, ponderous man who stood a good 6 feet, 2 inches, began the meeting after introductions were made.

"As I told you on the phone. Dr. McAbee is working on Father Billy's case. He wants us to be honest, so let's be so. Dr. McAbee?"

"Thank you, Monsignor McMahon. Let me say in advance that I have not come on behalf of Bishop O'Meara, Monsignor Duncan, or the lawyer for the Diocese, Mr. Blaine. I have been hired to look into the Taylor case by some very well-connected friends of his, and I am formally under contract with my brother's firm in New York City, which in turn is in an agreement with these friends of Father Taylor. I don't mean to sound obscure, but that's all I can say. As Monsignor McMahon knows, the Bishop has cleared me to speak with you."

The young priest, Father Spain, smiled and said, "I think we can guess fair enough about the engaging parties. Regardless of whom they are, I owe my vocation to Billy Taylor. I was an altar boy in his parish many years ago. I don't know this Antle fellow, but I can tell you of my experience with Taylor-never was there a person who treated me with the gracefulness and respect that I was treated by him. He could make a 10-year-old kid feel like an adult."

"Did he ever touch you … anywhere, Father Spain?" McAbee went right to the point.

"Wh…."

"Look. I'm not trying to put a noose around his neck, but I need to know how something could be confused in the mind of a child. Do you see what I mean?"

"Well. OK. I do remember his touching me-arm around the shoulder, pat on the back-about as nonsexual as imaginable. There was never the slightest hint of anything to these touches. This guy is a spiritual dynamo. I would stake my life on his word." Philip Spain was a very handsome man, dark hair cut short, and a highly athletic figure.

Joe Smith had a pugnacious visage, reminding McAbee of Socrates. He looked hard at McAbee and said, "Look. I take this seriously. Father Billy Taylor should have been Bishop of this Diocese. It would have been in another dimension by now. Our present Bishop is a mannequin with no sense of diversity, no sense of ambiguity, and no sense of genuine holiness. He's about as Irish in soul as a Serbian gunman or a Rwandan slaughterer. His DNA can be spelled out as IRA. This damn thing is a political trial in my mind. Taylor wouldn't touch anyone in a using way. Our good Bishop is leaving him to the wolves because Billy is somewhat liberal and theologically at odds with his assness." He pounded the table and looked up at McAbee as he lowered himself into a crouching position, seemingly ready to spring at McAbee if he disagreed. McAbee nodded his head to show Smith that he understood and let it stay at that.

Father Dan Van de Hyfte was an urbane man, quite thin with sharp features. He spoke through an artificial voice box, probably a victim of larynx cancer. McAbee felt bad for him because it was hard on Van de Hyfte to speak. He had yet to become comfortable with his disability. "I will ... keep my ... piece short. Billy Taylor ... is a saint. I have ... never trusted ... anyone like … him. It is ... unfair and ... scandalous. The Bishop ... and his Pancho are ... actively ... destroying ... the work ... of our diocese ... and our priests. I am ... so ... sad."

McAbee looked at the others. They lowered their heads and said nothing. McAbee wondered just what you could say. The only effort was made by McMahon, who patted Van de Hyfte lightly on his shoulder while saying nothing.

McMahon had a sense of humor about him, a gregarious, big-hearted man who reminded McAbee of the late Tip O'Neill, the former Speaker of the House of Representatives. "Well, I guess it's my turn. Look, Dr. McAbee, I really don't have anything to say that makes my conclusions different from my confederates. We all agree on one thing-he's innocent! Have you met him?"

"On a few social occasions. I know why you say what you say. But I also know that the world is full of surprises and just maybe he is guilty. I mean to say that all of us have our dirty little secrets."

"Oh, I'll concede that, and I'll concede that nothing is certain in this world. But we all live in a world of probabilities, and let me tell you in no uncertain terms, I don't think that there is a priest in this Diocese who feels that he is guilty. In fact, I can't believe that the Bishop and Monsignor Duncan really feel that way. But, on the assumption that they do, I can only say that they are terribly confused. You know, Dr. McAbee, between us and the wall, they are fairly isolated from the priests in this Diocese. I don't want this going further than this room, of course, but I'd say that there are substantial problems of judgment. The Bishop is not American, and he brings ... and I'm an Irishman, so I can say it ... a lot of baggage from that Godforsaken history. As to Duncan, have you met him?"

"Yes. About a week ago."

"Well, ... how should I phrase this? Well, a shrewd observer such as yourself must surely see what is involved with that one. His family is well connected, and thus the appointment to Chancellor. You know, he went around at our last diocesan conference asking about Billy, and of course we all know what he wanted us to say, but to a man, we told him to go to hell."

McAbee knew that McMahon figured that he was there on behalf of someone in Rome. He opined that it was known all over the Diocese that Taylor had been a classmate of Pope John Paul II. Perhaps the politically shrewd Irishman was hoping that some of this conversation would find its way back to Rome. He wondered if the Priests Council was not far from being a union.

McAbee looked at these four men and saw the intentness in their faces. These were men of God, whatever that meant, and they were dead serious. He knew enough about the modern-day priesthood to know that the strains and stresses were enormous on them and that they really only had each other and perhaps their families to fall back on.

"So, Dr. McAbee, what is your assessment of this thing?" The youngest of them asked, Father Spain.

"I don't know. Ostensibly Father Taylor appears to be innocent, but you have it correctly perceived. The top sees it differently. There are some interesting angles in this case that weren't obvious until I did some digging. You know, fathers, ultimately I'll respond to my brother with yes, no, or maybe, and I'll vote the probabilities from one to ten, but right now I just don't know. Like you, of course, I wish it to be so that he is innocent."

"Have ... you met ... with him ... yet?" Van de Hyfte asked in his halting manner.

"No. I'll do that tomorrow, hopefully. You know, this afternoon I'm going to St. Anne's to meet with Father Schaller and a few parishioners who can remember back to those days when Father Taylor was there."

Monsignor McMahon said, "I'll call him and tell him you are on your way. I'm sure that he will be very cooperative." McAbee wasn't sure, for a second, whether the big Irishman was going to make a preemptive threat against this priest, just in case he was inclined to be difficult.

The drive to St. Anne's parish took McAbee across 30 west to 67 south and then west on a rural road that took him to the parish. The history of the parish went back to the 19th century, one of many rural parishes throughout the Diocese. St. Anne's had a particular fame, especially in the days when Taylor was pastor. It had been voted as one of the most beautiful rural churches in the Midwest. It sat between two groves of trees, a simple white church, quietly elegant, with a pillarless interior. McAbee had been there once for a wedding in the late seventies and was impressed.

Like many, he was amazed when the Diocese, under Bishop O'Meara and the St. Anne's Council, had decided to donate the entire church building to the County of Scott and permit its usage as a non-sectarian chapel relocated about a half mile east of its present location. The argument went that the Church was simply too small to serve the needs of the people in the area, an area that had become crowded with the expanding growth of Davenport and surrounding towns.

And sure enough. The church had been moved and a new church was built, a very sleek, modern design that would not have any stigma associated with it, like being called a magnificent edifice in a rural setting. The church hall was also modernistic in design and together he was sure that they featured in some type of magazine read by church architects, perhaps the *Architectural Shakeup of Old Christian Churches* magazine.

Father Schaller wore thick glasses, had black, oily hair, and was quite somber. McAbee didn't want to get into a doctor thing and made it clear to Father Schaller that his name was Bertrand. He was taken into a spacious room where five people eyed him with varying facial expressions. He was introduced to each of them. After that, Schaller said, "Bertrand McAbee is investigating the Father Taylor case. He asked me to gather people from the period when Father Billy was the pastor. I'd like this session to be honest and helpful, and I'd like you to feel free to ask anything and say anything. It may be very important."

The average age had to be 65, with one woman probably in her 80s. The youngest was a man in his late 40s or early 50s. They looked at McAbee expectantly, reminding him of teaching and his first day of class for all those years he did it. After some initial comments and thanking them for coming, he went to work.

"My first question is this. Do any of you know of

records about this parish during Father Taylor's term of appointment?"

"I do. I do. They're stored in this very building over in Room B. We've always kept the weekly church bulletin. Oh, I edited it for over 15 years, and we had a strong custom of insisting that whoever took over the job of editing had the responsibility to save them. They're there all right." She was about 70 and had an admirable intensity in her gray eyes, which were enlarged by her thick glasses.

Father Schaller said, "I'll be happy to let you study them any time."

McAbee continued. "As you know, Father Taylor has been accused of molesting a John Antle while the boy served mass here for about a two-year period. Do any of you remember John Antle?"

A balding man with a reddish-purple nose, broken it seemed by too many shots of Jack Daniels, spoke up. "I was the head usher here for a bunch of those years, and I remember that kid. He was a pretty good kid. He was enthusiastic and had a sense of leadership to him."

This didn't square with the adult version that McAbee had perceived. McAbee asked, "Smallish, blonde hair?"

"Yeah. That's him. I remember him; good kid."

"And, of course, you all remember Taylor?"

Four of them spoke of him with kindness and about how shocked they were by the charges. But McAbee noticed that a woman, who seemed to be about 65, was quiet. He looked her way and said, "How about you, Ms... ?"

"Haden. Brenda Haden. Organist. Was then, am now. You want honesty?"

"Absolutely." Finally, a break was possible. Maybe Billy

Taylor had actually picked up an enemy besides those in the episcopal clique.

"Well, I know he seemed holy and all. And ... mind you I never saw him do anything ... but he was awful friendly and personable." She looked around at the other guests as if to stare them down. "I think that he was a flirt."

"Jesus! Brenda!" A man in his 70s pounded his cane on the floor as if he was a sergeant-at arms. "Brenda. You think that any man who looks at you is flirting. What would Father Taylor see in you, even if he was inclined in that direction? God save your miserable soul."

She took out a handkerchief and put it to her eyes and said, "See. I tried to be honest, but this is what happens."

Father Schaller went to her and placed an arm around her shoulder and consoled her. The old man with the cane ineffectively whispering, "Well, don't you look at me like that. She had it coming. She's lived in a world of gossip all her life."

The gray-eyed woman said to him simply: "There's no reason for this in a church hall, Alvin. After all, she was asked to be honest. Shame on you, Alvin."

McAbee said, "Brenda. I appreciate your honesty, and I may want to speak with you at a later date." He thought that there was probably little chance of that. "John Antle was at this parish for two years. He claimed that he was abused in a small room that altar boys' garments were stored. It was a room where altar boys changed into their robes. Does anyone remember that room?"

Vein nose said, "I do. It was in the basement of the old church. Alvin, you remember, don't you? It was behind the stairs."

"Yeah. I do."

The women were not offering on this one. They were probably kept out of those areas. And just as McAbee was set on this conclusion, the black and white clad nun said, "I remember it also. I did sewing and button repair and the like."

So, at least there were three who remembered the room. "Could Father Taylor have done anything down there, assuming that he was guilty? I mean to say, was it remote and secure enough?"

Alvin said, "If you put it that way, yes. But I don't remember his being down there. I don't think that he'd have that much cause to be there. After all, maybe he was flirting with Brenda."

"Now that's enough, Alvin. Really!" the gray-eyed woman thundered and as Brenda let out a new howl and rained tears.

Father Schaller said, "Alvin, that's enough please." Alvin didn't want to take on the priest. He was dutifully quiet.

"Between masses ... what could Father Taylor do?"

Purple nose responded, "He was a gadfly. Once a month, at least, we'd have breakfast for the congregation. It's hard for me to see him having the time even if he had the inclination. He was always hobnobbing with the parishioners. Is that when it was supposed to happen? Between masses?"

"Yes. The record is clear on that."

"Well, I just don't see the opportunity."

"Did anyone wear robes other than Father Taylor and the altar boy?"

Brenda said, "In those days we had a choir of three to maybe ten people. We were in the back of the church ... in the loft They were required ... but ... but ... the robes were kept up in the choir loft. Why?" Her mascara streaked varying paths down her cheek.

Alvin said, "The reader did as I recall. During those years ... oh ... am I right ... I think so ... we used to have a kind of regular reader. He'd read the selections from the Epistles or Gospel. It was Bob Hartwig. Don't you remember?"

The nun responded. "Yes. I do. We would spell each other. But other than him, I don't remember anyone else, except the choir."

Brenda said, "And that was only for the loft. They'd come down for Communion, but that was it."

McAbee said, "Bob Hartwig? That's a new name."

Purple nose said, "Bob! A good man. Been associated with this church all his life. But you don't want to go interviewing him. He's heavy into Alzheimer's."

Alvin, punching his cane down a few times, "Yeah. That guy is loonier than hell. He started slipping about four years ago. Nursing home rats probably have him now. Terrible thing. Warehousing the old. Better off shooting them."

McAbee knew that they didn't know why he was running this down, but he intended to chase it to the end. "Would Hartwig have had an opportunity?"

"We all could have," the gray-eyed woman said defensively.

"I understand that, but just help me. Could Hartwig have had an opportunity?"

"Yes. But he's an important man ... very good family. The family has a good 2000 acres," purple nose said.

McAbee was unimpressed with the wealth argument. It was totally irrelevant. He was highly interested in the robe feature since Antle was so fixated on that memory. He went back to the organist, Brenda. "Now, Mrs. Haden. You said that the choir members would robe and disrobe up in the choir loft which was in the back of the church and up a flight of stairs? You also said that they would come down to receive Communion and then go back to the loft. After the mass, would they disrobe there or would the come down and circulate among the congregation?"

"Of course they'd circulate. That was one of our missions. Without a choir, there is no true high service in my mind. It was important to me that they get out there and let people know who they were."

"They'd have their robes on all during this?"

"Oh heavens no. They'd have those things off lickety split." She laughed in a dismissing way.

"And what if one of them kept their robes on? If they went down and said goodby to the congregants in their robes?"

"No. Impossible. I wouldn't allow it. Only the priest gets to wear the robes beyond the mass."

"How about Hartwig?" McAbee looked at purple nose.

"Can't say. Just don't remember."

"I do," the nun said. "Between masses it was our job to clean the cruets, pour new wine, and re-lay the vestments, darken the candles, and so on. You see, it was more than just being a reader. We were the sacristans. I didn't have to wear robes because I was in my garb, but the … Hartwig did, and he did keep it on."

"And was Hartwig here when Antle was here?"

The gray-eyed woman said, "You can look that up. I would list all participants, choir, altar boys, and the like. Father Taylor was always one for giving credit."

"So, Sister, let me get this right. You would alternate weeks with Mr. Hartwig. You'd cover both masses?"

"Yes. I'm pretty sure that's how we operated, but it's long ago. But you could find that out in the bulletin I'm sure."

McAbee was brought into the records storage room by Schaller. He was pleased to see how well it was organized. He found the years in question. They had it right. Hartwig and the nun operated in tandem during the period, and John Antle was the altar boy. So, Bob Hartwig was a possibility, but Bob Hartwig was beset by Alzheimer's. Now what?

CHAPTER FIFTEEN

Iowa, August 1996

Jack Scholz didn't like coming to McAbee's office. He figured that it was being watched by big brother. He much preferred his clandestine sessions at Sophie's in the dregs of the lower west end of Davenport, home of Ralston Purina, Oscar Mayer, and assorted other breeding grounds for rats and blue-collar laborers. The fact that the bar was a police-protected medium for whoring, drug peddling, stolen goods, and whatever, made it interesting. Unfortunately, Sophie hated the ex military colonel, and he, admittedly, despised the sin-encrusted bitch. That the sensitive McAbee got along with her angered him. It had something to do with his teaching a niece or some such genetically impaired relation of hers.

Scholz had built up a productive business in nefarious doings. He had gotten into the employment of former Seals, special forces types, and other military specialists like himself. He was in touch with a network of them throughout the country. He also knew that at least one of the bastards that he employed was playing ball with the FBI, and for the last six months he had been diligently trying to set him up, but, as of yet, to no avail.

On occasion he had undertaken an assignment for Bertrand McAbee, not out of any particular like for him-a misplaced academic. However, he admired Bertrand's brother Bill whom he had studied from afar. Now there was a major league player. Because Bertrand was a potential link to Bill, he therefore had decided, several years ago, to do impeccable and noteworthy work for Bertrand on the hope that it would get back to Bill.

In his judgment, Bertrand should have been a psychiatrist, given his penchant for getting to the bottom of things. Bertrand was a ferret, he'd give him that, but his problem was that when he encountered the prey he had cornered, he couldn't kill. At heart, Bertrand was a seeker who needed others to do his killing. He was not a complete man in Scholz's world. In sum, Bertrand McAbee was quite bright, but he had one serious flaw. He wasn't a terminator. Scholz was.

McAbee had warned him that Barry Fisk was going to be at the meeting. Great! Shrimpboat the Deviant! Scholz saw Fisk as a fundamentalist, that is, a completely dedicated anarchist who, because of his profoundly lethal abilities with the computer, was a dangerous man. That the midget saw Scholz as a fascist only brought a sneering smile to his lips. In the world of Jack Scholz, the Fisks would be the first to go, and no one would really give a damn.

McAbee's saucy and impertinent secretary (or was she his whore), Pat Trump, looked him over carefully. It was not a sensuous look either; she was studying him to see whether or not he was packing a weapon. Of course, at all times, he was. He was two minutes early. She said, "Bertrand will be with you in a few minutes. Coffee?"

"No thanks," he said in his most military-like, speaking-to-a-subordinate voice. Boy, he'd like to slap her one and take that insolent look off her face. Oh, well, he thought, McAbee surrounds himself with still another watchdog. He heard the door open. It was Barry Fisk waddling his way into the waiting room. They nodded to each other as he noticed that red-haired Pat Trump got an even bitchier look on her tight-lipped face.

Finally, McAbee came out and said, "Barry. Jack. Come on in. Pat, no calls please, unless it's the Pope." He smiled but neither Fisk nor Scholz gave him anything.

McAbee briefed them on the status of the case. Fisk, it was clear, had already been working on background. This meant that McAbee needed ground surveillance or some heavy-handedness thus shoving aside the virtual world of Barry Fisk for the real world. The case was simple enough. He had been hired to exculpate some pedophile priest. He remembered reading about it in the newspaper. Some Catholic crap was his assessment. But to hear McAbee, there was a chance that the priest was already a possible saint instead of someone skulking around in some Trappist monastery justly hidden in the hills of absurd Dubuque.

Scholz saw that McAbee deferred to Fisk who had probably been bouncing up and down on his computer keys for the past week and who looked like a little boy who had just found his dick for the first time. He had heard this little Cretan before. He would parse out information like gold bars, always building up to the denouement, and McAbee, the former professor, sitting there pretending to be shocked at each new revelation that Fisk would dole out. He wondered if McAbee realized just how much the sycophant he looked. Scholz wanted to scream out: 'Get to the goddamn point, you little twerp!' But he knew that it would only aggravate an already touchy situation.

He noticed that the midget, sitting uncomfortably on the edge of his chair, wouldn't look at him. They had worked together, not as a team, but by accident, on several cases in which McAbee was involved. Fisk knew that Scholz was in the hard end of the business, and he didn't like it. Another one of these academic types: 'Don't let the real world intrude on fantasy.'

Fisk said, "First off, I checked the phone bills for Margaret Aaron. There were several from many months ago from her office to Youngquist's office in Minneapolis, so there's a connection. There were none in her residential calls."

McAbee said, "Well, we know of that connection between Aaron and Youngquist. The Antle case. So, I don't see that getting us anywhere, do you?"

"No. Not from what we know," Fisk answered

"And?" A good question, Scholz thought. You have to lead the midget on because his sawed-off little legs were moving around like beads of water on a hot skillet. Body language! The midget would give anyone a military position in a few seconds. It's a good thing that the military would have nothing to do with someone like this; on the other hand, give this oversized Arkansas satyr, Clinton, a chance, and the Fisks will be the Seals of the future.

"I did check on the nurse, Margi. There are calls to this Herb Scannell guy on an average of twice a month."

"Really? Length?"

"About 15 minutes per. It might be fair to assume that she was riding shotgun for Scannell, reporting on Aaron. She probably knew Aaron was in drug trouble and that Scannell was loading her up."

He wasn't finished with his revelations. His legs were still jumping around. Scholz observed that McAbee was all too aware of Fisk's big moment, and its tie in to further information.

"Do you want to hear about Scannell?" Fisk asked. McAbee hesitated and rightfully so. There was more information on this street, but the midget was holding back. That was going to be his killer surprise. McAbee wouldn't burst his bubble, and he went along.

"Sure."

"Scannell is an ex-Army man who did service in Vietnam. He was fluent in Vietnamese and was in ground intelligence." He gave a quick, disdainful look at Scholz and said, "As you can imagine, most of those characters were freaks who actively engaged in murder and torture."

Scholz could feel his blood pressure starting to rise, and some sweat was starting to accumulate on his upper lip. In a world without the restraints of society, he would have bodily picked up the little bastard and hurled him through the window of McAbee's suite. He took some deep breaths and said nothing. Someday he'd get the little fucker.

Fisk gave an employment summary of Scannell, ending up with his current work for Youngquist. He noted Scannell's career with the Minneapolis Police Department and his premature retirement, information that was not available in virtual reality. "It's a job for a groundhog, if you want it."

"I think," McAbee said, "I want to know anything I can know about him. Dr. Aaron's therapist saw him as being a primary cause in Aaron's fall from grace. Jack, do you think that you could get at this? His dismissal from the PD?"

"Consider it done," Scholz said dutifully.

"Now, Barry, I have a feeling that you have more," McAbee said coaxingly. Scholz was put off by McAbee's disingenuousness. It was unseemly, this one professor trying to potty train this other professor into emptying his bladder.

"Oh, yes. There is one other main detail." His feet were now kicking up a storm. "Margi called Scannell two nights before she and Dr. Aaron were murdered!" Suddenly the feet stopped! He had delivered the coup de grace.

McAbee said, "Marvelous! An incredible detail. Not conclusive, but powerful."

Fisk beamed. He had hit a home run ball, but while it had distance, it might still be foul. Anticlimactically Fisk said, "After the call, Scannell made three local calls. I have the addresses. I don't know if there is any connection, but I'll keep working on it."

McAbee looked at Scholz. "Jack, I need some ground men in Minneapolis, not just for Scannell's background, but also I think we need to trail him and also track these addresses in case there's some connection. I figure that we're ahead of the cops on this one, and I'd like to stay there. I'm especially interested in where he was on the day of the killings."

"That I can tell you," Fisk said. "He was charging clothes at the Southdale Daytons, and he was gambling at the casino. The times are 2:05 p.m. at Daytons, and then he was at the casino. Two cash withdrawals at 3:55p.m. and another at 4:51p.m."

"OK. He wasn't at the murder scene in all probability. Question. Does he show an inclination to go to casinos?"

"No. There were no withdrawals like those from a casino over the past five years, and that's as far as I can get"

"Alibi stuff?"

"If he was in on the murder in some way, no doubt about it," Fisk responded.

Shortly Fisk left, leaving behind his printouts. He handed a separate envelope to McAbee, probably his bill. Grudgingly, Scholz admired the work of this man, except for the one look his way during the description of Scannell. Fisk never looked at him again.

McAbee said to Scholz, "So, Jack, can you start this up ASAP?"

"Don't worry about it."

"Tell your guys that this Scannell is no fool."

"Neither are they. Two things, McAbee. Do you really think that this priest is innocent? And do you really think there's a connection between the murders in Iowa City and your case? Seems a bit farfetched," Scholz said, looking at McAbee with puzzlement.

"I'll give you that, but so far there's nothing coming between a possible connection. In fact, the more we get into this, the more I slide toward this conclusion. Scannell looks interesting, but Youngquist is still out there. As to Father Taylor's innocence, I don't know."

"I could bring Youngquist in and find out real quickly," Scholz said. He knew that McAbee would not resort to such an extreme tactic, at least at this stage of the investigation.

But there was a tantalizing piece to McAbee, a subterranean malevolence, pragmatism, and amorality that would come out under the right circumstances.

Scholz would have himself and men on Scannell by early evening. One of these days he would be led into the world of Bertrand's brother, Bill. Bertrand never verbally responded to Scholz's extreme measure request. That meant something other than a 'no.'

Iowa, August, 1996

Still another visitor. This time Bertrand McAbee. Father Taylor remembered him. McAbee had been a professor of classics at St. Anselm College. They had attended several social functions together. But Taylor also remembered him most especially from an honors colloquium in which McAbee had participated at the University of Iowa. McAbee had held forth on Plato's *The Laws* and had done a superb job.

Father Edward had initially refused McAbee's request until Bishop O'Meara, through Monsignor Duncan, had personally intervened. "Do you have any idea why this man would want to see you, and, and perhaps this is more curious, how did he get the Bishop's office to involve itself?" Taylor's response was one of ignorance.

He stood by the door of the visitors' entrance. McAbee would be driving from Davenport in all probability. Brother Joseph, who was writing a note, looked up from his desk and said, "Father Taylor. You seem anxious. Can I do anything for you?"

"No, Brother. I'm OK. This visit is a bit strange. I understood the other ones, but this one leaves me confused."

Taylor heard a vehicle, that slow crunching sound across the dirt road, the crushing of rocks, and the hum of the engine. It was a black Explorer.

From the vehicle came an athletic-looking man in his mid fifties. He hadn't aged that much from the lecture that he had attended a good 15 years ago. His pace was firm as he strode across the small visitors' parking lot. He wore khaki pants, a black, short-sleeved shirt, and a pair of white walking shoes. For a reason he couldn't explain, McAbee made him nervous. Taylor stepped back into the shadows to the right of the screen door. As expected, McAbee paused upon entry, trying to adjust his eyes to the contrasting darkness.

Father Taylor went up to him and extended his hand. "Dr. McAbee. You've come to visit me." Brother Joseph came forward and also introduced himself. Taylor hoped that this wasn't perceived as a monkish power play. McAbee appeared to be unfazed and shook the hands of both men.

"How was the drive?" Taylor asked.

"Not bad at all. I drove by the cross road on 61 and had to do a U-turn." He shook his head as it he was hopelessly foolish.

"Lots of people miss that. The DOT doesn't seem to like us particularly," Brother Joseph said. "I've been instructed by Father Edward to show you our visitor's room, or, of course, if you choose, you may walk the grounds. I'll leave the two of you to decide. If you need anything, just get me. I'll be here for the next few hours."

"What's your preference, Father?" McAbee queried.

"Well, I usually walk the grounds, and today is pretty cool. How about that?"

"Sounds great." Taylor told Brother Joseph that they would be walking the grounds, at least for a while.

As they walked, Father Taylor looked up to the second floor of the main building and noticed that the venetian blinds in the corner room moved ever so slightly. It was Father Edward's room.

They walked in silence for a few minutes. Finally, McAbee said, "You know, Father Taylor, I'm not just up here on a mission of curiosity, although it may seem as such. Your guilt or innocence is the issue."

"I understand that is the issue, but what is its bearing on your job as a classics professor at St. Anselm College?"

McAbee laughed, in a self-defacing way. "Oh, Father Taylor, I've been out of academia now for a number of years. I have my own investigation agency. I thought you knew. I'm so sorry. This must seem like the strangest thing to you." He laughed again, a quiet but full laugh. He liked absurdity, apparently, Taylor speculated.

"Well, I had my conjectures."

"I'll bet you did. Let me process a few things. First, I left St. Anselm's when the then President had become so aberrant and crooked that I had to get out of academia. Of course, the Board finally got the bum out, but by that time, I was enjoying the change of a pace. My brother in New York City runs a very successful international security firm. He throws me work, and then I have my clientele. It's really interesting work."

"Don't you miss teaching the classics? The Greeks? The Romans?"

"Of course I do, and I occasionally do a guest lecture, but St. Anselm's has become a business school, and I just don't know what the future holds for classics professors. When I got into administration, I lost touch with my research skills, and now, I'm not inclined in that direction. But I do well in this job." Taylor thought he picked up the slightest trace of defensiveness.

"So, how does all of this relate to Monsignor Duncan's request for a meeting? How involved are you with the Diocese?"

"I'm not. First, I bring you the highest regards of a friend of yours, and also of a friend of this man to you, from long ago." Father Taylor was suspicious. Just where was this going. "I'm relaying a message of goodwill from Guillermo Scarzi and Karol Wojtyla." He dropped this in a spectacular way. Taylor was stunned into silence as he gazed at McAbee. The two names brought a rush of gratitude to Taylor, who felt that these natural defenders had given up on him.

"Is this through Bishop O'Meara?" Taylor asked suspiciously.

"No. No. I met Bishop Scarzi in New York City in my brother's office. I've been having a run at this for several weeks now. I just didn't want to come to you until I had a grasp of this case."

The lane that they had entered several minutes previously looked as though it would never end. Flanked by rows and rows of corn, they trekked forward. Taylor had an ever-so-slight desire to sit down and cry. He led those thoughts out of his head.

"Are you here at the request of Guillermo?"

"Yes. His personal request. And he made it clear that the Pope himself is also seriously interested."

"And? What do you think?"

"Well, as a start, for every adversary, you have 100 friends. I have never seen a depth of support that I'm seeing in your case, Father. If innocence could be declared by proclamation, you'd be innocent, and this very conversation would be moot. Do you see?"

"Yes. But proclamations, like you say, mean nothing next to what I must deal with when it comes to Bishop O'Meara, Monsignor Duncan, and the diocesan lawyer, Chip Blaine. They want me to settle."

"But, Father, there's more to this. Are you innocent?"

"Yes."

"John Antle was being treated by a very capable psychiatrist before she was murdered."

Taylor was stunned. "Surely you don't think that there is an association between that murder and my case, do you?"

"I wouldn't count it out, Father."

Billy Taylor walked along the lane in stunned silence. He was horrified at McAbee's suggestion. McAbee had just blistered him in a few short minutes. He questioned his innocence. He told him that Antle was treated by a capable psychiatrist and that there had been a murder. What in God's name was going on here? He asked gingerly, "You are not asking me if I or one of my supporters did this, are you?"

"Well, not really, but answer it for me anyway, Father," McAbee said flatly.

Taylor was incensed and turned on McAbee as both men stopped. "I told you that I was innocent. Do you think I could be innocent of the sexual crime but authorize the murder of John Antle's psychiatrist? Please, think about what you are asking, Dr. McAbee!"

"Father Taylor, think about Jesus and Judas, or Socrates and Alcibiades. I'm not saying that you engineered or authorized it, and I'm not saying that one of your friends did it. I'm merely asking for your opinion. I have to rule out every possibility, you see, but I can't back away from my search."

McAbee's look was intense. His gray eyes worked their way into Taylor as the two men stared at each other. Taylor held his anger in check. It took great resolve. Had Bishop O'Meara talked Scarzi and the Pope into his being guilty? Was McAbee an alternate approach to the hardness of O'Meara and Chip Blaine? And what made him believe that this classics scholar was an easy approach anyway?

"Dr. McAbee," he said reservedly. "I am innocent of all these things, and I did not send anyone to murder or maim the psychiatrist or anyone else," he said with finality.

"Father," McAbee said speculatively. "Is there any chance that John Antle was abused while in your care at St. Anne's?"

Taylor stiffened at the question and wondered what McAbee was getting at. He answered slowly. "He was never under my care. His mother dropped him off at the church, usually, as I recall, about ten minutes before mass. He would go down to the altar boys' room, change, and be ready. He was about eight or nine years old. He could take care of himself. As I recall, he usually had a book of some kind with him. I never really saw much of him. After mass, he would go back and wait for the next mass, or if there was a doing at the parish, he would attend that; for example, a pancake breakfast. His mother would come back and would frequently attend the late mass. Then he would leave. Now I have to think that the psychiatrist talked him into my guilt."

They walked across a field of green grass, spotted with daffodils. The blue sky was cloudless, and the 80-degree temperature was a relief from the heat of the past few weeks. Even the tough Iowa humidity had abated.

McAbee said, "I met John Antle a few days ago. At first I thought he might be a hustler going after the deep pockets of the Church. I didn't leave him feeling that way anymore. Do you understand me, Father?"

"Of course I do. I never said that he was a liar. He's just wrong. I never touched him other than maybe touching his hair or patting him on the back. In those days that was not seen as a sexual act. In fact, it was seen as a manly and supportive gesture." They were at the visitors' entrance. Taylor asked, "Would you like a Coke? We can sit in the visitor's room. I'm sure that Brother Joseph will accommodate." McAbee nodded and they went into the visitor's room. Cokes were brought and Brother Joseph left them alone. There was a silence between them as they sipped the iced beverages.

"So," Taylor asked, "how is Guillermo?"

"Oh, fine. An impressive man, very caring, very … sensitive."

"You know that during World War II he was just in his early twenties, and he was tortured by the Nazis and the Italian Fascists. They suspected him of helping Jews. He has permanent nerve damage."

"Did he help them?"

"Oh, my. Yes, he did. He was given several awards in

Israel and from the Jewish community in Rome and Venice. He always said the Nazis were right about him, but they didn't break him."

"You know, he is definitely concerned about you. He thinks it is incomprehensible that you might have done anything that despicable. The Pope agrees with him."

"Dr. McAbee, you know for a while I wondered about you. Were you an enemy or a friend? You got under my skin for a few minutes," Taylor said with a look of consternation.

"Father Taylor, my job is to get at the truth. It doesn't pertain to your civil trial. They'll ask me how I feel about the whole thing, and I have to say things with some kind of finality. Unless I ask the questions that come to my mind, I will have reservations, naturally. Allow me back to the point." Taylor had not shaken him and knew that he wouldn't. McAbee was simply too concentrated and too focused a man. He rolled his left hand over so as to tell McAbee to continue.

"You say that you did touch John Antle, but that there was nothing sexual about it. Am I right?"

"Yes. I touch people all the time, men, boys, women, girls. I hug, I reassure, I pat. It is my nature. It is one of my ways of being a priest. It is inconceivable to me that there could be any association of that to sexuality. If there is, then I am a very promiscuous man." He couldn't help but smile, even though McAbee didn't flinch from his intense stare.

"Would you touch him again in this way, given today's climate?"

"Yes. I will never change. I am not fond of this society's newly found Puritanism. It doesn't come from the gospels;

rather, it comes from a furiously antiseptic and strained sense of self and otherness."

McAbee continued to gaze at him as if measuring every syllable and nuance that Taylor expressed. He had no idea how he was taken by this erstwhile professor.

McAbee said, "You say that Antle took care of himself. It seems that his exposure was between 9:00 and 11:00 a.m., between masses. What do you remember about that?"

"Dr. McAbee, I remember this. I would spend time with the people. Our parish hall was open. Once a month, at least, we had pancake breakfasts, and I'm sure that John Antle was invited. You do not understand, I think, Sunday is frenetic in a parish. I had no time-you would say opportunity-to abuse the boy. Don't you understand? Do you go to church?"

"Not if I can help it."

"Well, try it some Sunday. See what a priest is all about!" Taylor said emotionally.

McAbee persisted. "But you said that Antle pretty much took care of himself. Maybe it wasn't you, Father."

There was a long pause in the conversation. Taylor wondered where McAbee was going. He answered tentatively. "If you think that someone else might have violated him unbeknownst to me, I do not know."

"Don't know, or won't tell?" McAbee fired back at him.

"Do not know. And if it was a confessional matter, yes, could not tell." Taylor felt jittery. McAbee had something. Was he about to spring it? Or was he just guessing? "Dr. McAbee, the kind of therapy that John Antle was exposed to could lead to all sorts of conjectures or manipulations. Don't you agree?"

"Yes, there are a number of cases out there where it seems that serious injustices have resulted from hypnotically-based, repressed memory approaches. But I don't believe that all of them are merely the result of suggestion or some therapist leading people down the road to false memories. I can't buy that."

"Well ... I do not know really. I can just tell you of my innocence, Dr. McAbee." McAbee reminded Taylor of a watchdog. In this case he was watching Taylor's every move and probably listening to his every voice intonation. Taylor wanted him to believe him, but he couldn't get a read from him.

"Father," McAbee probed, "I have seen the psychiatrist's notes. Specific features of the abuser are pointed out by Antle to the psychiatrist. One of them referred to fingers, pudgy fingers. I've looked at yours. They are certainly not that. Your fingers are quite thin and small, so that's encouraging. Everything else could easily fit to you. And fingers? That's very relative, isn't it? Tell me, Father, about others. Who else was clothed in a cassock?"

Taylor tightened at this query. McAbee had again returned to this piece. He remained as non-committal as possible in his reply. "There was the choir, of course, and the gospel readers. That's it. Why do you ask?"

"That was a point of identification. The cassock, very detailed, very precise. Tell me about the choir. Would they have worn their cassocks outside the choir loft?"

Taylor was now quite alert to McAbee. He thought that McAbee was trying to go somewhere but at oblique angles. "No, I'm sure that they would have stayed there; in fact, there was a small changing area in the loft itself."

"And how about the reader?"

"Readers," Taylor corrected him and a bit too quickly.

"OK. Readers," McAbee pressed.

"One of them was a nun, as I recall, and the other was a man. The man would have changed in the altar boys room."

"Tell me, Father. What do you know about ...," McAbee looked down at a small notepad, and Taylor perceived this to be a ploy, and Taylor could see it coming, "... Bob Hartwig?"

Taylor was sure that he held his composure precisely, because McAbee was telegraphing where he was going. "Well, he was a very dedicated Catholic layman and a generous giver to St. Anne's. He was virtually a deacon without ever becoming one. Why do you ask about him?"

McAbee was giving the full gray-eyed stare across the three feet of table that separated the men. There was no letup in his concentration, and Taylor felt uncomfortable. "He had access, Father."

"And you think he abused John Antle?"

"If you didn't, he might have. Do you know of any incidents between him and John Antle?"

"No, I do not."

McAbee, who had been leaning forward through much of the meeting, now sat back in his chair. He rubbed his chin a few times and sat silently for a minute or so. Then he asked, "Is Hartwig still alive?"

"I do not know for sure, but I think he is. I am not aware of his death, let me put it that way." If McAbee had pressed him, Taylor would have revealed two other data. Bob Hartwig, if he had not died since Taylor's entry into the Trappist monastery, was in a home in Calamus, Iowa, suffering from advanced Alzheimer's, age about 87. For years

Taylor had been his confessor. Taylor, in fact, knew of no sexual incidents between Hartwig and John Antle. He had not lied to McAbee on any score, even though he wasn't exactly forthcoming to the classicist.

McAbee put his notebook into his pocket. He was finished, much to Taylor's joy. But the joy was short lived. The look of sadness that came over McAbee's face gave him pause. McAbee said gently, "Father Taylor, walk with me to my car."

They walked toward the dusty black Explorer in silence. McAbee took his car keys from his front trouser pocket and opened his door. He now turned toward Taylor and extended his hand. They shook and as they did, McAbee said very quietly, "Father, there's a piece missing, I'm sorry to say. I'm sure that I'll be here again. And ... you know ... I think you know that. Goodbye."

Father Taylor bowed his head slightly, the only concession to McAbee's prediction.

When he went back to the doorway, he found Brother Joseph standing there. The Brother said, "Seems like an interesting man."

"He is, Brother. He is an investigator."

"Really? He doesn't seem like one. He's too pensive. I thought for a moment that he was asking you about the entry requirements for this place." The Brother was not smiling.

Taylor went to his room and laid down on his cot. He was exhausted. He fell asleep.

CHAPTER SIXTEEN

Minnesota, August 1996

Herb Scannell took off the rubber band holding together the morning edition of the *Minneapolis Star Tribune.* He was in mid-chew of his English muffin when he turned to page three and saw the likeness of The Princess, along with a short story detailing the murders of a psychiatrist and nurse in Iowa City. The goddamn Princess had his cover blown, and even though it was due in part to Scannell's pressing him to do the job with a one-day's notice, it still posed a threat. There was linkage.

He was also, deep down in his gut, afraid of The Princess. This seemingly impotent, lisping, effeminate fairy was a killing machine. Scannell had never seen better. The disguises, the careful planning, and the precision murders were surgical compared to the kind of gross killing that Scannell preferred, and there was jealousy, perhaps, that he didn't have the emotional control and discipline that The Princess possessed.

He saw no good reason to go to Youngquist with his decision to murder The Princess. Once he saw the police artist's likeness, he knew what had to be done. But he also knew that The Princess probably read the same newspaper. He would calculate Scannell's choices and know that his assassination was high on a likely list. Any underrating of The Princess was insane. Furthermore, it would be essential that he gain access to The Princess' house in Edina to comb it for any incriminating evidence. While it was true that a professional gun-for-hire instinctively ridded himself of all traces of his work, there was something about Toby Leonard and his association with the antique business that gave him pause. There was, after all, a collector's frame of mind.

He would have to make it look like a gay-revenge killing. Mercurial fags make all sorts of enemies, and it was fair to assume that Toby, The Princess, was no different. So it would have to be a messy kill-his kind of kill. He called Toby, who picked up the phone on the first ring.

"Yes?"

"Herb here."

"I saw it. I think I'm going to do some antiquing out of the country."

"Good idea. But before you do, I have one more quick favor to ask of you. It's worth 50 gs. Can we talk?"

The Princess fell silent on the other end of the phone. He was probably turning over every possibility. Finally he responded to Scannell, "You've never been to my place. Why don't you come over at about 10:00 tonight. By then I'll be packed and will have my store covered and so on. I'll listen, but I won't promise on this. The paper has me jittery." He gave Scannell instructions as how to get to his house. Scannell pretended to be writing them down. The goddamn

Princess was falling right into tow. It shouldn't be all that hard to get the drop on him.

Minnesota, August 1996

Jack Scholz was in Minneapolis by 6:30p.m. He was picked up at the Northwest Airline's carousel by an ex-Marine named Abdul James, a black, 35-year-old who stood at 6 feet, 3 inches and weighed about 260 pounds. Scholz had worked with him once. There was mutual respect there, and the military underpinning brought a glue to the relationship.

Other than "hello," nothing was said until they were on 494 West. Scholz asked, "Got O'Brien and Melcher?"

"Melcher is on a job in Detroit. Got a brother I've been bringing along ... special forces ... super. OK with that?"

"Because you say so, yes." It was the highest compliment Scholz could give. "As I told you, we're around the clock on this. I'll begin. I'll drop you off and take this car. Are we all connected?"

"Twenty-four hours a day till you say stop. We looking for anything special?"

"Right now, no. But there's some danger in this. Ex-cop ... rotten Vietnam duty, ground intelligence. Seems like a mean bastard," Scholz said flatly.

Scholz was on duty by 8:15p.m. Scannell's apartment was above an ice cream store in the artsy section of Minneapolis called Old Town. Scholz thought such a location a bit unlikely for someone like Scannell, as he tucked his car behind a Volkswagen Beetle about a block and a half east of

Scannell's apartment. He saw the images of a TV set through the half-closed blinds of the apartment as he walked the rather crowded area full of assorted freaks and students from nearby University of Minnesota. Storefronts, pizza parlors, bars, and art shops were in abundance. He had Scannell's license plate tag, thanks to anal Barry Fisk. Scannell's car was in a small, private lot a block away. Perhaps Scannell was in for the night. He walked into the lot and looked around. He pretended to sneeze and cough and took out a handkerchief from his back pocket. A few quarters scattered on the blacktop surface near Scannell's car. He crouched to pick up the quarters and managed as unobtrusively as possible to place a homer under Scannell's car.

He was back in his car in a matter of minutes, setting the receiver to the homing device. Scannell, at least if he took his car, could be tracked. Scholz turned on the radio and listened to a pathetic Minnesota Twins game. They were losing to the Milwaukee Brewers by a score of 5-l. He had two pictures of Scannell that Fisk had provided in his folder, and he kept his eyes peeled on the entry door to the upstairs apartment.

Toby Leonard froze when he saw his picture on page three of the *Star Tribune*. He had been in the assassination business for 15 years, and he had never been identified. It had to be that guy who was near the doorway of the psychiatrist's office, the son-of-a-bitch. He had a one-second look, but it was good enough to lead the newspaper to say 'probably a female.' The word 'probably' really irked him. Toby was known around Minneapolis as a transvestite stripper, and he felt that the likeness was too close. One of his gay friends or a straight "oh-you-really-are-a-man" johns would give him up. It was just a matter of time.

He had always been careful, and the Iowa kill had been no different. No one knew that he had driven there. His antique shop was open only when he chose to open it, but he'd argue that he was in the back working. He had canceled his stage performance at the gay bar, because he had "strained a knee." He was back in the Twins by midnight. He and Scannell had met the next morning at a Starbucks, and the received $50,000 would soon be in a Mexican bank. So other than Scannell, the only person who could make him was that guy on the pathway in Iowa City. He would be a long-range project-he would have to die.

The Princess always knew the risk of his profession. In the 15 years he had murdered 23 people in the United States, Canada, and Mexico. He had never failed, although he had his delays. He had never been fingered, and he had always used a disguise-utility worker, UPS driver, postal employee, cop, model, maid, cook-the more, the merrier. Brutish Scannell had imposed himself into his world, and he had had to adjust and come to terms with him. But now the day that he had dreaded had come to be, and it was time to run the table.

He called a former lover who was also an antiquer. He told him he had to leave town for a few months and wanted him to look over the store. He'd straighten up with him on his return. They had talked about this eventuality on several occasions. "I have just the sweetest boy to do this. I'll pay him and you can straighten out with me when you get back. Just drop the keys in my box. Love!" One problem down, he thought.

He called the club. "Sorry, but I just had some bad news ... gotta leave town." He knew the club owner was thinking AIDS. Who cares? If the cops were asking around, it was a good cover.

He had a sister who lived in St. Paul. He told her that he had to leave ... would she watch over the house, pay the lawn service and utilities, pick up his mail, and so on-there was a $5,000 check in the mail. He'd be in touch. She had a key. All set.

He was starting to pack when Herb Scannell called. His plane was to leave tomorrow at 5:00 p.m. for Chicago and then on to his condo in Mexico City. The right thing to do became obvious. He would see Scannell tonight. When he finished his conversation with Scannell, he made one more call and managed, after threatening to bring his abuse case to someone else, to get a 10:00 a.m. appointment with Martin Youngquist. She had just been raped by three priests he had said. Her name was Barbara. He didn't wish to say anything else on the telephone. Youngquist was salivating.

Phil Garner, the Milwaukee Brewers' manager, was shouting at the umpire about a play at the plate. He'd already been tossed and was now getting his two cents worth. The score had moved up to 5-4, and it was the top of the seventh inning. The Minnesota announcers naturally were having a great time watching Garner spill his guts.

When the receiver started blipping, Scholz was caught off guard. On his surveillance he had gone behind the ice cream store and had noticed a back door out of the store, but he didn't think it likely that the upstairs apartment would have access to it. Scannell, for sure, had never come out of the front door. He followed Scannell at a very safe distance across Lake Street and onto 62, which brought him to Edina. He picked up the signal loud and clear on Glendale, and as he looked to his left, he saw the double garage door closing down behind Scannell's car. He drove on a block and parked. It was 10:00 p.m., and it was finally dark in Minneapolis. He decided to walk back by the large house, which stood about 100 feet from the sidewalk. The garage door opened again, and a Toyota Celica backed down the driveway. Scholz ducked behind the bushes that adjoined The Princess' property line, as the car got to the street and headed away. He did not get a clean look at the driver. Scholz ran back to his car and tried to catch the speeding Celica, but he lost him. He searched frantically in the curving and winding streets of Edina, but to no avail. He went back to the house. The Princess had left one light on in his den. Scholz looked through the narrow opening in the blinds and didn't see anyone. He walked behind the house and tripped a full array of lights, which caused him to move swiftly to his car and out of the neighborhood. His level of disgust with himself was at a record level. He would have fired himself if it was convenient to do so.

He went to a pay telephone at a convenience market and called McAbee, who had insisted on regular reports.

"Bertrand? Jack." Ever oblique on telephones, he continued. "Lost Scannell, I think. But have the men and will go on."

"Jack, Barry called this afternoon. You remember that three calls were made by Scannell off the nurse's call?"

"Yes."

"Well, two of them are to the same person. One, a Toby

Leonard at 3154 Glendale; the other to his antique shop. He's also a stripper at a gay night club to where the third call was made. Maybe it had something to do with this case. Or maybe they're friends, lovers ... who knows." McAbee said.

"The Glendale address is where I lost Scannell!" he said sourly.

The Vatican, August 1996

Bishop Guillermo Scarzi was late getting to his computer terminal. It was 4:30p.m. It was time for the weekly check on new priestly problem areas. It was a bad week: 23 names!. He muttered under his breath, "Maybe we should build a stalag and make these characters just disappear."

He was in the middle of the seventh incident when the door was tapped. It had to be Sister Catherine Siena. Only she had developed that knock of understated intensity.

"Avanti."

She came through the door with humble pushiness, that modest stride that it took a while to understand. "Bishop, I have a FedEx packet from the Bishop of Davenport in the States. I know that this is of importance to you." She handed him the stiff mailer and then stood there. Was she hoping that he'd open it and discuss its contents with her?

"Grazie," he said with finality.

"Prego." She left ... slower ... and with her ear slightly cocked to her right as if he'd call her back for the packet opening.

He slid the cardboard zipper across the thin package and found a two-page letter addressed to him, and then an

8 1/2-by-14-inch legal document that was six pages long. He shook his head. He didn't trust the judgment of the Irish Bishop. Studied prudence was simply absent in the man. The letter read:

> Dear Bishop Scarzi:
>
> We have labored in pain on the Father William Taylor matter. We know that it has caught your interest, given the letter of introduction by one Bertrand McAbee. We have accorded him cooperation and access to the clergy of the Diocese of Davenport as requested by you.
>
> Be that as it may, we have also conducted a study into the charges made against Father Taylor, who adamantly, to this day, tells of his innocence. Unfortunately, I have come to disagreement with him. I feel that he is guilty in all likelihood to the offense itself, or at the barest, to creating the appearance of such.
>
> We have spoken with our insurance carrier who has expressed fear at the financial exposure of the Diocese of Davenport in the litigation. The insurance company has agreed to pay $300,000 to end our exposure by having our name dropped from the suit. This would leave Father Taylor to his own devices, his own defense, and his own responsibility. We think this solution serves the common

good. My understanding is that Father Taylor is not financially secure, and thus he could declare personal bankruptcy, which would bring a judgement against him to naught. This is of no concern to us.

Enclosed, please find the temporary settlement made between Mr. Chip Blaine, our attorney, and Martin Youngquist, John Antle's attorney, detailing the above items. We are sending this to you as a matter of courtesy, and we intend to settle this on Friday morning of this week. We are sure of your concurrence.

In Christ,

Bishop Brendan O'Meara
The Diocese of Davenport, Iowa, USA

Scarzi was inflamed at the arrogance of the high-handedness of O'Meara. Well, the conservatives were having their day with the American Church. They were going to bring it to heel and probably create some massive schism down the way. Bishop O'Meara really belonged in some rural area of Ireland that saw the office of Bishop as the equivalent of kingship. The Irish, for all of their bluster, were basically monarchists themselves. He caught his unfairness, shook his head, and spread open the legal document. It was as O'Meara had said, an escape for the Diocese on the back of Billy Taylor.

He buzzed Sister Catherine and told her to call Bill McAbee in New York, and see if a three- way call was possible. He had heard nothing for too long from Bill except for two cryptic messages: "Bertrand pursuing Taylor matter full time," and "Bertrand still in air on matter."

Ten minutes later she came to his door, knocked, and entered. It was agreed, without ever being made explicit, that when she was on an immediate errand, she would not have to have his permission to enter his office.

"Bishop, the phone will ring into your office in a matter of minutes, and it will connect you with both the McAbees."

After the obligatory hellos, Scarzi was on the point of his call.

"Gentlemen, Bishop O'Meara has informed me of his intention to settle the case with John Antle. He will leave Father Taylor to fend for himself. I need some information on the investigation."

Bertrand McAbee reported on the progress of the case. Scarzi was puzzled as he listened, and when Bertrand was finished, Scarzi asked, "What are these murders that you speak of? Surely they are not relevant to this case."

"I'm not sure of that Bishop. There are many ins and outs on this case. Every time I come to the end, I see another door. The guilt or innocence of Father Taylor is quite unclear to me. I spent several hours with him just a few days ago. He swears to his innocence, and as you know, he's a very compelling man. It could be mistaken identity"

"How about his faculties?" Bill asked sharply.

"How do you mean?" Bertrand responded.

"Well, is he slipping? Is his memory blown? Could he be guilty in reality but in his own reality of faulty thinking, think that he's innocent?"

"No. Head-wise he's fine. He's quite intelligent and sharp. That's not an issue as far as I can see."

"Bertrand ... you say new doors open. You say that ... maybe it was a case of mistaken identity. But I have a problem here." The Bishop was speaking slowly and deliberately. "Why would you believe this John Antle ... that he was abused ... and yet hold out that he was confused about who did it? It seems that if you allow for confusions on the who, you should also allow for confusion on the what."

There was no reply for a few seconds. Finally Bertrand said, "Very good question, Bishop. I'm going on two things: the notes from the sessions taken by the psychiatrist, the vividness about clerical garb and the feel of the information, and two, I met him. There's a terribly honest quality about him. I can't describe it to you. It's a feel I get. Terrible things sexual happened to John Antle."

"And you don't get the same feel from Father Taylor?" the Bishop asked.

"I do and I don't. I'm inclined to think that he's innocent, but I also feel there's more to this.

"Bishop," Bill interjected, "why is Bishop O'Meara settling this? The case is far from proven against Father Taylor. Also, it will make Taylor's defense doubly hard, since it will be apparent by the Diocesan action of what its conclusions are."

"Bill, this is exactly why I'm calling you on this matter. I don't think that the Bishop is handling this very well. I'm trying to make a judgment on this matter. Bertrand, is it possible that he knows something about this, some incriminating piece that you don't know?"

"Possibly, but I have no way of knowing that. When I met with some priests, they were also sure of Father Taylor's innocence, but, more alarmingly, they were outraged by the Bishop and his Chancellor, Monsignor Duncan."

Scarzi put his hand to his head and shook both back and forth. He figured that some priests would use Bertrand as a water boy to get their message of discontent back to Scarzi. But, on the other hand, the discontent might be pervasive.

Bertrand continued. "Father Taylor enjoys an almost universal support and love by his fellow priests."

"You're saying that you would not settle this out of court with what you have been able to turn up. Is this right?" the Bishop asked.

"Yes, without a doubt."

Absentmindedly, Scarzi had scrawled the word "Pope" on his writing tablet. It was the thing to do, he concluded.

The Vatican, August 1996

Pope John Paul came to the desk of Monsignor Brezinski just as Brezinski, on the telephone, was denying access to still another priest. Brezinski had been told to put walls up for the beleaguered man, a severely introverted man who was in a constant state of exhaustion from the demands of the office. The Pope noticed the name scribbled by Brezinski and signaled to him to cover the mouthpiece. He said, "Is that Bishop Scarzi?"

"Yes, your Holiness."

"What does he want?"

"To see you. I've already told him no."

"Get him in this afternoon, any time, and it is always 'any time' for him. Squeeze a few minutes for him."

He heard Brezinski do some loops and schedule Scarzi at 2:15 in the Pope's apartment. The Pope wasn't superstitious, but he did believe in 'occurrences' and his being at that desk at that very minute was perhaps an omen of sorts. He had certainly experience enough of these moments over the 18 years of his reign.

At 2:15 p.m., Scarzi was shown into the apartment by an outwardly contrite Monsignor Brezinski. God knows what the pugilistic little man Brezinski was thinking in his heart.

"Ah, Guillermo. Do sit down." He hugged Scarzi and looked into his eyes. He remembered him as a man of deep passion and robust health. Now he seemed so vulnerable. "I sense this is about Billy Taylor."

"Yes. There are things that are occurring in the Davenport Diocese that are quite troubling. I need your counsel."

"Speak freely, Guillermo," the Pope ordered.

The Pontiff listened intently for the ten minutes that Scarzi needed for the briefing. The Pope said, "Something is wrong here, I agree. Either O'Meara has a piece of information that is unknown to us, and it affects the very crux of the matter, or he is being precipitous and imprudent. In a case like this, summon him here to Rome under my direction. I wish to talk with him and tell him not to sign any agreement to pay a lira on this case until I have spoken with him. Guillermo. Good to see you. Come by again."

Scarzi left. The Pope knelt at his prie dieu and prayed for Billy Taylor.

CHAPTER SEVENTEEN

Iowa, August f 996

Augusta Satin drove out on Rural Route 12 in Clinton County in Iowa trying to ascertain the whereabouts of Bob Hartwig's farm. She wondered if McAbee took joy in sending her out into rural areas where African-Americans were perceived as some type of exotic species on the one hand or demons from ghettos on the other hand. "Okay!" she said to herself. The Hartwig name showed up on a roadside mailbox. She turned into the lane and drove into the main yard and parked to the right of a large farmhouse with white shingles and green trim. There was a barn about 75 feet to the west and a long, low, brick building very close to this bam, a huge shed to the east housed the heavy equipment of the farm.

She sat in the car for a few minutes, and when no one came, she got out. She walked out to the shed where she thought that she had heard some noises. There was a fifty-ish, heavyset, balding man forging a metal spike over a flame. He was bent over and part of his ass showed as ill-fitting jeans slid down his waist. A country-western radio station was blaring away about some double crossing dude who had better watch his back next time she sees him.

She didn't want to startle him and thus walked around the fire until she stood opposite him at about 12 feet. When he saw her, he jumped ever so slightly. She smiled as innocently as she could. She didn't need him chasing her around the barn with a fiery spike.

He yelled, "Hey you! Lookin for someone?"

"Yes." She was almost at the top of her voice. "Mr. and Mrs. Hartwig. I'm a private investigator."

"Well you won't find him here, Miss. He's been in a home for years. Mrs. Hartwig is over there now. You can either come back or show me some ID and maybe I'll let you wait inside." When she reached for her purse, he said, "Here. Why don't we go outside." He placed the spike or whatever he was working on into a pail of water, and there was a loud hiss.

When they got outside, she showed him her PI identification. He studied it and matched the picture before saying, "I'm Mrs. Hartwig's youngest great-nephew, Eddie. I'm helping out on the farm. What exactly to you want?"

"Oh, I'm working a case. You might know of him. The priest, Father Taylor. Trying to find out some background when he was the pastor of St. Anne's. Do you remember anything?"

"Not really. Bob, my great-uncle, was a big cheese there, but hell, he's useless to you now. His wife, my great-aunt, was a Methodist, so I don't know what she could tell you. Seemed to me that the holier he got, the holier she got at two ends of the pole, if you see what I mean. Don't know how they ever got involved with each other ... night and day, if you know what I mean."

"I was wondering if Mr. Hartwig had any records of his work at St. Anne's."

"Records?"

"Oh, you know. Old church bulletins, diaries, that kind of thing."

"I don't know. The Alzheimer's has been a real curse. But I'll tell you something. She stands by him. You gotta give her credit for that. If you want, I can take you up to the attic where they have all of his stuff. I don't think that she'd mind. She always says that when he dies, she's just gonna have a big bon fire of the whole thing. No saying when she'll get back though. Let me show you up there. But I warn you, it'll be hot. And I don't want you taking anything without her permission. Agreed?"

"You're real obliging. I'll just poke around," she said, surprised with her luck.

They went into the house. It was dark. The curtains and shades were shut. It looked as though the place was set back in the fifties. They went up to the second floor, and the man pulled down a step ladder from the ceiling and slowly climbed up the ladder and pushed open the door to the attic. "I'll be back in a minute." He disappeared for a few minutes, and she heard him walking around before his face showed up in the ceiling door. "OK, you can come up now."

It was hot to say the least. She saw shafts of light in several areas of the dusty attic, which was filled with all sorts of odds and ends. He placed an arm around her waist and pointed to a comer filled with objects and three old steamer trunks. Augusta sighed to herself, 'Unwelcome

232

sexual advance,' but she didn't want to alienate him. She was having an unusual stroke of luck. She took his arm gently, pulled away from his grasp, and shook his hand with as much strength as she could muster. She said, "Thanks. You've been so kind. I'll be out of your hair quickly."

He looked down at his shoes. She figured that he was going to make this hard or easy. He made it easy for both of them by saying, "Well, I'll be in the barn, Miss, if you need me. In case I'm gone, I'll leave a note for her so that you don't scare the living hell out of her." He smiled shyly, touched his baseball cap, and climbed down the ladder.

She moved quickly and began to check over the abundant materials. In one trunk there was just clothing, an old army uniform, a tuxedo, shirts, a Boy Scout uniform, and other sundries. She closed that lid. In the second trunk she found tax records and bills going back to the 1940s. Bob Hartwig had been a meticulous businessman/farmer. There was nothing here, however. She saw that the other trunk was covered by several old rugs and decided to look at the unboxed materials before taking it on. There were several old birdcages, a box of old iron toys, and numerous puzzles (500, 1000 pieces). She wondered if they were missing pieces or whether anyone had ever done the damn things.

Finally, she went to the third trunk. She pulled off the rugs and much to her frustration, she found that it was locked. If there was anything pertinent to Hartwig and Taylor, it could be in here. She studied the clasp. It had decay, and if she could find a nice pry of some sort, she could spring it. She looked elsewhere in the attic. She was soaked in perspiration. She was also getting a tingling feeling. The seemingly innocent attic environment had turned sinister.

She stopped and listened but heard nothing except for aging creaks of the old house. Her work continued. She found a hammer at the back end of the attic, and on her way back to the trunk, she took a quick inventory of the boxes, trunks, and loose objects lying around the entire attic. She saw nothing had a lock on it except for the trunk.

She tested the strength of the clasp. It would need a serious pry from the pry part of the hammer, and she was reluctant. She looked at the lock. It was a simple iron lock. She took out her key tools and started to pick the lock. She was never adept at this art. Perspiration flowed across her intent face as she worked in the ill-lit attic.

She heard a vehicle drive up to the house. A minute later, the lock opened. She opened the trunk as she heard the great nephew, Eddie, yelling at what was probably Hartwig's wife. Other than the exchange of voices, she couldn't hear distinctly what was being said. The trunk was divided into two sections: newspapers and magazines, and letters and picture albums. The newspapers were yellowed. They were dated all the way back to the fifties. Beneath the papers were magazines. She said, "Jesus, Lord!" Some of them were four inches by six inches with black and white photos of naked children. Names like *Boy Love, Hot and Young, and Manly Delight* stunned her. It was a pedophile's trunk of goodies. She heard the creak of the steps. They were coming up from the first floor.

Quickly she looked at the letters and picture albums. She stood up and hid two magazines down inside her pants and took two letters at random and did the same. She heard the voice, "Miss ... Miss ... you'll have to come down now."

"OK. Coming. Sorry." She closed the trunk hurriedly,

put the lock back on, and threw the rugs over it. As she turned around, she could see his head just appearing out of the floor. She strode over quickly and said, "I couldn't find anything, but I was wondering ... there's a locked trunk.."

"We'll ask Auntie," he said tentatively.

Auntie was one mean-looking bitch. She had a stare about her that could go through a wall. Her mouth was stern, and her head was cocked to the side. Augusta figured that was her natural state. What would happen when her blackness sunk in? They stood gazing at each other on the second-floor landing. Augusta said, "Mrs. Hartwig, my name is Augusta Satin. I'm working on the Father Taylor case, and I'm...."

"Enough of that nonsense. I don't care what you're working on, brown lady. You stay out of our business! You have no right to be prying around my husband's possessions."

"Well, I was let in by your great-nephew. I. ..."

"Enough! You hear? I want you out of this house now! And if you come back, I'll blow your goddamn head off! And as to you ...," she turned to Eddie, "what in god's name has gotten into you?"

Augusta took the offensive. "Do you have something against Father Taylor? All I'm looking for is something to exonerate him. I'm not trying to embarrass your husband. I understand he was a big assistance to St. Anne's parish."

"Listen . . . Father Taylor, and actually that whole damn bunch of Romanist dogs, are beneath my contempt. Yes, beneath my contempt."

"There's a locked trunk up there. I'd really appreciate getting access to it."

"That trunk will not exist tonight! Now get out!"

Augusta walked down the stairs. She heard Mrs. Hartwig bark out a command to Eddie. "Take those three trunks down from there, put them in the yard, and burn the goddamn things. Now!"

Augusta felt the materials in her pants. She got in her car and drove away toward the town of DeWitt, where she picked up a garden salad for lunch at McDonald's. She slid the two letters out from her pants and grabbed a corner in the restaurant and looked at them. They were both addressed to Birdsong Inc., P.O. Box 91, DeWitt, Iowa. The postmark of the one, which was on light-blue stationery, read: "Canal Fulton, Ohio, February 6, 1968." She removed the notecard inside and read:

> Dear Birdsong,
>   Our mutual friend, Grape Jelly, will be in your neighborhood around Valentine's Day. Keep your Cupid's arrow ready for the little sharpie with him.
>
>   Donkey

Augusta looked around. A woman from across the room quickly looked down. It was the old story and the old question. Did she look down because Augusta was a black and in lily white DeWitt, or did she look down because she was trailing Augusta? She figured the former and went on to the next note, which was postmarked "Madison, Wisconsin, June 3, 1977."

> Birdsong,
>   Thanks for the contact with Chickenfingers. He gave me some grade-A

material. I can't get it out of my mind.
Forever indebted.

The Kidder

With no one sitting near her, she slid out the two
magazines. They were both dated from 1969. *Ah Kids* was
the title. One was from spring, the other the summer. She
was angry with herself. It wasn't a good cross selection of
the magazines, but she cut it as close as she could, and she
had been specifically warned by the great-nephew not to
take anything. The spring issue had 64 pages. There were
a number of ads for other literature, pen pals, and the like.

There was a column espousing the purity and beauty of
pedophilia with many references to Greek civilization. The
rest of the magazine had pictures of prepubescent children
in a variety of poses, some naked, some clothed.

She wondered about this little underground that she had
wandered into: How deep it was? How populated it was? And
the kids? Where did they find them? Did they abuse them?
Were their parents involved? But the letters that Hartwig
received were more troublesome. They appeared to suggest
a real trade in children among a hardcore underground, and
Bob Hartwig was right in the middle of it. She figured that
Bertrand would be elated, since there was an alternative to
Father Taylor as the perpetrator.

As Augusta got into her car, she was struck with one
more thought, however. What if Hartwig <u>and</u> Taylor were
in cahoots. Taylor was not free from suspicion yet after all.

She drove back by the Hartwig farm. There was a small
trace of smoke coming from the yard, and while she couldn't

see for sure, she figured that all three trunks had just been torched.

Minneapolis, August 1996

The Princess did not like to act quickly. It was the downfall of so many who made their living outside the pale of the law. He had always been a prodigious planner. When he had received his MBA from the University of Minnesota, he had been awarded a commendation by the Management Department for the best graduate paper of the year. It was a detailed piece on the cognitive processes that drive effective strategic planning. It was such a good effort that he had been offered scholarship entry into their doctoral program. By this time, however, he already had established his antique business, was fully engaged in a gay lifestyle, which included nightclub acts and, more importantly, had murdered two people on a contract basis. At the beginning, he charged only $5,000; now the figures were negotiable, but generally his minimum was $20,000 in cash, and there was nothing like tax-free money.

Toby Leonard was worth $2 million, money which stood in Switzerland, Mexico, and Bermuda. His greatest claims to pride were that he had never been identified (with the exception of Scannell and that creep in Iowa City) and his efficiency as a killer. His victims never knew they were dead. He took out of his MBA courses two insights into himself. In a Business Ethics course, the professor had spoken of Lawrence Kohlberg and the stages of moral development. The most elementary of these stages was that behavior was driven by fear of pain, and if that fear was not present, the person would act out. It was the profile of a psychopath; it was also the profile of Toby Leonard. In an Organizational Behavior class, there were references to self-monitoring. Some people were very unaware of how they affected others in contrast to high self-monitors who were acutely aware of how they affected others. This latter was Toby Leonard.

His parents were both professional actors, and before they divorced when he was 11, he had learned a great deal about disguises and makeup. It was so natural for him, and he knew that he was quite good. While attending St. Olaf College in St. Peter's, Minnesota, he was called Mister Makeup. He loved to fool people.

His ability to shoot a gun was learned from a lover who had been an ex-Army man, who had kept up his skills on a shooting range. Toby was a natural, he said.

While waiting for Scannell, he placed a large plastic lawn table cover in his car trunk. Scannell was a detested bastard who had Toby by his proverbial balls. But now was the time to change this. At 9:50p.m. he opened up his double garage door and the inside door leading to his house. He put on the lights all over the house, lit up his garage, and put on his stereo. He filled up a cocktail glass with ginger ale and watched for Scannell, a worthy adversary who, if he made a mistake, would kill him.

When he saw Scannell's car moving up the driveway, he came out of his house's entry door and into the garage proper, drink in hand, and waived Scannell into the garage. Scannell looked confused as he rolled down his window at the apron entry way. Scannell said, "What's going on?" "Oh, nothing. I have three friends who are just about to leave. Just a few minutes and we'll be able to talk. Why don't you drive in and have a drink." The party angle, the three friends, the music, the lighting all confused Scannell.

"Ok, but I don't want to be made by them."

"Well, you can stay in here, and I'll come out when they go. They'll be gone in a few minutes."

Scannell looked at The Princess warily and said, "OK." He drove in as the garage door descended. He started to get out of the car as Leonard went behind Scannell's door and reached down under his own car for a baseball bat. Toby Leonard was quick … always was … and by the time Scannell had come to his full height and was turning around to face Leonard, the bat was swinging across and square into Scannell's head. His last words were, "What the f…."

Toby watched him drop against his car and onto the floor. He muttered, "Didn't get the word 'fuck' out, did you, you slime ball?" There was more blood than he wanted. He immediately placed towels around Scannell's head to absorb the flow and took a two-gallon baggie and put it over Scannell's head and tied a knot with another towel to stop leakage. He placed the still-living Scannell into his trunk at considerable effort and began to watch Scannell's face turn blue as he smothered to death. "Voila! A new kind of kill!" He took a hose and washed the still-fresh blood down his drain. He threw the baseball bat and his bloodied sweatshirt into his car trunk, opened his garage door, and drove off. For a split second he thought he saw a movement near the bushes adjoining his property, but he decided to let it go. The main project was the disposal of Scannell's body.

He drove to a deserted landing in St. Paul that was built on the Mississippi River. He removed the body from his trunk, pulled off the baggie, took off the bloodied towels from around the head, and tossed all them into an outsized plastic bag, and dropped the body into the Mississippi, after removing all identification. He then drove to the campus of the University of St. Thomas, which was pretty deserted, found a dumpster that was half full and tossed all of the materials from the murder into the large container. Scannell, at last, was out of his life. On his way home, he saw a car parked about a block away from his house. Someone was in it, but he thought that it was probably just an innocent thing. He made the intention, however, to be extra alert tomorrow, just in case.

The very old lady with a cane and severe osteoporosis stepped out of Scannell's car and headed toward the elevator to Martin Youngquist's office. The old lady was preoccupied. She had been followed, but she made the car, that was the big thing. She carried a shopping bag with her.

When she got into Youngquist's offices, the receptionist took sympathy on her and helped her to a seat, saying, "You have an appointment with … ?"

"Martin Youngquist," she said shakily.

The secretary's eyes were knitted, but she said nothing. She was probably expecting a young sex kitten who was ravished by three priests. 'Stay puzzled, you little bitch,' The Princess said to himself.

Martin Youngquist came out shortly after the secretary had probably alerted him. He came over to her and asked demandingly and suspiciously, "Surely, Miss, you're not the one who called me yesterday. What is this?"

The Princess said, "I had her call you. I'm her grandmother. I know how good you are. She has cold feet.

She's in shock. I just want to give you the details and some names, and I'll be out of your way. OK?"

He hesitated before saying, "I'll give you a few minutes. Come in."

He brought her over to a round table and helped her sit down. He was an arrogant, officious, smarmy cock sucker. It would be a pleasure to murder the bastard.

"Now tell me what this is about?"

"I have a letter here. I need to be beside you when you read it. Please indulge me, young man. A real crime has been committed by these so-called Catholic priests." She noticed that Martin Youngquist enjoyed her take on priests.

She removed the letter from her purse and got up painfully and walked over to Youngquist, to whom she handed the letter. He took it and opened it, and as he did, she drew out her Walther cum silencer, and pressed the gun to Youngquist's head and fired. His brains exploded on the white wall. She didn't do her customary coup de grace. It was unnecessary. She kept the gun in her hand as she heard the secretary knock at his door and yell, "Mr. Youngquist? Is everything OK?" There had been enough of a noise to startle her.

The Princess opened the door and said to her, "He seems to have fainted. Help me." As she moved to help, the secretary was dead, two seconds later.

Quickly Toby Leonard went to the door, listened, and hearing nothing, left. He went to a bathroom and closeted himself in a stall where he washed off the specks of blood and changed into a pair of jeans and white tee shirt. He placed the old lady's clothes into his shopping bag and left for his car. Aware of the tail, which was parked about five cars from his, he moved behind the tail, whose eyes were riveted on Scannell's car. He was listening to some talk show on WCCO. The last thing the poor bastard ever heard in his open windowed car was, "Give us a call." He'd be looking for the old lady for an eternity.

Leonard hailed a cab and took it to the Edina Public Library, where he read for about a half hour. He picked up the bag and dumped it into a Burger King garbage can.

He walked home. He checked his place once again and called for a taxi. It had been an intense time, and he was pleased when the Northwest Airlines plane took off for Chicago where he transferred to a Mexicana flight and was in Mexico City by 7:00p.m.

His place had been opened and stocked, and he stood on his deck at 9:00p.m., looking over Mexico City, with a drink in his hand. He had only one regret. Who was the son-of-a-bitch who had made him in Iowa City? Someday he would kill him.

CHAPTER EIGHTEEN

Iowa, August 1996

Bertrand McAbee drove north and west toward the Samaritan Home in Calamus, Iowa, one of the countless small towns in Iowa. It would have its gas station, probably in combination with a small grocery store, a tavern, and not much else except for a dwindling population.

The past 24 hours had left him a bit harried. So many events around this one case made him think of it as being a tar baby-once touched, forever attached.

The news from Scholz was what first came to him. There had been four murders, and one of them had been in his own operation, a man by the name of O'Brien. Scholz was depressed and angry with himself. He felt that he had mishandled the Scannell situation, that he should have had all four men working on the case at one time. He had made a terrific error in judgment, and it had cost a man his life. "My reputation will be forever flawed now-1 lost a man." McAbee wondered whether he was grieving for O'Brien or for his own reputation. Whatever it was, Scholz was more vulnerable than McAbee had ever seen the man. "I won't send you a bill on this one, McAbee. I feel that I have to bear this, and don't argue with me," he said adamantly. McAbee didn't.

The deaths of Scannell and Youngquist, however, caused McAbee great confusion. Was this some type of revenge for what happened in Iowa City to Margaret Aaron and her nurse? Or was it a falling out in a hive of thieves and bottom feeders? And did it have anything to do with the pseudo UPS driver? If it did, she or he was one dangerous person.

Scholz went on to detail what he could turn up by way of a friend of a friend in the Minneapolis Police Department. Scannell had been murdered by asphyxiation after he had been clubbed with a piece of wood-ash-and thus probably a baseball bat. He had been murdered somewhere else and taken to the Mississippi River and dumped. Scholz had seen him drive into a garage in Edina, owned by an antique dealer named Toby Leonard, who has disappeared. He looks fairly close to the Iowa City assassin, from a picture of him in the *Star Tribune*.

The cops searched his house and found nothing as far as a Scannell presence and/or a murder. One of the investigators said that his house was decorated in 'sterile queer.'

"I saw Scannell come but saw, presumably, this Toby Leonard leave almost immediately after Scannell got there. I lost him. I reconnoitered the house but didn't see anything. Leonard got back around 12:30 a.m., and from what I could see, went to bed. I figured Scannell was there. His car was still in the garage. O'Brien relieved me at 6:00a.m. and tracked Scannell's car ... he called in ... to a parking garage under Youngquist's office building. He didn't know what to do, because he said that Scannell's car was being driven by an old lady! Scannell's car was impounded by the police. It had been left in the parking garage. The old lady stuff makes no sense. The cops are pressing. Everyone wants to talk with Toby Leonard, but he's gone … to Mexico. They're sending some cops down to talk with him."

"So now what happens?"

"I'll stay up here and be a presence for the O'Brien family, and I'll start looking into this Leonard guy. If he offed O'Brien, we'll take him out privately."

Of course, Augusta's news was more salient in terms of his investigation. She had found a smoking gun. Bob Hartwig was a pedophile of the first order, and now the question was, did he violate John Antle and did Antle confuse the robed Hartwig with the robed Father Taylor? Augusta reported that Hartwig had advanced Alzheimer's and that she had pretty much worn out her welcome at the Hartwig farm; in fact, she was convinced that Mrs. Hartwig would blow her away. "It's time for a sweet talker like you, Bertrand."

The Samaritan Home was on the western edge of Calamus, which went three blocks deep on it south side, one block deep on its north side, and about the equivalent of four blocks on an east west axis. It had a population of 297 according to the DOT sign. The Samaritan Home was a one story brick complex that sat about 200 feet off Highway 30, which severed the town. McAbee figured it held about 40 residents and was probably a nice little profit center sucking off Medicaid, Medicare, and the life savings of its residents.

The place smelled like Clorox as he entered it. It wasn't air conditioned. The windows were open and fans were beating the air. There were two visitor's rooms to his left, a row of three offices to his right, and then a long hallway with rooms on either side. Halfway up this narrow hallway, this wing of the building was bisected by still another long building which created a circle at its nexus. This was the dining room, TV room, and entertainment center. No one saw him, and he walked straight ahead up the corridor. The smell got stronger in the humid and warm environment. It was a battle between human waste and Clorox, with no clear winner and many clear losers. Some rooms seemed to be singles; however, some rooms had two beds which allowed for virtually no free space. It took an act of will for him to look at the names of the patients (AKA residents). He passed a nurse or an aide or whatever they were called. She said nothing. She looked to be in her sixties. She probably figured he was a doctor and that it was none of her business.

His gaze caught the eye of some of the patients, and their empty expressions seared through him. He heard his brother Bill's voice: 'Bertrand, you're a poet or something. Stay out of bad things you weren't made for there.' He wondered if they could see themselves from their youth and what they would say. He figured most of them would say, 'Kill me.' He hoped that when his time came, and no one has beaten the time, that he would not have to endure this stockpiling of futility. Perhaps you only realize that you've become one when you can't do anything about it.

At Room 17 he saw the name Bob Hartwig. He went in. Hartwig was tied to a wheelchair. He was looking out the window. The day was hot and cloudless as it probably appeared on his empty screen of a brain.

"Mr. Hartwig … Mr. Hartwig … Bob?" McAbee touched his shoulder. He wore a tee shirt and didn't have pants on or even underwear. He was sitting on a bowl that fit into the wheelchair. They probably let him sit there all day as long as he leaked out his body fluids in a proper way.

McAbee turned his wheelchair around and looked at him. 'Jesus,' he said to himself, 'abandon all hope all ye who enter here.' "Excuse me, Sir. Sir? Can I help you?" She was a large, red-haired woman. The name on her ID said 'Chris Worthy, RN.' She was more curious than anything else, it seemed.

McAbee walked to the doorway where she stood and said, "I'm Bertrand McAbee. I'm a private investigator. I wanted to ask Mr. Hartwig some questions."

She looked at him with an air of incredulity before responding. "Look. Nothing personal, but it's customary to stop into the office first before you see a patient. Secondly, Hartwig is beyond any conversation, believe me. He's in the zombie zone for good." She patted McAbee on the arm before continuing. "And lastly, it takes an adjustment of attitude to come into this place, mister, and, to be frank with you, you don't look too good. Whatever you hoped to get from him won't happen. Why don't you just go and get some fresh air." She smiled at him.

Bertrand McAbee had just been given the heave ho, Iowa style: polite, caring, but get the hell out of here. He had also been given a look into the future, and he wasn't handling it very well. He got into the Explorer and drove toward Hartwig's farm. Augusta's directions had been flawless.

He drove into the yard, not knowing what to expect. Would Mrs. Hartwig come out with a shotgun? Augusta saw her as being a screwball. He got out of the Explorer and walked up the stairs to the house and knocked at the screen door. After about 15 seconds, he rapped louder and heard from somewhere deep in the house: "Come in. I'll be with you in a minute."

He stayed in the hallway. The house was quite dark and the contrast with the sunlit day was powerful. He was shaken from his reverie by a "Yeah? What do you want?"

"Mrs. Hartwig? Bertrand McAbee."

He didn't extend his hand. Her icy look told him to keep his physical distance. "You had a visitor by the name of Augusta Satin, a licensed private investigator. Am I right?"

She cocked her head and said, "Yeah. What of it?"

"She said to give you her apologies," he lied.

"Yeah? And?"

"I'd like to talk with you if I could."

"Nothing to talk about. You want to know about my husband, go talk with him over in Calamus."

"I just came from there. We didn't have much of a conversation." He looked at her sadly.

After digesting his statement, she said, "And that's what you're going to get from me. There's nothing to tell you. And when that brownie got upstairs, I ordered Bob's trunks burned. So there ain't anything. Hear? So, I think that you should probably get moving on now."

McAbee figured he had a chance and played it. "Mrs. Hartwig, while she was up there, she found some stuff that said your husband was into child sex abuse."

She shot back, "Nonsense. There was nothing up there, and it's all gone."

"No, it isn't. She saw it and brought me a few pieces of it."

"Impossible. It was in a locked .... OK, mister, you best get your ass off of my land."

"Please, Mrs. Hartwig. Listen to me." She stopped in her steps as she was heading for her kitchen and turned toward McAbee. "It won't hurt you. Everything is settled. I just have to know something. Was Father Taylor involved?"

"Goddamn Romanists. They're all that way."

"No, that's not true. Do you have good reason to suspect Father Taylor in any of this? Please answer me."

She paused for a few seconds. "Look, mister, I'll say this once and that's it. I came onto Bob's other life by accident about 20 years ago. I never told him because I'm not a snoop. To this day, he doesn't know that I know. Now, of course, it's too late to say anything. As to Taylor, I don't know. I never saw his name on anything. But he's a priest, and he's probably into it. Now, get out and stay out!"

McAbee left. So, again, it came down to Billy Taylor. Was he or wasn't he?

Iowa, August 1996

Kim Rice sat in Chip Blaine's car as they drove to the Chancery. There was now a permanent strain in her relationship with him. She wondered about her future with the firm. At least Blaine had started to keep his hands off her, and he was curbing his sexist remarks. The downside to that was that he no longer trusted her. The mentoring relationship was shattered. She wondered what this meeting would come to with the authoritarian Bishop and his casuistic Chancellor. Rome had really dumped a pair of losers into the Diocese.

She was broken from her reverie by the harsh tone of Blaine's voice as they drove into a parking space in front of the chancery building. "Just be there today. I don't need your comments, and I don't need you getting these two pissed off. Don't forget. I got you into this as a favor to you. While this account doesn't earn me much money, it has cachet, and cachet is half the game-class, class, class!"

She figured that Blaine was telling her that she didn't have class or cachet or, at least, until she kissed his ass, apologized, and dropped her skirt. She didn't respond.

He stared at her as he pulled his keys from the ignition and said, "Well? Do I get a response, Miss Rice?"

"I won't say a word, I promise," she said with more sullenness than she wanted to transmit.

The Bishop and his flunky were already seated. Monsignor Duncan gave a big welcoming smile to Chip Blaine and pulled out a chair from the table for him. There was no eye contact for Kim and certainly no chair etiquette. He looked in her general direction and said "Hello" in his airiest and sweetest tone. If she had been a dog, it would be like a distracted pat on the head. The Bishop looked at her with his usual frown of intolerance. She felt that Duncan and O'Meara had already decided to call for her head if she made even a slight peep in their proceedings. Whether Blaine was in on this freeze or not, she didn't know.

"So, Chip," the Bishop intoned with his Irish brogue under control, "the news of the death of Martin Youngquist and his investigator, Scanlon ... no ... Scannell, an Irish name for shame, leaves Monsignor Duncan and me in a state of confusion. How does it affect the case?"

"The offer is still good. I called his associate, Wilbur Bevington, and he said the deal maintains until they take it off. They're going to review all of his files in the next few days. But let me add. They've all been recruited, in my judgment, because of their hatred of the Church. Martin Youngquist is being replaced by still another hater. Whether they'll be as successful with their hatred remains to be seen, but there's nothing like a bullet to the brain to cause a little hesitancy." All three smiled, even the Bishop whose smile made him look as though he was having a difficult bowel movement. "My recommendation is simple. Get out now! The insurance company is OK with this. The only problem is Taylor, and I feel we'll just let him swing. Of course," he looked at Kim Rice with a bit of concern, "I represent all of my clients sedulously." He pulled the cuff of each of his shirt sleeves.

The Bishop responded, "As you know, Bishop Scarzi has asked me to suspend these talks, and he wants me to come to Rome. I have no great love for Roman intervention in the affairs of this Diocese, but, of course, I will have to appear in Rome. What I need from you, Chip, is a clear and explicit recommendation to settle this case as soon as possible."

Blaine took out his folder, got up, and presented a packet to O'Meara. "I suggest that you and Monsignor George look these papers over as I talk about each." The letter to the Bishop corresponded to what the Bishop had just requested. Blaine then went on to speak of the settlement with the Youngquist firm, including the approved press release which read:

The Diocese of Davenport has settled a complaint of sexual abuse filed by John Antle against the Diocese of Davenport and Father William Taylor. Diocesan officials said that even the very perception of irregularities was unacceptable. The complaint by John Antle against Father Taylor remains in the litigation process.

The Martin Youngquist firm of Minneapolis said the case is still another example of "clerical hubris and irresponsibility." No sums were disclosed.

So, the Youngquist firm received a free ad, and the Diocese sort of apologized and protected its pocket book from a further hit. Poor Taylor was left out to rot and at the mercy of Chip Blaine, who probably would toss him to the wolves to show the sagacity of Bishop O'Meara and his chief poisoner, Monsignor Duncan. Everyone was coming up a winner except for Taylor, Margaret Aaron, her nurse, Youngquist, and Scannell. Would anyone ever put this whole mess together? Kim wondered about Bertrand McAbee and what he was up to. Ethically, she wanted to talk with him, but legally she couldn't. To do so would jeopardize her license to practice law and her word, but that consideration was offset by this den of thieves.

The Bishop said, "Well, it looks as though my hand is forced by your advice. I'm signing the papers authorizing the settlement."

Monsignor Duncan said, "Very courageous of you, Bishop. The easiest thing to do here is to accede to Scarzi and his ilk who have no knowledge of Diocesan conditions and problems. I'm sure that the Roman bureaucrats will see the wisdom of what you did when it's all explained to them."

"Here! Here!" Blaine intoned as the Bishop signed away a large piece of integrity. In Kim's judgment, they had just made a pact with the devil, and Father Taylor's head was the prize.

When O'Meara had finished signing the papers, Blaine looked at both him and Duncan and said, "I know that you'll inform Rome in due course. Obviously, I have nothing to advise on that matter. However, I do think that we owe a brief explanation to Bertrand McAbee since he has some semi-official status in this case. Do you want me to call him, or will you, Bishop?"

O'Meara reflected on Blaine's question for a full minute and said, "Why don't we call him right now? We'll both tell him. How's that?"

Blaine shrugged his shoulders as if to say that was as good a choice as any other. The Bishop walked to his desk and said to his secretary to find McAbee. She did and McAbee was on the telephone in less than 45 seconds. The Bishop said, "Dr. McAbee, just a word. As far as the Diocese is concerned, we have no real interest in the Taylor case anymore. We have just settled out of the case. Father Taylor is all that remains, and that, of course, is up to him."

He listened for a minute and Kim could see the blood rushing to his face as he said with too much control in his voice, "He got himself into this without the help of the Diocese, and he can get himself out of this without the help of the Diocese. Here is Mr. Blaine. I don't want you meddling any longer in the affairs of this Diocese, sir,"

He handed the phone to Blaine who said, "McAbee? Did you get this message? I will stay on and represent Father Taylor, but he's in the cold now."

Blaine listened and looked at Bishop O'Meara as if to say that he shared in the Bishop's exasperation with McAbee. He responded to McAbee, "OK. I understand your view. But the point is this. You're now working for a man who will probably have to declare bankruptcy. He's a dead fish, McAbee, and there's nothing else to say."

He listened some more and said, "Well, whomever you're working for, I don't want to hear anything you have to say. Look, this isn't going to go away until he goes public with his guilt, begs for forgiveness, and, in this case, goes bankrupt. Come on. You know the drill. It's the American way!" He laughed mirthlessly and hung up. "Watch out for that pest, Bishop, Monsignor. He's pretty convinced that Taylor is innocent. Something about mistaken identity. Well, gotta go. It's been a real pleasure." They shook hands and patted each other on the back. Kim was excluded.

When Blaine and she got back to the car, Blaine said, "You did well today, Kim." He put his hand on her knee and squeezed.

She said, "Take your hand off my knee."

He gave her a long glowering look and said, "A little testy today, aren't we?"

Kim figured that she was dead at the firm and then said, "I can't believe what just happened in there. Why is it assumed that Father Taylor is guilty?"

"Kim," he shot back, "I'll say this once to you and that's it. It doesn't matter whether the old bastard is guilty or not.

The point is its eenie-meenie-minie-moe, and he's out, and when you're out, you're out," he said ominously. That was a message that was meant for her as much as it was meant for Taylor, she concluded.

CHAPTER NINETEEN

Iowa, September 1996

Bertrand McAbee was starting to run again. Scorpio was as excited as a three-month-old Puppy as they started back out on the country roads of Scott County. He had been warned to stretch, start slowly, stop at the slightest hint of pain or muscle tightening, and figure that it would take two months before getting near where he was. "And. McAbee, it's time to face up the fact that you're never getting back to where you were. You simply cannot and should not run every day. Seven miles, eventually. OK? But only three times a week, and back of the racquetball. Understand? It's coming to grips with your age. I've seen a lot of guys hit a wall. They get angry, they hurt themselves, and then they stop altogether. Before long, they are 50 pounds heavier, and they spend the rest of their athletic time in a golf cart. I can't stress this any clearer," his orthopedist stated flatly.

And while McAbee wasn't a particularly obedient person, he was, as people go, pretty obedient to doctors whom he respected. So, he ran three miles and huffed and puffed and tried to keep between a heart beat of 150 to

160 with the help of his Polar heart band. His legs seemed fine, but he had no breath. That would have to come. Even Scorpio was doing a little gasping as they hit the front door of the house. He was taking off Scorpio's leash when Gloria came across his lawn. Scorpio didn't even bother to give her a suspicious look, as he headed for his water bowl on the kitchen floor,

"Gloria?" McAbee wasn't anxious to deal with Gloria Now, but he was still feeling guilty about the beating that she took in a previous case and which subsequently enabled him to catch a murderer.

"Betrand, I have a letter for you." It was thick and had on it the Diocese of Davenport seal. "A man came with it 15 minutes ago. I saw leaving with Scorpio. I'm happy to see you off running again. I came over and he gave it to me. He said it was quite important."

"Thanks, Gloria." Scorpio had now come back to the door and was pressing his white head against Gloria's fingers, demanding attention and petting in exchange for his continued good will.

"I don't see much of you anymore, it seems. Are you on a big case?"

"Yes. A really interesting one. This letter is relevant to it, I'm sure. I'm not a pen pal of the Bishop."

She smiled. She knew enough of his habits to know that Bertrand was no church goer. "Well, have a good day, Bertrand. I have some stew if you'd like some." She patted him on the arm.

"No, that's OK." They both knew that Bertrand was an unusual eater. Fortunately, she had backed off from pressing him on the issue.

He didn't read the letter until he had showered and shave and shaved and went into his kitchen for some toast and coffee. Not for the first time, he thought back on Bob Hartwig sitting on his porta-potty looking out the window whit his dead Alzheimer's eyes. McAbee, always too impersonal for those near him, telephoned Gloria and caught her answering machine. "Gloria, maybe I was short with you before. I really appreciate your getting that letter for me, and of course, all the other things that you do. Don't ever forget that." He hung up. She was probably in her garden. He was slightly relieved that she wasn't in her house. This way he didn't have to speak with her. 'Proof, stupid, of just how locked in you are,' he said to himself disdainfully as he opened the Diocesan letter.

Dear Dr. McAbee:

This is to notify you that the Diocese of Davenport has settled its case with John Antle. Father Taylor is now his own agent and can continue to use the services of the Blaine Law Firm if he so chooses. In addition, we command that you seek our approval for all further interviews of any Diocesan employees up to and including Father Taylor himself. Feel free to call Monsignor George Duncan should you need any further clarification.

In Christ,
Bishop Brendan O'Meara

P.S. Enclosed please find a copy of the Antle settlement.

McAbee perused the settlement. The monetary figures were blacked out. What was left was the usual nonsense, that the Diocese does not admit to guilt in the matter and that Antle forever hold the Diocese free of any further action in the matter. Billy Taylor was carrion from here on in as far as the Diocese was concerned.

McAbee wondered whether Rome had approved this or whether they even knew about it. According to the document, a cashier's check had already been drawn and delivered to the Youngquist firm acting on behalf of John Antle.

What was of greater concern was the effort by O'Mera, probably at the behest of Chip Blaine, to freeze McAbee, and indirectly Scarzi, out of the case. Bishop Scarzi was not the kind of person to trifle with, and O'Meara appeared to be doing just that.

He called his brother in New York City. Bill was not available unless there was an absolute emergency. Bertrand left a detailed message with his secretary and started to drive to Iowa City. It was time to speah with John Antle again. Antle was not at McDonald's. He drove to his apartment, which was situated in downtown Iowa City. Formerly a large house, it now had five different apartments with tangled entrances. Antle rented apartment #4, as best as McAbee could tell. He knocked and the door was opened almost immediately. Antle seemed to be waiting for someone.

"What do you want?" he asked hesitatingly. He wore sandals, tan cutoffs, and a T-shirt.

"May I come in for a few minutes?" McAbee asked.

Antle hesitated and then moved his arm with a slight inviting flourish. The apartment was bare except for a bed in the corner, a small table and three wooden chairs. He had a bemused smile on his face. "Like the décor?" he asked.

"A bit bare for my taste, but whatever works for you," McAbee said with a smile. "Perhaps with the settlement you can go upscale."

The look on Antle's face was confusing. This wasn't the demeanor of a man who had just hit a small jackpot. McAbee sat on one of the slatted chairs and looked up at Antle, who eventually retreated to the far corner of his efficiency unit and sat on the edge of his bed.

"I don't feel good about all of this, but they tell me it's due to the abuse that I underwent. I guess that makes sense."

"They?" McAbee said.

"Oh, the firm up in Minneapolis, Younquist's people. There sure are a lot of people getting killed. I guess it's just bad karma."

"Yeah, that's one take on it," McAbee said cautiously. He gave him plenty of time to respond, but Antle didn't. McAbee said, "I've been on the trail of this, and I found out a few things. May I share them with you?'

He took his non answer as a permission to go forward. He removed five items from a small folder that he carried with him and walked toward John Antle's bed. "Do you mind if I sit?" Antle flexed his fingers outward and McAbee sat. He took a picture that he had retrieved from the St. Anne's records. It was a group picture taken at Easter of 1972 after a mass. There were 20 people in it, including Taylor, Hartwig, and Antle. He passed it over to Antle who looked at it for about two minutes before passing it back to McAbee.

"John, who's Father Taylor in this?" Antle pointed to Taylor correctly.

"And who is Mr. Hartwig? Do you remember him?"

He looked at McAbee with a puzzled explression before saying, "I don't know a Hartwig."

"How could you forget him? He was a big cheese there for years. He's the shorter, pudgy guy in the second row on the left."

He took hold of the picture again and studied it. "What can I say? I don't remember him."

McAbee saw no reason to disbelieve him as he took back the picture and handed over the first of the notes recovered by Augusta. "Would you read this?"

He looked at the address and slid out the note addressed to Hartwig and read it. He looked away to some corner of the room and then back to McAbee. "I don't see what you're getting at."

"Look, John, the money you have from the Diocese is secure. It can't be taken away from you. I'm not here to hurt you of trick you, but I do have very sincere doubts that Father Taylor molested you."

"Jesus," he said with tears in his eyes, "I can't believe you're saying this. I can feel his filthy hands on me… oh, Jesus!" He put his head down, shook it back and forth and cried.

"John I don't doubt that you were molested. I never did after meeting with you. Nor do I doubt that something happened to you at St. Anne's. But perhaps it wasn't Father Taylor. There's just no evidence on this. A man's life can be found in every corner of all the possible sins that are out there. I can't find Father Taylor in most of these sins, and especially in this kind of sin. Father Taylor might not be a saint, in fact, I think that he'd get very upset if he heard someone say that, but I don't think he's a pedophile. Hartwig, however, is another matter. What does that letter tell you?"

"Then why did the Diocese settle?" he asked with gentle defensiveness.

"Because the Diocese was afraid, that's all I can fathom." Antle just sat there staring ahead. McAbee gave him the second note, which he read, shaking his head ever so slightly. "My investigator, Augusta Satin, spoke with two other altar boys around your time. To the best of their memories, they adamantly deny any sexual experience."

"So did I before I went to Dr. Aaron. It's way down there, you know?"

"I'm sure." There was a long delay again. McAbee could hear blues music coming from somewhere in the partitioned house. McAbee took out both of the child porn magazines and handed them to Antle, who looked at them for a brief minute before tossing them back at McAbee.

"So, I guess you found these under Hartwig's pillow?

"Not quite. In a trunk in his attic. He's in a home now... Alzheimer's ... there are no lights on in his head. I tried to speak with him. There's no doubt in my mind that he's the one who violated you, John, but I can't offer you any proof. I can only offer you the little that I have."

"But if ... if .. . what you say is true, how come . .. well ... the other altar boys are probably repressing.'

"Or he didn't touch them because there was some interference," McAbee responded.

"Interference?"

"Perhaps Taylor became aware of Hartwig and stopped it. I don't know. Maybe Hartwig was into types and you were one of them and the others weren't."

"And? Now what? What do you want from me? I didn't even want to get into this stuff. Dr. Aaron pushed me and then this firm... Scannell ... they were brutal. I couldn't get out without declaring bankruptcy. And now you tell me I hit the wrong guy. And you know what? I'm inclined to believe you. I never felt right about the damn thing, and when they called me and suggested that I take $300,000, I said fine. I would have said fine just to be let out of the thing. I feel so terribly dirty and used ... used again." McAbee sympathized with Antle. His vulnerability was almost raw.

"OK. I know this is hard, but Father Taylor has been dragged through the coals on this. You do see that don't you? There are plenty of victims to go around, John. You're not the only one. But maybe it's time to end it. After all, Hartwig was an agent of the Diocese, therefore the money is proper for the damages done to you. But I hardly think that Taylor is a necessary victim also. All you would have to do is call the Minneapolis firm and insist that they drop the matter against Father Taylor and issue a statement to the effect that Taylor is not guilty, or, at least, that you're not sure." McAbee had played all of his cards, and many of the cards were beyond his mission, which was to ascertain Taylor's guilt or innocence and not to manipulate the case proceedings or become an advocate for Taylor. However, he felt, who would press for Taylor? The Diocese had given up on him, and Chip Blaine had been a willing agent in the settlement between Antle and the Diocese, thus exposing Taylor.

"I've got to think about this."

"Would you be willing to meet with Father Taylor?"

"No! Under no circumstances will I meet with him. I think that if he's innocent, I'd be too ashamed, and if he is guilty, I'd be too upset. You see, sir, whatever happens here, I think I lose. Would you please go now."

"McAbee collected the items on the bed and left his card on Antle's pillow. On his way out, he felt depressed and said to himself, 'What a rotten case.'

He decided to drive to Dubuque. He had unfinished business with Father Billy Taylor, as he thought that Taylor was not out of the woods yet in this matter.

The Vatican, September 1996

Sister Catherine Siena knew Bishop Guillermo Scarzi like a hand knows a glove. She had worked for him for almost 20 years. Yes, he was a bit soft, a bit of the aesthete, too much a lover of the things of the Renaissance; yes, he was a lover of fine food and wine, a bit of the hedonist; and yes, he was a chauvinist, a bit of the old ways, of male dominance. But he was also a true man of God, a man of prayer, and diligence. She knew that her obsessive ways frustrated him sometimes, but those very obsessive ways enabled him to run a competent and efficient office, admired all through the Vatican bureaucracy.

She had rarely seen him angry. He had a coolness to him, a savoir-faire, that would not allow for such a plebeian weakness. Only once or twice in the many whiles of a year would she see the fire in the 75-year-old Bishop who was kept out of the retirement ranks by a papal order. This particular fire had been burning low, but intensely, for weeks, and it involved an American Diocese in Davenport, Iowa, and a Bishop named Brendan O'Meara. It was clearly correlated with the Father William Taylor case that had come before her weeks previous.

Although Scarzi had kept things from her, she knew enough to know that Taylor, the Pope, and Scarzi had been friends at the 'Angelicum' and had stayed in touch with each other over the years. This wasn't just a Scarzi matter. It involved the Pope himself, and no one in the Vatican was unaware of the Pope's Vesuvian temper. The Irish Bishop in Davenport had clearly stepped over the line.

When Scarzi received the packet from O'Meara, he went over to the Pope, and as clear testimony to his clout and the Pope's interest in the case, he got right through that rottweiler Monsignor Brezinski. Although Scarzi trusted her to a degree, he did so in a somewhat arrogant manner by keeping details to himself. Sister Catherine Siena, however, was charged with maintaining the efficiency of the office, and thus felt only a smidgen of guilt at perusing the personal materials of the Bishop. After all, she reasoned, in the event of the sudden death of Scarzi, it would be her job to pick up the pieces and continue the flow of the office uninterrupted.

Bishop O'Meara had informed Scarzi of the settlement and had told Scarzi that it really was none of his affair. That's when the low burning anger started to erupt. He had her call Bishop O'Meara and summon him to Rome about the Taylor matter. It was clear that O'Meara should desist from executing the settlement. A day later a very brief E-mail message came across her computer: "On the advice of counsel, the Diocese has executed an agreement with John Antle. We are no longer respondents. Father Taylor is still exposed however."

When she relayed the message to Scarzi, his smoldering temper blew in a way that she had never seen in all her 20 years of service. "The Irish fool has pissed on the Pope and me! The bastard! I will take his crozier and stick it through his mouth by way of his ass! When is this damn fool supposed to be here?"

The tirade lasted, intermittently, for two days. Scarzi was beside himself as he ordered her to call the Davenport Chancery and find out just when "the stupid ass" was coming. The Diocesan secretary informed her that Bishop Brendan O'Meara and Chancellor George Duncan were in Chicago and would be landing at Da Vinci Airport at 8:00a.m. tomorrow morning, Rome time. Bishop O'Meara would be staying at San Clemente, the Irish Dominican Church in Rome. O'Meara and Duncan would be in touch when they adjusted to Italian time. The secretary added, perhaps with a light touch, perhaps not, that Bishop O'Meara was needed back in the Diocese and that she hoped his trip to Rome would be short.

Sister Catherine relayed the news to Bishop Scarzi, who upon hearing it sat down and stared at her in disbelief. Dutifully, she left his office. She learned something else. Although she had been careful in her snooping efforts and diligent about not getting caught, she decided to be extra careful from hereon in in any further encroachment into Scarzi's personal materials. She had seen a side of Guillermo Scarzi that she would never want set loose on her. She said a quiet devotional prayer for Bishop O'Meara.

Minutes later, Guillermo Scarzi came out from his office and stopped at her desk. "Telephone Bill McAbee in New York and see if it's possible for him and his brother Bertrand to come to Rome in the next few days. Stay on this, Sister, and keep me informed. I will be at the Papal apartments." He pointed to his valise and left.

She went into his office and looked in the file drawer where he kept his most immediate concerns. The Taylor file was gone. It was in his valise, she conjectured. She said still another devotional prayer for this Irish Bishop whom she felt was either very naive or very stupid, or both. And his Chancellor? It was the job of a Chancellor to keep his Bishop out of hot water. This one-Duncan-put him into scalding water. Two fools!

CHAPTER TWENTY

Iowa, September 1996

McAbee didn't announce his visit to the Trappist monastery, which its builder seemed to be have meant to be austere, but when bathed in the hot sun of early September, took on a welcoming and almost warm appearance. It was 2:15 and silence massaged the grounds more so than the last time he had visited. Even the birds were quiet. Was it siesta time? Just as he was thinking about that, he heard a lawnmower start up in the distance. That staccato noise made the entire place pick up a pulse.

He entered the visitor's doorway and saw the same wary-eyed monk from before. He came over to McAbee and said, "I'm Brother Joseph. Can I help you, sir?" He stood less than six inches from McAbee. He reminded McAbee of some Irish cop from the movies of the thirties and the forties, a set chin, opinionated, but a peace keeper in his own way.

"Bertrand McAbee, I have some unfinished business with Father Taylor. Is he available?"

"It's customary to schedule an appointment, and Father

Edward is in Des Moines on business. Father Edward, you see, must approve any visits."

McAbee wondered if the monastery had received word from Bishop O'Meara to lock him out of any contact with Taylor. The Brother wasn't hostile, but he had a stubborn look on his face. McAbee said, "I was here just a while ago. I have Diocesan permission to work with Father Taylor."

"No, sir, you don't. According to Father Edward, you must be approved at each visit by Bishop O'Meara. I've seen the letter. It's quite clear."

"Brother Joseph, do you know about the problems around Father Taylor?"

"I do."

"I intend this to be my last visit. I think I know what has happened. It's important that I confirm it with Father Taylor. I'm an advocate of his-not an enemy."

"I cannot disobey my superiors, sir," Brother Joseph said with just the slightest touch of irony.

McAbee recalled an old colleague of his who was a medievalist. These Trappists, if anything, were out of the middle ages. The medievalist argued that the scholastic philosophers and theologians of that age were a very dialectical group who were logicians of the first order. He maintained that there was an old axiom that provided the key to their thought, and McAbee was reaching back into his memory for it. It finally kicked in: 'Seldom affirm, never deny, always distinguish,' and the emphasis is always on distinguish. So McAbee needed a distinction, perhaps, to break down this protective monk.

"Brother Joseph, if I may, the letter from Bishop O'Meara has no weight in this monastery for two reasons. One, you're not part of the Diocese of Davenport and therefore he has no authority here, and two, if my memory serves me right, your true controls are within the Trappist order. So, perhaps, one could say that his letter is an advisement, but no more."

Brother Joseph smiled and rubbed his hands together. After a while, he said, "Well stated. I believed you to be a classics professor, but I sense a lawyer."

McAbee laughed aloud as the monk looked at him whimsically. "Hardly."

"But Dr. McAbee, you are still stuck with Father Edward, don't you see? And he is hardly an advisement when he speaks." He looked at McAbee with expectation.

McAbee reflected that the monk would let him access Father Taylor, but only if he could get him by the authority of Father Edward. Old Brother Joseph hungered for an excuse, a cover, to change Father Edward's rule. So, Bertrand needed a distinction. "Well, Brother, he's not here, or surely I would be at his door seeking his permission. Now things have been discovered that need the attention of Father Taylor.

"New things?"

"Points that lead me to the assessment that Father Taylor is innocent." He looked at Brother Joseph and saw in the Brother's eyes relief. Brother Joseph also wanted Taylor to be unquestionably innocent for his own peace of mind. "And since Father Taylor is an extern here and presumably under your direct charge, and since you run visitors, it appears that in the absence of Father Edward that the decision is yours to make. And, Brother, why do I feel that I'm in Egypt dealing with the sphinx?"

Brother Joseph laughed very quietly and rejoindered, "Maybe because Father Edward is the Pharaoh." He paused for what seemed to be long enough for Father Edward to make it back from Des Moines before saying, "Very well. I will see if I can find Father Taylor. But I have a warning for you."

"What's that?"

"I think that he will become one of ours," he smiled enigmatically as he left for unknown corners of the monastery.

Within a few minutes Father Taylor showed up in the visitor's room. He wore black pants, a black tee shirt, and a pair of blue sneakers. He looked at McAbee sadly as he shook McAbee's hand and pointed to a chair. The session would be held indoors, which was fine with McAbee because he wanted to study this man closely.

"Well, Bertrand, you predicted another meeting. It's probably God's will that Father Edward is in Des Moines today, because I don't think he would look at Bishop O'Meara's letter as a ... what an interesting word ... *advisement*. But the good Brother Joseph rules and I obey." He smiled stoically. Clearly, he didn't want this meeting. "So how can I help you?"

"Father Taylor, the question is, how can you help yourself, don't you think? I assume that you're aware of the deal made by your Diocese, a deal that I see as an abandonment of you."

"I am aware of the *deal*, as you refer to it," he said cautiously.

"Father, I am going to be frank with you. I get the feeling that this may be my last chance with you, perhaps ever."

Taylor continued to look at him flatly and with a degree

of suspicion. McAbee was not a welcome presence in this Trappist world that Taylor had discovered.

McAbee had been considering his approach all through the hour-and-a-half drive from Iowa City to Dubuque and decided that only a hypothetical approach would work. "Father, I'm going to ask you to do some supposing with me. Is that OK?" Taylor gave only the slightest hint of a nod to him. "If you were my confessor and I told you something, would you hold it to your heart?"

"I would be God's agent and whatever is said to me, stays with me, of course."

"And if I told you that I was a murderer and sought your forgiveness?"

"I do not and cannot forgive anything. But I can offer God's forgiveness if you are truly sorry and intend not to sin again," he said with a sharpened look in his eyes.

That look spoke much to McAbee. This was why the man was so leery the last time McAbee met with him. McAbee felt that a fog was starting to lift. "And if I commit murder again after getting your absolution? Do I find forgiveness again, Father?"

"If you meet the conditions, yes."

"And when do you turn me into the police?"

"Never! I can't," he said sharply.

"But a psychiatrist would, wouldn't he?"

"I would think so," Taylor answered speculatively.

"But what about a future action? What if I told you that I intended to murder someone?"

"No. I would not give you absolution, of course. There is no intent to reform, to refrain," he said adamantly.

"But, Father, I'm not talking about absolution. I'm

talking about foreknowledge of an event! What would you do with that?"

"It would be in the boundary of the confessional."

"Meaning?"

"Meaning I would plead with you to not go forward with the crime, but I could not tell others. I would never under any circumstance break the bonds of the confessional. There are no exceptions!" He was adamant.

McAbee was encouraged. By now he thought that Taylor would have broken this hypothetical game, but he didn't, and that meant that this all-too-shrewd man would perhaps give him the answer by indirection.

"And, Father, If I were an assistant to you in a church, let's say a reader and sacristan, the equivalent of a deacon, you might say, and I was into some very bad things, what would you do?"

"Bad things?" He eyed McAbee with full suspicion.

"Let's say I was sexually abusing one of your altar boys."

Taylor lowered his head and looked at his fingernails and shook his head, almost imperceptibly. "Bertrand! I have no direct knowledge of any crime like that being committed under my watch!"

McAbee saw no reason to doubt this holy man's statement, which at face value rested on the important words-"direct knowledge" and "under my watch." McAbee said quietly, "Father, if you knew that I was an assassin in Tunisia, for example, would you be concerned that I might be an assassin in Iowa?"

Father Taylor put his thumb to his mouth and bit off a loose piece of skin, and his eyes went to some distant corner of the room. There was a long pause. "Of course I would."

"And if in a confessional I told you I was a pedophile, would you not be concerned about my being in the parish and having access to children?"

"Of course! And if this knowledge came my way, and I didn't insist that there be no hint of any activity like this in my parish, I would be a horrible pastor!"

"But what if the boy in question was already gone?"

"Then I would go from there and keep all tempting areas of the Church off-limits to this sinner, and if he violated my mandate, I would have him removed from the Church. And I have gone far enough with these hypotheticals and this run at a Platonic dialogue," he said snappishly.

"Father Taylor, let me remind you of my charge. I'm here on behalf of Bishop Scarzi and," he lowered his voice to a whisper, "the Pope. The curtain is open part way. Don't stop now, please," he said.

"You are in territory that is very, very dangerous; very, very critical to what a priest is all about. Do you not see this?"

"Father, you haven't violated anything. This is a hypothetical discussion."

"McAbee! Do not be a casuist with me."

"Why not, Father Taylor. It seems to be a language you're familiar with." McAbee regretted saying this to this man, but he also felt that Taylor had a part in this tragedy, and even though his motives were good, the effect of his confessional theology was disastrous.

Father Taylor gazed at him painfully. He had been hurt by McAbee's verbal arrow. "I will repeat, and now to the point of this, I had and have no direct knowledge of any sexual crime being committed against John Antle." He said this in staccato fashion.

"I'm not saying that you actually saw it directly, Father, or that Antle came to you and spoke about it, or that anyone even confessed it directly to you, Father-yes-in that sense you have no direct knowledge of the abuse. But quite frankly, I don't think that you're clean on this. Father, we've spoken to other altar boys in the period around Antle's presence. There was adamant denial of any sexual abuse. My assumption is that you placed the altar boys' change room off limits to Hartwig and that you felt that this made your Church sufficiently safe. In fact, other altar boys around Antle's time don't recall an adult ever being in the change room. So, it appears, you heightened your vigilance. But John Antle was another matter. I take your word on this. You had no direct knowledge, but you had plenty of indirect knowledge that abuse was possible."

"No, sir. Awareness comes when awareness comes. John Antle was gone by a month or so when I became aware of clouds. These clouds are confessional in nature, and then I took to severe measures. I never knew that John Antle," he looked so intently and pleadingly at McAbee, "had been violated." He sat there and put his head down in resignation. He removed a handkerchief from his back pocket and dabbed at his eyes. He looked back up at McAbee and said in a sincerity that shook McAbee's soul. "Bertrand McAbee, I have sinned, perhaps, in the way that I handled this matter, and I have no doubt this whole thing is a story being written by a just God. But, I do feel a bit like Job in this."

McAbee sat and reflected before saying, "Father, Bob Hartwig is alive. I went to visit him in Calamus. That plant in the comer has more life to it than he does with his advanced Alzheimers. But I have indisputable materials that make him out to be a first-class pedophile who was actively engaged in a ring. So, why not declaim him?"

"McAbee? Are you really saying this to me? Back to your hypotheticals, what advantage is it to anyone to expose a man similar to the one you describe? He was a man of high repute. He served his church well, and like all of us, he was a sinner. Are there not sins that you have committed against others? Would you want them exposed now? *Cui bono*, McAbee. And, as to Antle. He will have me to punish. I will fight it, but I expect to lose now that the Diocese has set me adrift."

"Father, I just came from visiting with John Antle. I pleaded with him to drop the suit against you. I think that he will. I explained about Hartwig, and I think he sees the truth, that it wasn't you but rather another, another dressed in the garb of the Church, a man who could so easily overwhelm a little boy. A man, now as good as dead. He looks out his window at a lawn and cornfield sitting atop his own waste. What can you do?"

"So, McAbee, what now?"

"Tell me again, Father, that you're innocent."

"I am, but your point is taken. I wasn't diligent enough. You know we just were not that alert to these things back then. It was a matter of not being aware, a sort of ignorance. That is where the fault is on my part, most assuredly."

"Socrates spoke to this, I think, Father. Knowledge is a combination of knowing something intellectually and by will; when we don't know both ways we're ignorant. We really don't know."

"That is a Christ thing, too, McAbee," he said. "So, how can I make it up to John Antle?"

"He won't meet with you, Father. He's very messed up, I'm afraid. Maybe a note ... I don't know. But you, Father. What happens now?"

"Oh, surely, you remember your Epictetus. We are all in a play, Bertrand; each has a part, some long, some short. Parts change. Mine has for sure. John Antle has done me a good turn as God's agent."

"Meaning?"

"Oh, don't you see? I have no intention of ever leaving here again, unless I have to by some order or whatever by higher authorities. I have finally found a place where I am at great peace and among other men of like views. This is an existential outpost and I am thrilled. I cannot see this in any other way than it is. It is God's plan. He brought me here by a most circuitous route. I have no other way of describing what has happened over these past few months. Do you?"

"Yeah, but it sounds so pedestrian next to what you say and how you put it. But what about the others? There are three dead men and three dead women. Is God's hand there too?"

"Bertrand, that is the question of evil you are inquiring about. That is way beyond me I am afraid. I will say this, however, there is more to death than the cessation of physical life. I am trying to say to you that this puts the whole thing at the level of mystery." He looked at Bertrand with an air of finality. Then Taylor smiled at McAbee gently.

Brother Joseph came to the doorway. "Can I get anything for either of you?"

Taylor turned and said, "Yes, Brother. Would you bring a Coke and three glasses?"

When he came back with the coke and glasses, Father Taylor asked Brother Joseph to sit as he filled up the three glasses and said, "To the happiness of all of us. May we find our peace."

McAbee said, "Amen," without thinking. He looked around embarrassed. He didn't mean to say anything that outrightly religious.

Father Billy Taylor and Brother Joseph laughed as they tried to drink their Coke. They understood McAbee, even if he didn't understand himself, McAbee conjectured.

Iowa, September 1996

The next day Pat buzzed McAbee to tell him that Chip Blaine was on the telephone.

"Yes, Chip. What can I do for you?"

"What did you give Antle?" Blaine demanded.

"Are you trying to say something, Chip, or is this 'Twenty Questions'?" McAbee asked sharply.

"I just got a call from the Youngquist firm. John Antle withdrew his action against Taylor. This statement was just faxed to me, as well as to the media. Want to hear?" He sounded depressed.

"Please."

Blaine cleared his voice and intoned, "John Antle, after much reflection, can no longer say with good conscience that Father William Taylor was his abuser. That he was abused in a Diocesan facility is clear, but new information suggests other possibilities. For the sake of everyone, it is felt that the matter be put to rest. No further comments will be made from this quarter." There was silence.

"McAbee? You still there?"

"Yeah."

"And?"

"Did you relay this to your client-Father Taylor?"

"Well, no, not yet. I wanted to know what you put on this little bastard Antle."

"Something you'd never understand, Blaine, you stupid big bastard." He hung up.

New York, September 1996

After Blaine had called about the suit being withdrawn by Antle, McAbee gave a full oral report of his findings to his brother Bill. Father Billy Taylor was innocent. It wasn't more than two hours later that he was ordered by Bill to be at JFK for an Alitalia flight to Rome that was departing at 6:05p.m. "And bring your very best dark suit. I don't want to see one of those goddamn tweedy professor-horseshit coats where you're going," Bill rampaged on.

Bertrand was met at the United Airlines gate and whisked off to Alitalia where he was seated on the 747 next to his impatient brother in the first-class section of the plane. Bill was dressed in a suit and was working on his PC.

Bertrand asked, "Another day at the office?"

Bill said, "Did you bring a presentable, conservative suit?" He was in a foul mood.

"Of course. I did. Now, before I walk off this plane and tell you to go straight to hell, what's going on?"

He looked up from his PC and said, "Bertrand, this has been a long day, it's going to be a long night, and tomorrow is going to be exhausting. I had to cancel three critical meetings, and Mary has the stomach flu, so back off. Let me just say this. Tomorrow just might be the most interesting day of your life." Eventually they talked and it involved the Taylor case only. "But, Bertrand, there's something terribly wrong in this. I know your charge was the innocence or guilt of Taylor, but all the murders? What's that all about?"

"Bill, I'm not getting into that. That's a police matter."

"What about the female UPS driver? Did they find her?"

"No."

"You know you missed being murdered by probably 20 seconds, and yet you continue to walk around unarmed! And who's this old lady in Minneapolis who guns down Youngquist, about whom I could give a damn, an innocent secretary, and one of this Scholz's men?"

"Bill, it's not my case."

"Well, let me just say this. You probably were within a foot of the murderer in Iowa City. You could identify her. You may be the only one out there who can. File it away, Bertrand. You could be on this murderer's short list."

The Vatican, September 1996

He ached all over, not that it was anything new. But some days were worse than others, and this was a bad day. Scarzi's thorough memorandum convinced him to call a meeting in his office. He wanted all of the principals except Taylor. It shouldn't take long.

As usual, Monsignor Brezinski saw to it that they were all seated, and he gave the Pope a card telling him everyone's name, exactly where they were seated, and a thumbnail description. Scarzi's name had nothing next to it, of course. Next to Bill McAbee's name was the following: "Investigation firm, New York City, Knight of Malta, extraordinary friend of the Vatican, irreplaceable asset." Bertrand's read: "Brother of Bill, former classics professor, chief investigator." Bishop O'Meara and Monsignor Duncan would also be present, as well as Brezinski. The Pope was relieved to know that Billy Taylor had been exonerated and applauded Taylor's inclination to become a Trappist. 'God's will be done, Billy,' he said to himself. He also knew from his conversation with Brezinski that Scarzi had put O'Meara and Duncan into the deep freeze of bureaucratic avoidance. Scarzi was getting a bit personal with the two, but from what he could see, they had it corning to them.

Brezinski came to his private parlor and said, "They are all seated, Your Holiness, and have been for the past 15 minutes."

If they didn't stand when he entered the room, he would notice, otherwise all of the pomp around his papacy went largely unnoticed. He was a Polish peasant after all, and this Italian flair got on his nerves, even after 50 years of dealing with it. He sat behind his desk and looked at them: his old friend Scarzi who looked too firm in his jaw, the foppish Duncan who exhibited a dimwit's half smile, O'Meara, the stern Irishman who had the look of a man who was fully self-justified, Bill McAbee who had a pair of warrior eyes that had seen everything, and this Bertrand, who looked at him as if he were an item for study, as if he were some kind of museum piece.

"Gentlemen, we will speak English. You will excuse us. We don't get much practice, but we will do our best." It was humility that spoke. He knew his English vocabulary was better than most native speakers. "We will keep this short. We thank you all for appearing." The ibuprofen was kicking in, thank God. "Thanks to the oversight of Bishop Scarzi and the work of the McAbees, it appears that Father Taylor is innocent. Bishop O'Meara is that your understanding?"

"Your Holiness, I was just informed some three hours ago by my secretary, who had trouble reaching me at San Clemente, that John Antle, the complainant, that is, the one suing, has withdrawn his lawsuit."

The Pope took in what was said, including O'Meara's patronizing translation of what a "complainant" was. More importantly, he noticed that he hadn't answered his question. He looked down at his gnarled fingers and decided to give the man one more chance. "Bishop O'Meara, please comment on the guilt or innocence of Father Taylor?" The Pope looked down at his card when he saw the priest next to O'Meara lean over and whisper in O'Meara's ear. Monsignor Duncan. The Pope didn't like the look of him. He reminded him of a pair of patent leather shoes, only in this case it would be patent plastic. The whispering went back and forth for about 20 seconds. He caught the looks of Brezinski and Scarzi and the McAbees, all of whom were surprised by the impudence. He looked at his card again. The one on the end. Bertrand. Was that a slight smile on his face?

Finally, O'Meara cleared his throat and said, "Well, Your Holiness, there is the law and in that sense, he's innocent."

Well that said it all. Bishop O'Meara clearly had something on Taylor and the final report submitted by Bertrand McAbee to his brother and then on to Scarzi was wrong. He had to find out. "Bishop O'Meara, you must know something that the investigator doesn't know, some secret information that leads you in this direction. We want to hear it. Now!" The Pope was convinced that O'Meara had to have something otherwise his position was outlandish.

The Bishop looked at Duncan who looked away and gave that silly fawning look to the Pope. When the Pope would read of Roman Emperors who would arbitrarily order the murder of individuals who got on the wrong side of them, he would shutter at the whimsy of the whole thing. Every once in a while though, when his pain was intense ... the day had been long, and the world looked to be beyond hope ... he would very briefly, under the right stimulus, relate to one of these emperors. For a millisecond, he ordered a savage execution for Monsignor Duncan before catching himself and saying to himself, 'Jesus, grant me patience.' The slightest tremor in his right hand began, once again.

Finally, the Bishop responded, "I have no secret knowledge in this matter, Your Holiness. I have always felt that just the appearance of such a crime is enough to convict. Father Taylor allowed for that appearance; therefore, I can find him morally guilty regardless of the law. This is why I ordered a settlement with John Antle on behalf of the Diocese. The greatest good, you know," he spoke with his Irish brogue.

"The appearance?" the Pope asked tentatively.

"Well, yes, Your Holiness. The charge could be made that truth or falsity is not important. I'm not saying that he actually did it, but he created the conditions for the appearance of such." There was a clear shade of belligerence and self-righteousness in the Bishop's pronouncement.

"Would you say, Bishop, that our meeting now could be construed by someone as being an orgy . . . if they were standing below in St. Peter's Square?"

"No . . . yes . . . I suppose so," O'Meara answered speculatively.

"And are we guilty?" The Pope tried to keep the edge off his voice, and he wondered how this man ever cleared the hurdles that had been put in place for appointments to the Episcopate.

"Well, of course not. But this is different. He had the care of his parishioners to manage, and he didn't."

"We don't see the difference. We ...."

"But there ...."

"Stop!" The Pope stood up. The Bishop had triggered him. "Don't come to us and parade some standard that falls beyond common sense. You have allowed for the loss of reputation of one of the holiest men we have ever met! And now you have lost him to your Diocese, since he wishes to become a Trappist monk! If it wasn't for this man and his efforts," he pointed to Bertrand, "you would have crushed the man's reputation. And you-Monsignor ..." he looked down at his notecard, "... Duncan, where were you in this matter?"

Duncan squirmed and said, "As Chancellor I urged care and judiciousness. But, of course, I heeded my Bishop."

O'Meara's face went beet red, and his large hands tightened into a fist.

"Reverends! You are both dismissed! And you are not to leave Rome until you hear from Bishop Scarzi! Goodnight!"

When the two left, he sat there and wrote for three minutes. He motioned to Brezinski, who took the note and gave it to Scarzi.

"Friends, we must go now. We are beset by many enemies, but we don't need them to be aided by our own." He arose and looked out at them and made the sign of the Cross. They all blessed themselves, except for that Bertrand McAbee, who now had a quizzical look on his face. He wondered if even God knew what that man was thinking.

AFTERWARD

- Bishop O'Meara was transferred from the Diocese of Davenport to Rome. His responsibility is to oversee the raising of money in the Catholic Churches of Western Africa in support of Papal charities. It was a newly created post, with no staff assistance.
- Ex-Chancellor Monsignor Duncan is currently a pastor of three rural churches on the western edge of the Diocese of Davenport. He has gained 20 pounds.
- Father William Taylor entered into a one-year covenant with the Trappists, after which time, both being pleased, he would become a priest-monk in the Trappist order. Papal intervention shortened the time of the covenant.
- John Antle committed suicide in Iowa City two months to the date of the Pope's meeting with Bertrand McAbee, et alia.
- The Princess was not indicted by a grand jury in Minneapolis or in Iowa City. He could not be placed at the scene of the crime. And even though safe for the time being, Bertrand McAbee, the one

untidy piece, is the only name on his short list of eventual victims.

- Bertrand McAbee injured his leg again. He is now taking long walks with Scorpio, but both of them are unhappy with this option. He continues to be struck by how one incident in one's life can affect the lives of so many others.

END

04167750-00966864

Printed in the United States
By Bookmasters